A Shell for Angela

Ofelia Dumas Lachtman

Arte Público Press
Houston, Texas
1995

This volume is made possible through grants from the National Endowment for the Arts (a federal agency), the Lila Wallace-Reader's Digest Fund, and the Andrew W. Mellon Foundation.

Recovering the past, creating the future

Arte Público Press
University of Houston
Houston, Texas 77204-2090

Cover design by Gladys Ramírez

Lachtman, Ofelia Dumas.
   A shell for Angela / by Ofelia Dumas Lachtman.
      p.   cm.
   ISBN 1-55885-123-2
   1. Mexican American women—California, Southern—Fiction. 2. Married women—California, Southern—Fiction. 3. Suburban life—California, Southern—Fiction. I. Title.
   PS3562.A2453S54   1995
   813'.54—dc20   94-36140
                                           CIP

The paper used in this publication meets the requirements of the American National Standard for Permanence of Paper for Printed Library Materials Z39.48-1984. ∞

For Marta and Steve
who were part of it all

A Shell for Angela

Chapter One

It was one of those remarkable April afternoons in Los Angeles, made clear and smogless by a heavy rain that had fallen during the night and warmed by a sun that had been out since mid-morning. At two-thirty there was just enough breeze to set the trees on El Mar Drive to quivering. The street was empty of traffic except for a gardener's truck that turned the corner, rolled leisurely to the Raine house, and rumbled to a noisy stop. A dog barked and rattled a high iron gate.

Angela Raine blocked out the sounds. She shifted the suitcase she was carrying from one hand to the other and closed the den door firmly. Then, skirting rain water that had collected in a low spot on the patio, she walked toward the garage. She glanced back at the puddle and thought, those flagstones never have been right. A blue jay landed near the gate to which she was heading, picked and pulled at a twig, and flew with it over the garden to his nest. All around her was the promise of new life: the warm, wet scent of lemon blossoms, the swollen leaf buds on the elm tree, and, bursting beyond the fence, the birthday-party pink of a flowering peach. She alone, it seemed, was at the end, not the beginning.

A cold sweat broke out on her palms and she tightened her hold on the suitcase. In the last couple of months she had lost weight, and strength too. Maybe more. She pulled back the gate. A Cadillac, this year's model, waited by the closed garage door, the trunk open. Its 1974 license plate spelled out ANGELA. Bending her knees, she lifted the case into the trunk and turned to find her gardener walking down the drive.

Over the years, whatever the weather might be, Emilio kept a daily commitment to the garden that had, to all intents and purposes, become his. He was untiring, uncomplicated and gentle. Often she came across him cupping a flower and talking softly to it. In Spanish, of course. With her he spoke careful English, lapsing only occasionally into a Spanish phrase.

"Mrs. Raine," he called now, "if you have a minute, may we talk?" He took off an ancient grass hat as he reached her. "Is this not a day for miracles? A day in which one enjoys working." He chuckled. "A miracle in itself, no?"

She nodded. "I have no time to talk now, Emilio. Is it important?"

"Maybe not, maybe not. It's about the marigolds you wanted me to plant."

She avoided his eyes as she settled herself behind the wheel. "Not marigolds, Emilio. Let's have something that will last. Make it...oh, make it geraniums." She glanced at him and caught the raised eyebrow, the questioning look. "Pink geraniums," she said firmly.

"Well, why not?" he said, and as she backed down the driveway, he waved his hat and called, "*Vaya con Dios.*"

She curved into the street then sat up rigidly, her hands on the automatic shift. She would allow herself one last look. A quick look. There were memories here that would pull her. She couldn't afford that. Her eyes moved from the broad expanse of well-fed green lawn that fronted her house to the home of her neighbors, Maggie and Don Paul.

Across the street a delivery truck slammed on its brakes and swerved into a driveway, and the Pauls' two Dalmatians once again started barking, the iron gate clanging at their insistent thrusts. Her neighbors were traveling. Basking on a beach in Ibizia about now, she thought. But the dogs and the security patrol would keep their place safe.

All in all, this had been a good, safe place to live. The neighborhood had matured gracefully, passing from its young years into a self-satisfied older age that was green and clean and well-protected. It had been a good place for her children. Her eyes strayed to the jacaranda tree on the front lawn and, remembering Gloria's picnics there, she stiffened. Quickly, she put the car in drive and swung around the corner. Within minutes she was at the Sepulveda Boulevard on-ramp to the San Diego Freeway.

A big gray truck puffed diesel fumes into the air as it climbed slowly in front of her. Pressing down on the accelerator, she passed the truck and merged with the fast-moving traffic. She had no more patience for obstacles. She had had enough of them. In the last week, they had all been brought up by her husband Walt.

First, there was his disbelief. "Mexico, Angela? *You*? And *now*?" She envisioned Walt as he looked when she told him she was going, his lean frame sinking slightly, his face covered with confusion. Poor Walt. She wanted to reach out and touch him, but that would have defeated her. "Yes, Walt, Mexico," she said. "Yes, Walt, me. And now." Then there was his compromise. "I'll come with you," he said. "I can manage that." She said quietly, "I'm going alone." Finally, there was his resistance. "I won't let you go," he said. She turned around to challenge him, but stopped, shrugging in a gesture of resignation. Walt didn't understand. She wondered how he planned to stop her, and on the following day she had found out. Her son Ken and daughter Gloria arrived to back up their dad.

They all sat in the living room stiffly, the unusual silence putting distance between them. She sent Walt a swift knowing glance, and he nodded as if admitting to an accusation, but said nothing. The talk, when it started, was awkward. Gloria kept tossing her head like a nervous pony, her hazel eyes alert. In her Dutch-boy haircut and jeans she looked like a little girl. Angela had to remind herself that she wasn't. Gloria was someone's wife. Ken sat across the room—reasonable, logical Ken, uncomfortable on the low couch, his arms dangling between his knees.

She smiled at him and he said, "All we're asking, Mom, is that you talk to someone who'll be objective. It's obvious we can't be."

It must be hard for them, Angela thought. Of course they think I don't know what I'm doing. Running off to some God-forsaken desert town in Mexico where there's no hotel, no post office, not even a landing strip. Her hands began to tremble and she held them tightly. I understand how they feel, but they don't know how little time I have. Damn it, what I do now is for me to decide. "I have to go," she said. "I already explained...the best I can. If I can't make you see it, no one else will see it either."

And then Gloria said, "I guess what mother does at this point is up to her, Ken. Let's not hound her anymore today." It had been a soap opera.

In the car Angela squirmed. What Walt and Ken had asked in essence was, is this...this going really necessary? The answer was a definite yes. Necessary. But only to her. That was the thing that troubled her. She had been for years a wife and mother devoted to looking out for her family's comfort and interests. Now she had to forget all that. There was something more important to do. She gripped the steering wheel tightly and its padded cover gave beneath her fingers. Maybe it was the memory of that discussion last Sunday. She felt hot, flushed. She fumbled for the air conditioning. The cool air touched her almost immediately and she sighed.

Walt had been right about the car. It *was* a prize. When he had given it to her on their last anniversary, she hadn't felt a need for it. Today she was glad for its conveniences. Crossing the Mexican desert could be a trial. She had done it once before with her mother.

Frowning, she eased off the accelerator and glanced at the sky. Gray clouds were swelling directly ahead. Would it rain again? That would hold her back, and it was already Wednesday. She wanted to get to Punta de Cruces. She wanted to discover what was drawing her there. And she didn't want to waste any more time. She had kept the promise the three of them had wangled out of her last Sunday. She had waited three days to see that shrink, and it had done no good. She glanced at the clock. I'm glad I left his office early, she thought. It means I'll make it to San Diego by nightfall. And in another day, I'll be there.

Punta de Cruces was all-important to her now. More important than it had been during that long ago summer. "The summer of the fruit picking," her brother Ricardo later called it whenever he felt it necessary to talk about it. And that wasn't very often. She wished he had talked more. She wished she knew more. All that she knew was what had happened to her father...and what that had done to her.

Chapter Two

Angela was almost nine-years old the summer of the fruit-picking. Her brother Ricardo, who was thirteen, later said that the fruit-picking and the Padilla thing wouldn't have happened except for their father's losing his job in the dairy. But Ricardo also said that it was a matter of economics, that the Depression had finally hit Los Angeles and made everything go wrong. That was difficult for Angela to understand. As far as she was concerned, everything was all right until a certain Monday in June.

That was the day when Padilla made a proposition to her father, when the news came about her grandmother, and when the boys called her that name.

Things first started to go wrong that Monday when Miss Jennings, her teacher, told her not to talk Spanish, that she must speak English only. Angela didn't tell Miss Jennings that she *had* to talk Spanish at home because her mother couldn't understand English. Instead she said, "Yes, I know," and looked longingly at the cloakroom door. There she would be safe from embarrassment. She would be where she couldn't see the smiles or hear the giggles. She would hide with the sweaters and forgotten umbrellas and lunch sacks that smelled of pickles and bananas. But she didn't move.

Miss Jennings said, "I'm glad you know. But do you know why?"

"No, ma'am."

"It's because you were born in Los Angeles, in the United States, and that makes you American, not Mexican."

Angela nodded, but she was completely confused. Her father, mother, and two brothers had come from Mexico. But she and her eleven-year-old sister Bonita (whose real name was Estela) had been born in Los Angeles. But her father said he was Mexican and she wanted to be whatever he was. For the rest of the day she sat glumly, wanting more than anything to be at home.

When the last bell rang, she didn't wait for Bonita. She ran across the school yard and out the gate in the chain-link fence. When she heard footsteps behind her, she thought they were her sister's. But they weren't. Two boys from her class were racing after her.

One of them hollered, "Angela's mad at the teacher!" Then they stopped and began to chant, "Angela's mad and I am glad, and I know what will please her. A bottle of ink to make her stink, and someone to call her a greaser!"

What did that mean? She whirled around and shouted, "Stoppit!" When she started to run again, one of the boys grabbed at her dress. "Let go!" she hollered. And then, "See? You've torn my dress! You dumb old greasers!"

Her eyes filled with hot angry tears, but the boys just laughed. She could hear them laughing as she ran through the crossing tunnel at the end of the block. And although no one was following her, she ran all the way home to Twenty-eighth Street. When she saw the green siding of her house above the neighbor's ragged hedge, she slowed down. She was in no hurry to explain to her mother about the torn dress.

On the front porch, she dropped into an old blue rocking chair. She gave herself a push and the rockers grunted loudly against the uneven wooden floor. In a moment she leaned forward to look past a pepper tree by the side fence to the house where their neighbor Rosa lived alone. Sometimes Rosa sat on the steps to brush her long black hair and they talked. But today the steps were empty.

Angela wished that *somebody*—other than her mother—was at home. But the car was gone, so that meant that her father was still away, and Ricardo and Alberto were almost always gone in the afternoons. Bonita would soon be dragging home, pouting because Angela had left her behind. "Slowpoke Estela," Angela said out loud, but it didn't sound right. Bonita had really become her sister's name. It was the only nickname in the family that had taken, and that was because Estela loved that her nickname meant pretty. Her brother Alberto didn't like to be called Flaco because that meant skinny, and

Ricardo fumed when anyone referred to him as El Guapo, even if it did mean handsome. She, Angela, had never had a nickname, and only Papá called her Angelita. Well, she thought, I'd better go in and see Mamá before Bonita gets home. But instead of getting up, she continued rocking slowly.

Finally, she became aware of a rich smell drifting through the screen door and she went inside. Potato soup, that's what it was, and she was hungry. She hurried down the hall to the kitchen, but, remembering the torn dress, hesitated in the doorway.

The kitchen was a high-ceilinged room with a square of patterned green linoleum covering most of the pine floor. A heavy glass tumbler held spoons on an oilcloth-covered table, and a pot with boiled beans waited by the window on the drainboard. Today, the gray enameled coffee pot that was always on the stove had been moved to a back burner to accommodate a large kettle.

A slim, small-boned woman was at the stove. Her cheeks were flushed as she leaned over the steaming pot, giving her pallid face a rouged look. A crease grew between her eyes as, sighing, she turned away from the bubbling soup.

The crying look, Angela thought, and then shrugged. What could she expect? Mamá nearly always looked that way. She stepped into the room. "I'm home, Mamá."

"Ay, Angela," the woman said, "what have you done to your dress? The fences again?"

"No, señora. I wasn't climbing fences."

"Then how did it happen?"

"It got pulled." Angela backed away. "I think I'll go over to Rosa's."

"Don't you move. You know I don't want you over there so much."

"Why?" Angela knew she wouldn't get an answer. Mamá said Rosa was a good neighbor, but there was something else about her that she wouldn't say. "Why?" she insisted.

"Because I..." Her mother stopped and glanced toward the hall door. "Ah, Manuel, you are home."

Angela swung around. Her father was in the doorway dressed in his gray suit, his hat in his hand. He grinned, and his face, which was the color of the clay pot for the beans, lit up. He patted Angela's head. "What has this one done now?" he asked.

"What she has done," his wife said, sighing, "is nothing that I cannot repair." She sat down by the table and pulled a needle from a sewing basket on the floor. "Come here, Angela."

"*Andale*," Manuel said, giving Angela a little push. "Go. Your mother will make your dress like new. There are so many things that she knows how to do."

His wife looked up at him as she pushed the needle into the pink cotton of Angela's skirt. "There are so many things," she said sharply," that I *have* to do. Not like in Mexico. Here we have no servants, not even a cook. *Bueno*, and for what would we need one? There is very little to cook...only promises."

"Patience, Dolores," Manuel said softly.

Dolores shrugged, tightened the pink thread she was using, and bit it off close to the fabric. "There. That is the best I can do." She closed the sewing basket and said, "You promised me better things, Manuel."

Manuel stiffened. "Wait outside, Angela. If your mother agrees, you will go with me to the Plaza."

"The Plaza?" Dolores said. "You're not going to look for that man Padilla are you? We're not that desperate. I still have the mattress money."

"I'm not going to look for him, Dolores, no. But if I see Padilla, I think I will talk to him."

His wife shook her head and returned to the stove. "If only you knew the right people here as you did in Mexico."

Angela went to the sink and got a glass of water. Something was being said underneath the words that she didn't understand. But whatever it was, was something she didn't like.

"Things will improve," Manuel said as Angela walked up the hall to the front door. "Have patience, señora. The Depression cannot go on forever."

For the next ten minutes Manuel's voice drifted from the kitchen into the living room, past the light bulb that dangled from the ceiling, past the iron hooks on the coat rack in the front hall, at last sifting through the sagging screen to where Angela sat in the rocking chair, her straight brown hair pushed behind her ears, her black eyes staring out into the street. Finally, she got up and walked around the side of the house to the garage. She would wait for her father in the car.

The Model T in the garage was older than Alberto, who was fifteen. He called it "the old wreck," and that sparked Ricardo to defend it. Ricardo said that it didn't matter how old an automobile was if you could keep it running. And the fact was that their father could take that Ford apart and put it back together in better shape than before and even have some parts left over. That didn't make sense to Angela, but she figured that if Ricardo said so, it was probably true.

She climbed into the car and sat behind the steering wheel. The first thing she would do when her father came was to ask him why the boys had called her that name. She might even ask him to explain what Miss Jennings meant. But the first thing she did when he showed up was to help him start the car.

Thu-h-h-h, thu-h-h-h, thu-h-h-h! He turned the crank. When he signaled her, she moved a lever near the steering wheel up. And when he called to her, she moved it down. Hee-ic, hee-ee-ic, hi-ic, hic, hic, hic! The car began to rattle. She moved over and her father got in behind the wheel. They drove down Twenty-eighth Street and turned north on Main Street. Angela looked happily at the familiar buildings they passed.

First, there was the Mellinis' grocery store, which had a wonderful smell of Italian cheeses and a row of shining jars with candy. Then came the shoe-repair shop and, after a rock-strewn empty lot, Keller's Hardware Store. Ever since she could remember, the same keg spilled nails out onto the floor of its display window.

Where Adams Boulevard intersected Main, the four corners were taken up by a gray brick bank building, a motorcycle salesroom, a furniture store, and an accounting supply firm. Now Angela knew that she was out of her neighborhood, her comfortable *barrio*, and into the distant and uncertain familiarity of the city.

At Pico Boulevard, the arm of a traffic signal came down red and they stopped. A long line of men, women, some with children, stretched from around the corner into a storefront. The people in the line wore clothes that were old and faded, and they seemed tired and unhappy. Some of the men had hats pulled down over their ears, shadowing their faces.

A bread line. Angela moved closer to her father. "Why does Mamá think those bread lines are so bad?" she asked.

He gave her a sidelong glance. "It's because bread lines are for hungry people. Your mother is afraid that if I don't find work, we too won't have enough to eat."

"You will, won't you?" she asked quickly. "Find work, I mean."

"You will never go hungry, Angelita," he said, and patted her knee. "I will see to that."

But Angela noticed a furrow deepen between her father's eyes as he spoke. He was unusually quiet the rest of the way.

When they parked near the Old Plaza, she felt excitement starting up inside of her. The tree-scattered square, she had long ago decided, was especially hers and Papá's. Here everybody talked in Spanish, and the signs were in Spanish, and the men and women and the other children laughed in a different way that was Spanish, too: "¡Ay, qué chula! ¡Qué lindo!" And their eyes seemed to look in Spanish. She looked up at a tree that hung over a crumbling adobe fence and wondered if it was a Mexican tree or an American tree? And how about the birds?

"Do you think the birds are singing in Spanish?" she asked.

"What do you think?"

She shrugged. Sometimes her father wasn't very good at answers. Still, she would ask him now what the boys had meant. But before she could say anything, he said, "Come," and headed toward four men standing under a tree.

"Pablo Padilla," he called as he neared them, "is that you? You were leaving for Fresno when I last saw you."

The man called Padilla turned. He was heavy and short, with unusually narrow shoulders which he shrugged as he said, "As you can see, Manuel Martín, I am back. Come here. I have a proposition to make to you."

Her father's arm came around her and he said, "Wait for me here." Then he joined the men under the tree.

Angela waited. She sat on a stone bench at the edge of the walkway and waited. She edged closer and sat on a stone wall and waited. The man called Padilla talked and talked and the other men listened. Once she heard her father say, "...never followed the crops," and something unpleasant struck her about those words. She stared at Padilla's unshaven face, at the smile that, like a flickering light bulb, came and went, and decided that she didn't like him.

But her father kept on listening to him. Finally, he slapped Padilla on the back. "I will let you know, *hombre*," he said. "*Adiós*."

Back in the car she asked, "What's a proposition? Like Padilla said."

"Like *Señor* Padilla said, Angela. The man's made me an offer, that's all. That's what a proposition is."

"You mean he's going to give you something?"

"Perhaps. Yes...something like that."

So her father had really come to the Plaza to see Señor Padilla. But why hadn't he told her mother that? And why didn't Mamá like Señor Padilla either?

When the car turned south, her father said, "We have one more errand."

"Grand Central Market?" she asked, and he nodded. She was glad they were going there, even though she would have to put up with her father's little game. And didn't he know she was much too old for that kind of thing now?

Whenever they went to the market, he parked the Ford on the street above it and they rode down the steep hill by Third Street in a small red cable car. The game always started when her father said that they were going for a ride in *her* streetcar. She would complain that it wasn't hers, and he would say, "Then why is it called Angela's Flight?" And she always said that it said angel, not Angela. Then he'd say something silly like she really was an angel, and her face would grow hot as they faced the ticket seller.

Today's game was no different, but faster, because her father's mind, she could tell, was somewhere else. As the car slithered down the incline, she shivered with pleasure. Even so, she was glad when they were at the bottom of the hill at the noisy turn-around, and even gladder when they crossed the street to the market.

She liked the spicy, damp, food-and-people smell of the block-long market. She liked to walk by the stalls piled high with fruits and vegetables and listen to the men behind them call out bargains and make jokes. There were the long meat counters, too, that stretched out one after the other. And then there were all the places where you could buy coffee beans and flour and dried fruits. Today they bought dry beans, lard, rice, and a jar of apricot jam. Then they started back to Twenty-eighth Street.

They went into the house through the kitchen door. Before it had closed behind them, she heard her mother calling, "Manuel? Is that you? Come quickly, please."

Manuel dropped the groceries on the kitchen table and strode into the living room. Angela, suddenly very hungry, dug in the bag for the apricot jam.

Chapter Three

For a few minutes Angela chewed on the bread and jam in lazy contentment. Then she became aware of her parents' voices and her contentment came to an end. Something was wrong. But the sounds were too low to tell her what it was. She stuffed the last bite of bread in her mouth and went into the front hall where she could both see and hear.

Her father was standing by the front window, a square of yellow paper in his hand. He blew his nose and said, "My mother is dying, Dolores. I must go to her right away. Here, read the telegram yourself."

Dolores dropped the telegram on a chair and put her arms around him. "Ay, Manuel, I am so sorry." Then she stepped back and nodded sadly. "You will want the money I have saved."

"No, no, Dolores, that is yours. There must be another way."

"What other way, Manuel?" She left the room. In a moment she was back, a coffee can in her hand. She held it out to him.

Manuel took the can then lifted a hand to touch her cheek. "You will have every penny back, Dolores. I promise you."

"Please, Manuel," his wife said, shaking her head. "No more promises."

Her father let out his breath in a sharp gust, and Angela turned and left. The room she shared with Bonita was empty. Angela sat cross-legged on her bed, trying to understand. Her grandmother, Mamela, was dying. Dying. It was something that happened to cowboys and gangsters in the moving pictures, but that wasn't real. It happened to birds too. She remembered finding a sparrow, stiff and flattened, lying under a tree. She had dug a hole beside it and pushed it in with the toe of her shoe. But that couldn't happen to her grandmother. She was round and warm and soft. All of a sudden Angela couldn't bear to be alone.

In the kitchen she found her mother and Bonita packing a box with food. "Wash your hands, Angela," her mother said. "Wrap the tortillas in wax paper."

Alberto, his large-boned face serious under thick black hair, plowed in from the backyard and ordered, "Angela, go tell Rico to get his nose out of his books. We need him."

"Go, Angela," her mother said.

In a moment Ricardo padded through the kitchen in bare feet, slammed the back door, and went outside to help Alberto check the Ford. Angela followed. She watched as her brothers looked at the tires, counted the tools under the seat, and then, with a stick, measured the gasoline in the tank. In less than an hour her father started the Ford again and drove it away from Twenty-eighth Street.

Three days after he left for Mexico, a special delivery letter came from Manuel saying that he had arrived safely and that his mother was still alive. "...waiting for me in immaculate serenity," Dolores read from the letter. Angela wanted to know what that was, but everyone was so serious that she couldn't bring herself to ask. Besides, Tía Lupe was there.

Tía Lupe was always at their house when there was trouble. She had a round face with black hair pulled tight away from it. Curly white hairs poked out from the black, and Angela wondered how they dared not lie flat when Tía brushed them. Today Tía Lupe sipped coffee, said her rosary, and nodded all the time that Dolores was reading. The letter reminded Angela of her unanswered questions. Ricardo could answer them...if he wanted to.

Ricardo was reading in his favorite corner of the front porch, almost hidden by the rocker. Angela hesitated behind the screen door, listening to the quiet sounds her brother made: the rubbed whispers of the pages he turned; a grunt, a mumbled comment; the creak of the floorboards as he stretched and sat again. Finally, she pulled open the door. "Ricardo," she said, "I want to know something. What's a greaser?"

His head shot around the rocker. "Where'd you hear that?"

She told him about the boys.

He scowled at her. "Don't pay them mind when people call you names, Angela. And don't run!" A strand of hair fell over his eyes and he pushed it away angrily. "It doesn't do any good. Anyway, most times there's no place to run to."

"All right. But what's a greaser?"

Ricardo turned and glared out at the street with such intentness that Angela peered over the shrubbery to see what he was looking at. All that she saw was a man putting a "For Sale" sign on a seedy apartment building directly across the street. Finally, Ricardo let out his breath and said, "That's just a lousy word dumb people use for 'Mexican.' Probably means you're big and fat from all the grease you're supposed to eat. Dumb. Really dumb. Look at you. Skinny. Don't even fit in your clothes." He picked up a book. "Okay, now. Go away."

❦

One week after her father left, Angela was awakened in the middle of the night by a whirring, squealing sound. When she recognized the sound of the front doorbell, she sat up. She slid out of bed and opened her bedroom door in time to see her mother going down the hall in a long white nightgown. Alberto was buttoning up his pants as he followed her, and behind him came Ricardo.

Angela felt Bonita's breath on the back of her neck. "What's wrong?" her sister whispered.

"How do I know? Sh-h-h."

They heard the front door open and close. Across the dim length of the hall, Angela saw her mother hand a yellow envelope to Alberto. "Read it to me," she said in a shaky voice.

Alberto tore open the envelope. "It is from father. Mamela died today."

Angela closed the door and the two girls got into their beds. They were silent for a while and then Bonita whispered, "We'll never see her again."

"How do you know?"

"Because... because..."

"Because you don't know," Angela said. "Anyway, Papá will be coming home soon."

"Not for a long, long time," Bonita said smugly. "He's gotta stay for the funeral and at least a million other things." She turned in her bed and tugged at the blankets. Within minutes she was making the fluttering little noises that meant she was asleep.

Angela couldn't sleep. There were restless rustlings beneath her window and the light from the lamppost threw unfamiliar shadows into the dark corners of her room. She listened to the soft murmur of voices coming from the kitchen where her brothers and her mother were talking. She was still awake when the voices stopped. Then the floor creaked as Ricardo walked down the hall. The window in his room groaned as he lowered it, and the springs of his bed squeaked. Now the night had comfortable sounds. She slid under her blanket and closed her eyes.

When she awakened the next morning, it was raining. Her father had said that it rarely rained in June, but that if it did this year, it would be a good thing for their vegetable garden. Angela stared out the window at the big drops falling and wished that the garden was growing today.

Her father had started it in May, a few days after he lost his job in the dairy. She had helped him pace off a plot in the space between the sunflowers by the garage and the side fence. After he marked off a rectangle of "sufficient size," her father had leaned against the incinerator and described how the garden would be. Rows of corn and string beans near the fence; squash "near the edge, so that it can spread and embrace the incinerator"; and root vegetables near the garage. But that had been a month ago. Today, her father was still gone and the garden wasn't planted.

It rained again the following day. For two more days the sky was cloudy, and on the fourth, Angela awakened to a morning that was bright and sunny.

As she dressed, a bird whistled on the lamppost outside her window. She whistled, too, short, breath-filled notes. Bonita groaned and buried her head in her pillow. And then Angela stopped whistling and laughed out loud. Now all the

morning noises, the clinks and clangs of dishes and pans, the
footsteps, the whispers, and the whine of the hinges on the
bathroom door, became a part of the bird's song. She had
heard a car in the night. Her father was home!

She ran barefoot into the kitchen. Her mother was pouring coffee at the stove. Ricardo was sitting at the table.

"Where's Papá?" Angela asked.

Ricardo glared at her over a bowl of oatmeal. "Be quiet!
I'm talking to Mamá." He swung around toward the stove.
"The message is from Señor Padilla. It could be about work.
We should tell him right away."

Dolores sighed as she placed the steaming cup by Ricardo.
"He is sleeping, son, and he is tired. I cannot be so unkind."

Angela pursed her lips. The crying look. There would be
no use in arguing with that. She was going to have to go to
school without seeing her father.

It was a long day at school, but finally the last bell rang
and Angela raced home. In the kitchen, she dropped her
papers on the table and brushed a kiss across her mother's
cheek. "Where is he?"

"You haven't spoken to Tía Lupe," Dolores said.

"Go, go," Tía Lupe said kindly. "Your father is outside."

Dolores gave Angela a warning look. "Your father is tired,"
she said. "Don't ask him foolish questions."

Angela nodded and rushed out the back door. At the end
of the yard a large square of ground had been turned over and
her father was standing in the center of it, a shovel in his
hand. She ran to him and threw her arms around him. He
looked the same and he felt the same, and she was so glad
that she choked when she said, "You're back! All the way from
Mexico!"

He grinned. "Yes, I'm back. All the way from Guaymas—
which isn't that far away. Now, tell me. Have you been a good
girl?"

"Yes-s-s." She could think of nothing else to say. He had
been on a strange and frightening errand, one that had begun
with a torn yellow envelope, one that she still didn't understand. She looked down at the ground and then up at her

"Papá," she asked, "what is it to die?"

He rubbed the back of his neck as he leaned the shovel on the garage wall. Then he sat on a pile of bricks. "*Ven, Angelita*," he said. She sat on the ground beside him and he squeezed her shoulder. "To die, little one, is to sleep forever."

"But won't Mamela ever wake up?"

"Never."

"Oh. That's bad."

"It is neither bad nor good," he said. "It is simply the way that it is."

"But where is Mamela? Will you ever see her again?"

"I don't really know," he said, and dropped his hands between his knees. "I will miss her. But the real sadness is not in what I will miss, but that my mother will no longer enjoy the old rooster that crows by her window or the sunflowers that grow by the side of her house."

Angela looked to where their sunflowers were growing and a terrible fear filled her. "Papá," she whispered, "you won't ever leave me, will you?"

He smiled down at her. "You tell me. Am I not always in your heart?"

She nodded.

"Well, then, I will always be with you, no? And how could it be otherwise?"

She rubbed her hand across the roughness of his pants' leg. He was here, close beside her, and that's where he would always be. He had promised.

At one moment she was sitting on the ground and in the next her father was pulling her up and they were dancing. Around and around the backyard he twirled her, whistling a tune.

A hummingbird, exploring the honeysuckle on the back fence, flew to the garage roof, perched there for a moment, and then returned to the vine. The cat, Don Juan, napping on the back steps, opened one eye, yawned, and closed it again.

When they stopped, Angela was breathless. "What was that?" she gasped, meaning the song.

"That, my girl, was a happy waltz. Because one should not dwell on sad things." Her father reached for the shovel. "Besides, we are all together again."

Chapter Four

On the San Diego Freeway that April afternoon, Angela Raine was approaching the Los Angeles Harbor Junction. The broad highway, a stone wall dividing its two-way traffic, curved sharply to the east, and in a few minutes she passed the turn-off. From here to Signal Hill the outlines and billowing exhaust of electric power plants and oil refineries dominated the skyline and the air. This was the stretch of freeway that Walt disliked so much.

She flipped on the radio. The speakers poured out a Strauss waltz. It was familiar and sweet—and troubling. Troubling because she was thinking of Walt again. A younger Walt at a younger, lighter time of their lives. She had been twenty when they were married...

Walt and she were bubbling with excitement and a little bit silly on the day they got their marriage license, but as Walt brought the car to a stop in front of the house on Twenty-eighth Street, they both became more sober.

The late spring sun was high in a clear sky and fell pitilessly on the house, illuminating the deteriorated green siding and the dipping porch steps. Angela looked at the house with the eyes of a stranger, acutely aware of its shabbiness. In a few more days, she thought, I will no longer live here.

"Three more days," Walt said after a short silence. "How about it, Gypsy? Sure you're not going to wish you'd waited to have a regular wedding? You know, with all the trimmings: flowers, bridesmaids, and a long white dress?"

"I love my short blue dress," Angela said. "When I got it, I figured maybe I'd be married in it. Anyway, I'm glad we're spending what money we have on a honeymoon. Even if it's only a weekend."

Walt squeezed her hand. "I am, too. Besides, blue's my favorite color."

But Angela wasn't married in blue.

Two days before her wedding she was in the kitchen show-ing the blue dress to Alberto's wife Raquela when Alberto walked in the back door. Angela turned, ready to leave the room. She didn't want to discuss her marriage to Walt with either of her brothers. They had told her that it was a serious mistake. She had refused to listen.

"Angela," Alberto called to her, "don't leave. I want to talk with you."

She faced him, wondering what was to come. "All right. What?"

Alberto looked at his wife, and Raquela nodded encourag-ingly. "It's about Saturday," he said, "the day you're going to be married." He cleared his throat. "I've been thinking about it, and I realize that since our father is not here, it's my duty to see you married."

Angela stared at him in shocked surprise. *What's going on here?*

Alberto shrugged. "I know I said I wouldn't be there, but Rico can't—he's taking that examination—and your marriage should be properly witnessed."

"If that's what you want to do, Alberto," she said, "that's fine. It will please Walt."

"Of course, Raquela will come too," Alberto said.

"Of course."

"No one else, though. Mamá isn't up to it."

"Yes, I know."

Alberto looked at the wall to one side of Angela. "Tell me," he said, "the man who is marrying you. Is he a minister?"

"Yes, Alberto," Angela said. "It may be a wedding chapel, not a church, but the man is a real minister."

"Well, then, it's settled." He glanced at the dress draped over her arm. "You're not planning to be married in that!"

"Yes." She held it up. "What's wrong with it?"

"It's...it's not white," he said, and his color rose.

"No, it's blue." She sensed what was going on in his mind: his tradition demanded to know if she was still a virgin. But they had never talked about personal things. Nor could they now. "I don't have a white dress," she said, "and I don't have the money to buy one. Why should it matter?"

Alberto dug in his pants pocket and came up with a crumpled twenty-dollar bill. He tossed it on the kitchen table. "There. Go buy a white dress."

"I can't take your money," Angela said. "You two need it."

Raquela picked up the bill and pressed it into Angela's hand. "Take it," she whispered. "It will heal his injured pride."

The twenty-dollar bill felt hot in Angela's hand as she glanced at her brother. "All right," she said. "For your sake, I'll look for another dress."

She found a white shirtwaist dress at Sears. It had a full skirt that hung softly, and the long-stemmed pink carnations that Walt brought her made a delicate contrast against it. During the ceremony, Alberto stood stiffly to one side of Walt, looking skeptical as the minister read the wedding service. Afterwards, Raquela tossed rice from a little bag that the chapel had provided. Angela kissed her warmly just before she got into the car.

Walt and she drove to a cottage on the ocean near Malibu for their short honeymoon. One night after lovemaking, Angela awakened and lay quietly, listening to the ocean below their window. It seemed to her that never again would the rhythm of the surf be the same, that its union with the sand would be changed, just as she was changed by the knowledge of Walt's body, the consuming sensation of closeness and warmth, and the acute awareness that her life was, at last, beginning.

Walt stirred beside her and she whispered, "Walt? You won't ever leave me, will you?"

He pushed up on one elbow. "God, no, Gypsy. And don't you ever try to leave me, because I won't let you go." Then, as if to make up for the intensity of his words, he kissed her softly. "I love you. Now, go to sleep."

"Um-hum," she said, but rather than sleeping, she lay awake wondering why she had asked that question. And then she stopped wondering and thought about The House. There would be a house, she was sure of that. She was sure, too, that it would be on a plot on a high hill overlooking the ocean. But what was important about The House was that it and the land would be theirs. She would own a part of America. She would be a part of America. *Oh, beautiful for spacious skies, for amber waves of grain...*

"Mrs. Walter Raine," she said softly into the ocean-filled night. "Mrs. Walter Raine." She had pressed herself against Walt, circled her arm around him, and nuzzled her face into the back of his neck.

❦

They started their lives together in a small two-bedroom apartment over a garage in West Los Angeles. Walt was completing his engineering degree at U.C.L.A. and holding down a swing-shift job at Douglas Aircraft. She was a clerk-typist in the office of a machine shop. Their days were short on time, but, with two modest incomes and no time to spend them, long on money. Angela, her eye on a well-defined future, saved and planned.

She didn't scrimp, she assured Walt, just bought wisely. On Saturdays, while he poured over his books, she poured over ads and then searched in second-hand stores for the furniture they needed. Piece by piece, their apartment was outfitted. The small second bedroom was off limits to Angela. But that was all right. She understood that it was Walt's and that it was important to their future.

That room was furnished only with a card table, an old upholstered chair, a reading lamp, and books piled against the walls and scattered on the floor. Walt spent long hours there. But once his studies were done the job offers rolled in. It wasn't just that Walt was at the top of his class, it was also that engineers were at a premium.

One day he returned home from an interview and announced, "I've made up my mind. I'm going with Garrison-Melner." He slammed the door behind him, tossed the newspaper on the couch, and kissed her.

Angela said, "Isn't that...isn't it a very *little* company?"

Walt grinned and shook his head. "Don't think of Garrison-Melner as little, Gypsy. Think of it as new. New, with a great future. The people there are exciting. They have a real feel for what's coming."

"But what about all those other places? Aren't you even going to consider them?"

"Not anymore." He gave her a steady look and then said, "Hell, Gypsy, I know what I'm doing!"

Two weeks later he began his work at Garrison-Melner and Associates.

On her way home from her job that day, Angela splurged. The bus had been crowded and hot, and she left it gratefully, walking briskly toward home. There was a light afternoon breeze blowing. It was that breeze, she told herself, that pushed her to the door of Jack's Deli. Twenty minutes later she was climbing up the steps to her own door, a paper sack filled with the makings of a celebration: cold cuts, potato salad, French bread, and champagne.

When she heard Walt come in the door, she called from the kitchen, "Hi, honey, how'd it go?" Getting no answer, she went into the living room and found him sprawled in a chair, his legs stretched out in front of him, his tie loosened, an embarrassed smile twitching his mouth.

"They think I'm spectacular," he said. "And all I did was make a couple of suggestions. Would you believe the luck? They were having a problem with something I know a little about."

Angela didn't have to ask what. Walt was already launched on an explanation, most of which she didn't understand but to which she listened patiently. They didn't open the champagne until after nine o'clock. And they were already in bed when they remembered they hadn't eaten anything but the French bread...

ও

A long blast from a horn shook Angela out of her thoughts. In the rearview mirror she saw the truck she had passed earlier following closely. She pressed on the accelerator at the same time that she glanced at the speedometer. Thirty-five miles an hour. She was crawling. If she was to get to San Diego by dark, she had better pay attention to her driving.

Less than an hour later she was passing through the
Irvine Ranch area. On her left, four or five miles beyond the
freeway, were rolling hills covered with dark green groves of
citrus trees. The same hills, maybe, that Walt and she had
driven through long before freeways had crisscrossed Orange
County. Over the years, old landmarks had disappeared.
Those that remained were pressed into new shapes by the different angles of the highway. She felt a rush of homesickness
for the old road that Walt and she had known so well.

As she watched the traffic and her speed, Angela envisioned those early years as a gleaming string of months, softly
scented and lemon-yellow. What had made them so? She
knew, of course. A glowing belief that the good part of her life
had just begun, and that it would get better and better. It was
much later that the small unrecallable erosions of her happiness had begun.

She stiffened behind the wheel. This wouldn't do. All that
was in the past. Why dredge it up? Maybe, she told herself, it's
my "troubled and unusual state of mind." That was the psy-
chological jargon she had heard earlier today from Doctor Verdon. She had told him immediately that she was there under
protest, that there was really nothing a psychiatrist could do
for her. And he nodded, and somehow she had felt he understood. Still, now she had the uncomfortable feeling that she
had made a fool of herself. He had been kind through it all,
which was small comfort. She thought of his eyes, steady
behind gold-rimmed glasses, when he had spoken of the way
an animal, after exhausting its powers to save itself from a
predator, gives in to death. Fear leaves, he had said, and an
unresisting calm takes its place.

In spite of the sun that poured through the windshield,
Angela felt chilled. Calm? What rot! She pulled at her purse
on the seat beside her, dug in it, and pressed a small green
pill into her mouth. She let the saliva gather and gulped it
down. As the road made a broad curve inland, she determined
to keep her mind on anything but herself. She scanned the
billboards, playing a guessing game. An automobile ad on that
one, and over there, the Las Vegas Hilton. The next should be
an ad for liquor. But it wasn't.

The next one was a brilliant orange billboard with the blurred outlines of a familiar face. How unreal it felt to see her brother's face staring down at her. In a month or two that sign would be peeled away. The primary elections would be over and, if the pollsters were right, Ricardo Martín would be leading the pack for State senator. As Ricardo's face drew closer, she thought uncomfortably of their meeting a couple of months before. Maybe it was too much to say that she had had a premonition, a warning of some heavy blow to come. In any case, she hadn't wanted to go to that fund raiser. Neither had Walt, for that matter. But her neighbor Maggie, in her own persuasive style, had called in a favor due her. From its beginning, the evening had held an uncomfortable note. Even as they had driven there...

❦

Walt had grimaced as he tightened his hands on the steering wheel. "I'd rather be sitting in my chair at home," he said. "Preferably in my robe and slippers."

Angela threw him a look and said, "I'm sure you would." Behind a book or a newspaper, she thought. That way you don't have to talk. She wasn't looking forward to the evening either. A buffet dinner party in the home of strangers—to accommodate Maggie who was accommodating a friend who was accommodating the reelection of Matt Hedrick for Supervisor—was not her favorite thing. Not that there were many choices. The comfortless truth was that she had few favorite things, if any. She shrugged the thought away and said, "It's a favor for Maggie. Let's make the best of it."

"Sure," Walt said, "I will. If we ever find the place. I hate the Palos Verdes Hills."

"It's Rolling Hills," Angela said quietly.

"What's the difference?" Walt let out his breath in slow exasperation and hunched over the wheel.

They made two or three wrong turns in the maze of narrow roads that wound up and around the hills, but eventually found the address for which they were searching. The house was large. Angela had expected that. It clung in four levels to the side of a terraced hill that rose high above the ocean. A red-coated attendant took their car, and they went down a short flight of stairs to an iron-grilled door.

"Good evening," a smiling bright-eyed brunette said to them from behind a small linen-covered table. "May I check off your names?"

"Yes," Walt said. "I'm Walter Raine. This is my wife Angela. We're guests of the Pauls."

"Oh, yes, Mr. Raine. Go right on in." She swung around and pointed. "The bar's under that canopy in the patio. And Supervisor Hedrick—last I heard—is holding court in the big room beyond it."

Walt gave the girl a grin, and Angela and he moved slowly through the crowd. The loudness of the talk and laughter said that the happy hour was well under way. Angela glanced at her watch. Technically, they weren't late, but it was close to the announced time for dinner.

"Get me a drink, will you, Walt?"

"That's my intent, if I can figure out how to reach the bar." He moved into the crowd, jostling his way toward the orange and white stripes of the canopy.

Angela looked around. She couldn't see Maggie in this part of the house, but in a far corner she saw Maggie's husband, Don, nodding and grinning as he listened to a gray-haired woman wearing huge dangling earrings. Angela looked for a place to wait for Walt and found one in a corner beside a pillar and a potted azalea.

She took one step toward the pillar and was bumped into from behind so sharply that she gasped. There was no apology, but suddenly a stark, white-painted face appeared from around her shoulder. Below that face was a thin man clad in a black body suit and a long bright scarf. He patted his hip, then pointed to hers and sighed. Then he pressed his hands against his cheeks and shook his head sorrowfully.

A mime. Angela grinned and said, "It's okay. No harm done."

The mime blew her a kiss then gave her a broad sweeping bow. She started for the pillar. And there he was again, in front of her now, persuading the laughing people to make way for her. He disappeared into the crowd and Angela settled back against the post to wait.

"Angela."

She turned. Standing against the wall behind the pillar, a glass in his hand, stood her brother. He was smiling softly, a warm remembered look that tugged at her heart.

Rico! "Ricardo," she whispered, and then quickly bit her lip.

"It's been a long time, Angela," he said.

"Yes, yes, I know. What are you doing here?" As she heard her words, she stiffened. *What a dumb thing to ask.*

The color in Ricardo's face heightened. "I'm here to say a few words about Matt," he said mildly. "To introduce him, actually."

Of course. Ricardo was a VIP now. Angela looked at him unsteadily, trying to find something to say. Her brother had weathered the years...more than two decades...well. He still had a full head of hair, gray now, and a few lines around his eyes, but that was all that had changed. All, except for a sharp-cut impression of strength.

Ricardo spoke. "How are you, Angela?"

"Good. And you?"

"Fine. Look, I know this isn't the time or the place for it," he said, "but seeing you has convinced me that I have to have a talk with you."

Angela looked at him in surprise. "I don't think we have anything to talk about."

"Yes, we do. At least, I do. And it's something I think you would want to know."

She shrugged. "I can't imagine what."

"Angela, Angela," Ricardo said, his tone softening once more. "I wish things were different between us, then it wouldn't..." He stopped and threw back his head as he glanced beyond her. "Someone's looking for one of us."

Angela turned. Maggie was a step or two away, pushing her way toward them. *Had she heard?*

"For heaven's sake, Angie," Maggie said breathlessly, "I've been looking all over for you." She looked from Ricardo to Angela with sharp interest and then she frowned. "Well, at least you're in good company." All at once she frowned. "Am I interrupting something? Do you two know each other?"

Angela shot Ricardo a look. He looked back and waited. She took a deep breath. "No," she said, "you're not interrupting anything. We just stumbled into the same corner."

Ricardo downed the liquid in his glass in one gulp and put the glass beside the potted plant. He edged his way by the two women. "Excuse me, please. I'm being signalled from across the room."

Angela watched him go. The floor beneath her shifted uneasily and she pressed herself against the pillar for support. *How could I have done that?*

"What is it?" Maggie said.

"Nothing. A little dizzy spell. I'll be okay."

Across the room, the mime was standing on a chair giving an impassioned but silent political speech. When he saw Ricardo approaching, he jumped down, bowed, and proceeded to roll out a red carpet for his passage. Ricardo seemed unaware of the mime's attention until the people around him applauded. Then with an abashed grin, he indicated the mime for the applause and had disappeared into the other room.

Scanning her brother's face on the billboard against the sky, Angela shuddered and thought of The Dream. When she first had it, she was barely ten. And in The Dream the faces looming down at her all belonged to her father. Later, they had belonged to a boy named Armando, to Walt, and to her brothers. Sometimes they had no features at all, but she knew they were men. In the dream, the huge faces pushed down on her, blotting out the light. As she fought for air, she felt herself shrinking and knew that she would disappear completely unless she could escape the ominous eyes and noses, the colossal mouths and towering teeth. No matter how benign the landscape of her dream, by the time she had shrunk to the size of a pin it had become a vast and airless desert. There was nowhere to go for safety and she was being pulled in by the sand. In the last few weeks, Ricardo's face had dominated her dream. And as always, he had been trying to tell her something.

Now, staring blankly at a red car in front of her, Angela shrugged off the memory. Ahead of her the road had broadened, curving to join the Santa Ana Freeway in a six-lane swath of southbound traffic. In a matter of minutes she was traveling by the Laguna hills. The hills are so green, she thought, so bursting with spring, so *young*. If she were young again... She looked away from the hills, glanced instead at a cluster of high-rise hotels that jutted sharply into the sky ahead.

Everywhere in Southern California hotels sprang up unexpectedly, bordering the highways like a new giant plant species. Ice-cube machines and instant coffee. It occurred to her that she could use a cup of coffee. But when she reached the juncture at Ortega Highway, she sped by the restaurants that marked it. She had changed her mind. She frowned, thinking it must be classic—the syndrome, that is: indecision; vacillation; talking to myself and answering back. Doctor Verdon probably has a name for this, too. But I don't want to think of him—or any other doctor. I'm tired of them. Sick and tired. And with good reason.

For the last few months she had been shuttled back and forth from one medical appointment to another, with decisions made and actions designed for her by ominous machines attended by rosy-cheeked technicians. The machines had no answers. It was a relief when seven weeks before, her internist and the surgeon, Doctor Eichar, had advised surgery. At last, she thought, someone was doing something, and she had gone to the hospital almost eagerly.

After the operation, she awakened to the blurred and gradual awareness of people and objects surrounding her. She turned her head slowly. The people wore green and floated above and around her. The objects lay immobile on wheeled carts. There were bottles and intricate tubing attached to the carts in magnificent Rube Goldberg designs.

"Wake up, Angela, wake up. It's over." The voice that cut through the layers of clouds pressing down on her was mechanical and persistent. "Wake up, Angela," it said again. "You're in the recovery room. Your surgery is finished."

The operation. Angela awakened fully for a moment. Her hand swung to the bandage that covered her abdomen. She moved it across the taut square of tape, but she could tell nothing. She would have to wait until she saw Doctor Eichar. The waiting had been long. The rest of that day and night and some of the next morning were lost to fitful sleeps and jumbled images: three faces, Walt's, Ken's, and Gloria's, appearing and disappearing; a hand with a plain wedding band shaking an IV bottle; Doctor Eichar's glasses blurring into his smile; the curtains by her bed sliding back and forth; and far, far away, a laugh track blaring behind a TV show.

But finally she was awake enough to talk to Doctor Eichar. He was standing in the doorway talking to a nurse who was plump and pink and blue-eyed under a mass of blonde curls. Now, she remembered. This was the person who had chirped, "Oh, no, not water. We'll just moisten your lips with this nice washcloth. You wouldn't want to get nauseated and vomit, now, would you," and had left her to die of thirst.

The nurse disappeared from the doorway and Doctor Eichar walked to her bedside. He was crisp and fresh in a white shirt and a gray suit that *had* to be starched to hold such sharp creases. He looked so comfortable, and she was so miserable. "How are you feeling?" he asked, his brown eyes crinkling. "Pain?"

"Only when I laugh," she said. And then, "Sorry for the lousy humor, but then I guess that's what I'm in, lousy humor."

He picked up her hand, pressing her fingernails gently. "Are you cold?"

"No. Scared. How did it go, Doctor Eichar?"

"You came through it splendidly," he said, nodding.

"Thank God!" She had been dreading this moment. The biopsy had told her it was cancer, but the surgery would tell her what she *had* to know: How good her chances were.

"Everything is fine," Doctor Eichar said. "But we're going to keep you around for a few days to make absolutely sure."

Oh, God, what did that mean? "That sounds like doubletalk," she said. "How about the facts?"

"The fact is that we think it was all contained and, in that case, Angela, you're clean. You'll have a little therapy, and that'll be it."

"If I'm so clean, why the therapy?"

"It's a routine procedure," he said, patting her hand. "Stop worrying, Angela. You worry too much."

"What if it wasn't? All contained, I mean. What then?"

"We'll cross that bridge when we come to it," he said, his brown eyes softening in a way that terrified her. *Oh, my God, he said when, not if, we come to it. I really am going to die.*

"So I'm not out of the woods yet," she said.

He looked surprised, then blank. "You're jumping to conclusions. We're simply taking things in an orderly sequence."

"You promised to tell me the truth," she said, "and you're skirting it as if it'll explode in your face. It's my face it'll explode in, remember? Tell me."

"I have."

"No games, please, Doctor Eichar." She took a deep breath and leaped into the center of her desperation. "On a scale of one to ten, ten being best, where do you rank my chances?"

He made a gesture of impatience, stared at the bedclothes, and then looked up. And she saw it in his eyes: a certainty mixed with so much kindness that she had to look away.

"That's no way to make a scientific evaluation," he said. "We do have some questions left, but the tests will answer those."

He went on talking, but she had heard enough. She turned her face to hide the tears that were dribbling from her eyes. *Not me! It can't be me! Dear God, let him be wrong.* She twisted in the bed and pain jabbed her, and she wanted to hit back. How dare they! How dare they interfere with my life! There must be something I can do to stop this! But what? Who? What can I do? She brushed the tears from her cheeks and turned to Doctor Eichar. "Have you talked to Walt?" she asked.

"He's waiting to see you." He filled a glass with water. "Here now, take your medication. You'll be more comfortable."

After he left, she closed her eyes. The usual hospital noises, the soft flap, flap of rubber-soled shoes, the rhythmic rubbing of turning wheels, the muffled voices and inconsistent clatter of metal and glass, all sounded hollow and echoing to her. She thought she was in a vast damp cave, dark and shadowy and deeply cold. She was shivering when she opened her eyes.

And Walt was there, sitting in a stiff wooden chair by her bed. "Hello, dear," he said.

She tried for a smile and said, "Doctor Eichar's been here. Don't be so gloomy. It's not all that bad, you know."

"Right," he said, and squeezed her hand. His chair creaked as he leaned back.

He stayed by her bedside for a long time. She sensed his presence even through the fuzzy cocoon of her sedation. After a while she realized that Ken was there too. He was leaning against the wall behind Walt, arms crossed, staring at the ceiling. Her eyes were heavy, but through the spidery lace of her lashes, she watched her men. And she knew that if she was near enough, they would both smell of a spicy after-shave. The thought annoyed her. She wanted to nestle the young man with the worn face against her breast and smell sun and sweat and dust on his head as she had when he was a little boy.

The bedclothes rustled softly as she rolled toward them. "Hello, Ken," she said.

"How are you feeling, Mom?"

"I'm not feeling much, but I probably will later." She looked him up and down. "You look good, son."

"My new job agrees with me."

"Yes," she said, "yes. Is your sister..."

"Gloria's having something to eat. She should be here any minute."

And then there she was, standing in the doorway, her hands pushed into the pockets of her jeans. The striped knit shirt she wore was loose on her tiny frame. A large leather bag hung from her sloping shoulders. She hesitated for an instant, a question on her face, and then said, "Hi, mother. God, what lousy food they have in this hospital. Hope you fare better." She continued to the foot of the bed. "I'm next in line to get near you once the men move out of the way."

Walt stood up. "Honey," he said, smiling, "any time you wear a pair of shoes, you command my respect. Here, take my chair."

"Or my wall," Ken said, and moved to the door with his father.

Gloria edged along the bed to the chair and angled it so that she could look directly into her mother's eyes. "You're going to be fine, Mom," she said. And then with a grin, "Maggie's been spreading the good news."

"Leave it to Maggie," Angela said. "The eternal optimist."

"Oh, c'mon, Mom. You're going to be fine."

"That's what Doctor Eichar says," Angela said, and closed her eyes.

When she opened them, she realized that she had fallen asleep. Gloria was gone, but Walt was there. He kissed her on the forehead and said, "Rest now. You need to rest. I'll be back soon."

She watched him walk out the door, a dejected Walt, crumpled, just like his blue suit. Funny. Walt's always so neat. She looked away from the empty doorway. Beside her bed was a bowl of yellow daisies. "Aren't these pretty," the curly blonde nurse had said. "From your husband. And do you want some cold, cold ginger ale to sip now? Slowly, though, you wouldn't want to throw up again." The daisies became a yellow blurr as she stared at them. He loves me, he loves me not, he... What did it matter? She was going to die. And soon. The daisies melted like butter and dribbled down the bedside stand; her pillowcase was wet. She covered her face with her hands.

On the fourth day of her hospital stay, Angela was ready to go home. Maybe there her crazy dreams would disappear. Besides, flower-filled rooms depressed her. On the ledge of the window, three baskets of spring flowers crowded one against the other, and on the night stand, daffodils had replaced the daisies. She would ask someone to take them away. She pushed up on the pillow, staring at the doorway, inviting someone to come in. And when someone did, it was Doctor Eichar.

"Well, good morning, Angela." He scanned her face. "You look good today."

"That's nice. But am I good? Really? Inside where it counts?"

"Everything's good. I told you it would be. What are you doing? Worrying again?"

"Why not? There's nothing better to do." She looked fixedly into his eyes, but he turned his head aside and spoke to the nurse.

"Shall we tell her?" He turned back to Angela and patted her arm. "We're letting you go. Tomorrow."

"That's great," she said, and her voice broke. There had been a gentleness to the touch on her arm that frightened her. Had he told her everything? She had to know. True, Doctor Eichar had answered all her questions. So why did it seem to her that something had been left unsaid?

❦

Angela told herself that she should be recovering more rapidly. It was two weeks since her return from the hospital, and the energy she was used to calling on had disappeared. Her strength was returning, she sensed that. She moved more easily and more quickly, but she had lost spontaneity. Each movement required a mandate from her mind. She spent a great deal of time lying on a wicker chaise longue under her elm tree.

This afternoon, the late March weather was summerlike and her walled patio should have been a haven. But Angela felt anything but protected. She put aside the book she was attempting to read and swung her feet to the ground.

Slipping off her sandals, she rubbed her bare feet across the grass. Nothing was more comforting than its cool touch, or the steady hum of an airplane above her, or the perfume of the flowering shrub beside her. They reassured her that she was still alive. But for how much longer? She wriggled her toes in the soft blades of grass. How much time do I have? Suddenly there was urgency to her thought. Time. I need time. And then, no, it's not a matter of time. It's a matter of...it's... There is something that I have to do. Yes, yes! *But what?*

"Hey!" The call shook Angela out of her thoughts. Maggie was across the yard, the gate closing slowly behind her. "Is something the matter?" she said as she dropped on the grass near Angela.

"Not really, Maggie. Why?"

"Because you jumped a foot when I called. You're as quivery as a quarter horse."

Angela smiled at her friend. "Whatever that is."

"Doesn't matter. You know what I mean. There's something important going on in your mind. What is it?"

"I don't know."

"*You?* I don't believe it. I can always count on you to know just where you are and what your next step is going to be." Maggie studied her for a moment. "But something *is* bugging you. Tell me about it, Angie."

Angela stared at the grass at her feet. Ricardo's face, grim as it had been two months before, and the sorrowful mime's swung there crazily. But it was more than her last meeting with Ricardo. A lot more. She sighed and finally glanced up at her friend. "Have you ever regretted something so much, Maggie, that it weighs down every step you take? So much that you have trouble sleeping? And you have to sleep, because being awake is the nightmare."

"Angie, come on. What do you have to regret that could be that bad? What could *be* that bad? A vicious murder, I suppose. Or maybe betraying your country." She grinned. "Have you been selling secrets to the Russians?"

"No," Angela answered absently. And then suddenly, "I guess I'm just blabbering. Anyway, I don't know what I can do about it."

"For God's sake, Angie, *what?* What are you talking about?"

Angela turned her eyes away. This woman across from her, an old friend with whom she had shared many confidences, would listen without argument if she could tell her more. But she couldn't talk about it. "I'm sorry, Maggie," she said. "Maybe later."

After Maggie left, Angela stayed in the patio. My life has been a fraud, she thought. A mockery. *My God, why did I do it?*

She got up and walked quickly to the end of the wall. Her hands were clammy. "They're gone," she muttered. "It's too late. Too late for all of us." And then, as if the certainty had always been there, she knew what she would do.

Her heart raced as she returned to the garden chair. Her lips were dry. She ran her tongue over them and shook her head. She was crazy, she told herself. This was where she belonged, not somewhere far from Walt and the kids. You can't do it, she argued. Yes, I can. But it will seem bizarre to everyone. That doesn't matter. In the marrow of my bones, deep where I really live, I know it's right. She rose once more and walked steadily toward the house. It was clear at last. She had to make amends.

A day or so later she told Walt that she was going and where, and he had looked at her incredulously.

Chapter Five

The summer of the fruit picking was also the summer of the vegetable garden.

Although she was the youngest in the family, there were some things that Angela understood well. She understood, no matter what Tía Lupe said, that almost nine was not really very old; that some of the laughter had gone from her father's eyes; and that she didn't know what to do about it. She also understood that the vegetable garden had become important to everyone.

Her mother said that she looked forward to rich red tomatoes, leaf lettuce, and beets "to pick young and serve cold with lemon juice" as Lucinda, her cook, had prepared them in Mexico. Alberto helped move the piles of bricks so that the garden could be larger and without grumbling too much turned over some of the earth. Later that same day he told his friend, Gordo Ramos, that the garden was his idea. Bonita bragged to her friends that she was going to have a real farm in her back yard. Ricardo brought home little packets of vegetable seeds and discussed them with his father. The garden was most of all important to Manuel because it gave him something to do. Angela understood that, too. Every morning her father drove off to look for a job. Every noon he came home without having found one. Every afternoon he weeded and hoed.

In the first week of July, a miracle occurred in the vegetable garden. Green shoots thrust through the earth. The seeds were reaching for the sun! And the tomato plants that Ricardo had set in the ground early in the spring were doubled over under the weight of their fruit.

Other miracles occurred on Twenty-eighth Street. One morning Alberto looked closely in the mirror, rubbed his face approvingly, and reached for his father's razor. Miss Todd, the librarian, gave Ricardo five books. And Bonita stopped demanding that Angela wait and walk with her wherever they went.

For a few days Angela was glad. Then she became curious. When she discovered that what Bonita wanted was to walk home from school with the older boys, she felt deserted. That day when Angela got home, she went straight to the vegetable garden. She needed to be with her father.

He was kneeling on the ground, staking up the tomato plants. She knelt beside him. She said, "I'm home." And then, "Look, Papá! Look right there!"

Her father grinned and lifted a thick green worm from a branch, dropping it on the ground. "Is he not a pretty one? More like a dragon, no?"

She shrugged and said to herself that he was just a worm.

Her father crushed the tomato worm and covered it with a clod of moist earth. "It is sad to kill such handsome creatures," he said," but they will eat our fruit before it has had a chance to ripen." He wiped his forehead on his arm and turned to look at her. "You and your sister must take care of this garden for a while, Angelita."

"*Us*? Why?"

"Because your brothers and I will be going away in the morning, and someone must water and weed and watch over the seedlings."

"*Going away*? Why?"

"Patience, patience. I will tell you."

"But why can't *we* go?"

"Because this is business for men only."

"But I want to go."

"Impossible," he said sharply. "The work is too hard. I won't take my wife and daughters, no matter what other men do." He turned away from her then, bending over another tomato plant.

Angela felt tears fill her eyes. "When are you coming back?" she asked.

"Before the summer is over."

"*All that time*, Papá?"

He frowned and adjusted a twig, but said nothing.

"But where are you going? And what are you going to do?"

Now he raised his head and smiled at her. "Your brothers and I are going to pick fruit. We will travel over the mountains to a town called Fresno. There we will be told which orchards we are to pick. Perhaps it will be walnuts, or pears, or maybe peaches."

"Bonita and I could pick peaches. We're..."

"Angela!" he said loudly. "You will remain here." Then he patted her head and spoke more softly. "You are not old enough to go."

But I'm strong, she said to herself. I'm very strong. It isn't fair.

Manuel wiped his hands on his pants' leg and stood up. "Go look for Bonita while I talk with your mother."

She nodded sadly. The idea of his returning before he had even gone was unreal. The idea of the empty summer was not.

Manuel climbed the back steps thoughtfully. Angela was not the only one who needed to be reassured.

He found Dolores seated at the dining table, socks piled high around her sewing basket. As the July sun filtered through the starched white curtains and shone on her hair, it seemed to him that she sparkled like a crystal. He was married to a woman who was industrious, immaculate, and still beautiful after bearing his four children. Could he ask for more? She looked up as he walked in.

"It isn't right to separate us," she said as if continuing a conversation. "Even waiting in line for soup is better than that."

"No, Dolores. We will not beg." What was happening to her? She had never contradicted him this way before. Still, he must be patient. Even to suggest the bread lines showed her desperation. How would Dolores, who was so dependent, manage without him and the boys?

The girl he had first seen seventeen years before in the plaza of Guaymas was a flower, a lily, slight and willowy, grown in a sheltered garden. "*Amigo*," he had said on that day to his good friend, "I swear to you as your name is Ramón Salgado, that there goes the girl I will marry." He had succeeded in overcoming obstacles to make his prediction come true. He persuaded Dolores' concerned father that he would provide well for his daughter. He had tried, yes, to cherish and protect and provide, but life had presented him with a revolution in Mexico and a great depression in the United States that had brought him to this day.

He rubbed his chin. How could he convince her? "It is time that Alberto and Ricardo learn more about a man's world," he said. The frown deepened on her face. He pulled a chair close to hers. "Come, Dolores, a little smile," he said, rubbing her knee. "I will bring you a pretty nightgown, one with flowers around the neck. A little smile?"

"No, no, Manuel, do not play."

For a moment he felt anger, but only for a moment. Perhaps she was right. This was not the time for foolishness. This was the time for a common-sense argument. "If we are to eat, Dolores," he said slowly and deliberately, "the boys and I must go. Still, you can be comforted by this: there will be no question about our pay. Padilla tells me that Señor Kirk owns many ranches above Fresno. He is a wealthy man, a man of much influence. And there is this. Padilla tells me that the yield of fruits and vegetables is the heaviest in years. Not only will we have money, but we will help save the harvest. You see, Dolores, this is a matter of great importance."

Dolores nodded as she rummaged in the sewing basket. "As you say," she said, and slid the darning egg into another sock.

Manuel sat back, and she looked up and smiled nervously at him. He wanted to reach out and pat her hand but held back. I'm talking to myself as much as I am to her, he thought. Of course I want to ease her, but I also want that for myself. Yes, he was trying to convince himself that good fortune had led him to Padilla that day in the Plaza. And later, when Padilla had explained proudly that he was a crew leader and assured him that the summer would be a good one for all, he had not hesitated to accept jobs for himself and the boys. Eighteen cents an hour for him and twelve for Alberto and Ricardo. One-hundred dollars in two months. How could a man in good conscience refuse such an offer? He got up. There was more that he should say, but it had all been said before.

Dolores would have to forget her notions about "suitable work" and be grateful for what he had.

She was silent as he rose, but when he turned to leave, she mumbled, "How can you trust that man? He has such a smell about him and a way of not looking straight at one that..."

Manuel slammed the table with his hand. "I will hear no more!" He heard her draw in her breath at the same moment that he saw Alberto and Ricardo. They were standing in the doorway looking at him in surprise. He felt his face grow hot. Dolores should not dispute his judgment. And not before his sons. He walked into the kitchen and to the back-porch door where he stood hands in pockets staring at Angela who was still sitting in the garden where he had left her. She had not made a move to find Bonita.

How different those two girls were. Bonita would be upset about his leaving, yes, but her disappointment would be short-lived. Her interest would be diverted quickly. All it would take would be the radio, a magazine, or the chatter of the little girls who, like a covey of quail, often landed on their front porch calling for her. On the other hand, Angela would work with her concern. It would stay with her as a brain-teasing puzzle does, annoying and frustrating her. And Dolores, who so easily "drowned in a glass of water," would not be able to help her.

Now Manuel's eye was caught by a movement near the pepper tree. Their neighbor Rosa, in a bright yellow dress, was leaning over the wooden fence. She tossed a wad of paper at Angela, and when Angela looked up, smiled.

"*Hola*, kiddo," she said. "Your sad face is making me unhappy. Come here. I have something in my hand to make you smile."

Angela ran to Rosa.

Manuel nodded slowly and turned away from the door. Now there was a woman who wouldn't drown even if an ocean engulfed her. He grinned. *No hay duda.* No doubt about it, Rosa is a woman who uses what she has.

That night Dolores ironed and mended and rolled the men's clothes into tight bundles. Bonita and Angela went to bed sulking because they were being left behind.

During the night the fog rolled in. It hovered close to the earth, clinging to rooftops and treetops, window ledges and leaves, until the moisture that built up on them spilled over drop by drop, interrupting the rhythmic breathing of the night with its uneven patter.

Angela heard the drops and was instantly awake, but she stayed in bed until she heard her parents get up. Then she went into the kitchen and watched the preparations for breakfast and listened to the pieces of advice her father kept listing for Bonita and her.

Dolores set out the dishes, served the cereal, poured the coffee, picked up the dishes and rinsed them, all automatically. Angela kept looking for the crying look, but it wasn't there. Her mother seemed to be wearing a mask with a painted-on smile and dark hollows for eyes.

Then it was time to go out on the porch and wait for Padilla and his truck. "It is only because Señor Padilla is my friend that we have this convenience," Manuel said. "The others will be waiting for him at the Plaza."

The screen door slammed as Alberto and Ricardo came out. They dropped two large bundles on the porch floor. Alberto put his arms around his mother.

"You are not to worry," he said. "We know what we're doing."

The smile on Dolores' mask trembled a little as she kissed him. Then she hugged Ricardo. "Take care of yourself. It will be a long, hard summer."

"I know." Ricardo's face was somber. "Yes...I...I know."

The boys said goodbye to their sisters and carried their bundles out to the curb.

Manuel talked quietly with Dolores. Then he put his arms around Bonita and Angela and said, "I'm counting on you both. Help your mother all you can."

That was when a creaking flatbed truck rumbled up and stopped. Señor Padilla jumped to the sidewalk and hurried to the porch, his hand outstretched. "*Bueno*, Martín. So these are your sons."

Manuel said yes and quickly introduced Dolores, who only nodded. When the handshaking was over, Padilla pointed to the bundles and said, "Load them quickly. We must hurry. We have the Ridge Route to worry about and the truck will be heavy. Let's get an early start."

Alberto and Ricardo yelled goodbye again and scrambled onto the bed of the truck. Manuel got into the cab beside Padilla.

Angela pressed close to her mother and watched until the truck had vanished. "Mamá," she complained, "the summer is so long."

"They will return, God willing."

Angela heard something in her mother's voice that she didn't like. When Don Juan, the cat, rubbed against her legs and meowed for attention, she shoved him away. Almost immediately she bent down and picked him up. "I'm sorry," she whispered, and pushed her face into his warm fur.

Chapter Six

The Ridge Route to Bakersfield which had concerned Pablo Padilla had a notorious reputation. It was a mountain road that gave no respite, except for a moment at the summit before the start of a new ordeal. It was a thrill ride carved into three ranges of mountains. The mountains themselves had forced the abrupt curves on those who cut into their sides. They had resisted with unexpected pockets of unyielding rock and hidden caches of sand that shifted underneath the road-building equipment. But the Ridge Route was the main connection between Los Angeles and the Central Valley, and hundreds of cars struggled from the south to its summit to be faced with "The Grapevine," a downgrade on which automobiles careened dangerously and heavy trucks often lost control.

As they rode to the Plaza, Manuel was thinking of the Ridge Route, especially of The Grapevine. He had heard many stories, some of them even believable, about the horrors that happened there. *Basta*, he thought. Enough. One does not need to add to the error of having listened by dwelling on the stories.

Nearing the Plaza, Padilla muttered, "It is already hot and we're late.

Manuel shot a glance at him. The morning was just starting, six-thirty at the most, and the sun, hidden by the buildings to the east, had only a promise of heat.

They circled the Plaza and parked under the same tree where Manuel had met Padilla on that June Monday. Manuel climbed into the back of the truck with his sons, and by the time all the members of the crew had shown up, he understood Padilla's worry. There were over twenty men and women crowded on the splintering flatbed floor when the truck groaned its way up Sunset Boulevard. In spite of that, Manuel felt ease of mind. It flowed through him, soothing like a steaming cup of Dolores' beef broth on a cold day. It will be all right, he said to himself. Padilla is a man to be trusted where his own interests are concerned, and it is his body behind the wheel. He sat back and relaxed.

Directly across from him a thin young man tuned a guitar while a girl with a round black eyes crowded close against him, as if to hide her pregnant belly. The young couple caught his eye and smiled, the girl hesitantly. Manuel thought, Dolores had that shy look, too. She had been like a doe, cornered, looking for escape, when her time came with Alberto. And when the boy was born and the midwife gone, together they had been like children, awkward and clumsy, struck by fear and wonderment. Now, quickly, he turned his look to others in the truck, afraid that those round black eyes might have read his mind. But of course not. He listened now to Alberto, who was talking loudly to the man at his side.

"*Sí, señor*, I attend school. So does my brother. My father sees to that." He grinned and threw a glance over his shoulder at Manuel. "But I've had enough learning. I may be through with school."

"We shall see," Manuel muttered, and nudged Alberto in the ribs. It was true that at fifteen Alberto did not look like a schoolboy. He looked like a seasoned man. His bones were large and his frame sturdy. Only a close look into his eyes or along the line of his chin showed a boyish softness, and that would soon be gone. Manuel glanced at Ricardo. That one was still a child. He needed to ripen. The problem with Rico, Manuel thought, is that he is always huddled over books. Yes, the summer will be good for him. The decision I made in the Plaza will be a good one for all of us.

In an hour they were driving through the San Fernando Valley. Here and there in clusters of trees were small neat houses. When Manuel saw vegetable gardens alongside some of them, he thought of home. Somehow he had to come up with a comfortable untroubled existence for Dolores, and the children, of course. No more causes to champion. Instead, what he needed were some acres of land to plant in beets. Sugar beets. A good crop for a new rancher. "Look at the green fields," he said to the boys. "See how irrigation has made a garden of this place."

At Castaic they said goodbye to the flat lap of the San Fernando Valley and began a slow climb. They were at the Ridge Route. The rolling hills on either side of the road were covered with dry grasses and dark green clumps of scrub oak. Far on the higher ridges Manuel saw pines, and he longed for their cool shade. The sun suddenly was not only fierce, but almost inescapable. Alberto untied his bedroll and Ricardo helped him to string up a blanket to shade them. Others did the same.

The man with the guitar, who introduced himself as Carlos Vasquez, played a few chords. In a few moments Conchita, his wife, began to sing in a thin, childish voice. Manuel grinned and nodded with pleasure...and something like pride. Where, he asked himself, could you gather together five or six Mexicans that there was not a guitar and singing?

> *"Cuatro milpas tan sola han quedado
> en el rancho que era mío, ay-y-y..."*

Conchita's voice was sweet; the lament seemed real. Soon there were seven or eight singing with her.

> *"...Y aquella casita, tan blanca y bonita
> lo triste que esta-a-a-a..."*

They had all joined in now. The crowding and the heat were forgotten. They sang two or three more songs, and then the truck came to a sudden stop, jarring the singers into silence.

Padilla shouted at them through the broken rear window. "Everyone off! The radiator is boiling!"

It was plain to Manuel that it was fear, not respect, that pushed them all into action. They were somewhere below the summit and the truck jutted out from the rocky wall of the mountain. At this point the road curved along a narrow ridge, and a descending car would have no warning that a truck was there. In seconds, they had all scrambled off the flat bed and pressed themselves against the side of the hill.

Padilla beckoned to Alberto and Ricardo. Manuel nodded his approval when Padilla sent them back down the road they had traveled to alert oncoming cars. He sent a young man called Lalo ahead of the truck to do the same.

For a while there was silence and then muscles relaxed and talk began. A few endured the full blast of the sun to inspect the countryside from the edge of the road. A few sang again. Padilla sat on the ground at a distance from the others and smoked. The cars that passed them in the hour that followed did so carefully; the three boys were doing their jobs. In that hour the radiator had cooled enough to be filled with water, and when that was done, Padilla leaned on the horn and the boys returned.

When they started to climb into the truck, he stopped them. "We're not going to load up that truck again," he said. "You saw what happened. You're all going to walk to the top of the grade." He pulled himself into the cab.

"Padilla!" Carlos shouted. "My wife shouldn't have to climb in this heat!"

"What? What? Wasn't it you who said no special favors?"

Conchita pulled at her husband's arm. "I will be fine. I am strong as a...a...I am very strong."

Carlos shook his head. "*Bueno, hombre*. What kind of a favor is this? She weighs nothing, even now."

Padilla leaned across the passenger's seat and threw open the door. "Get in, Conchita. The rest of you, move! Move!"

It was a sullen, sweating bunch that reached the waiting truck on the road's high point. Conchita was sitting on a flat rock, her skirt spread out around her. When she saw them, she ran to meet Carlos. Padilla took a last drag on a cigarette, flipped it into the road, and stood up.

Ricardo sank to the ground in the shade of the truck. Alberto dropped next to him, and the dust rose in a yellow fog above them. Ricardo lay with his eyes closed, his breathing shallow and quick. There were damp ringlets on his forehead. Manuel raised his hand to smooth them away, but stopped in midair. Instead he reached for his canteen. They each took a swallow of water, then pulled themselves onto the truck.

Manuel leaned against the sideboards and grasped his bent knees. When he heard the engine start, he straightened up and slapped Ricardo's thigh. "The worst is over," he said, but his voice was unconvincing. The Grapevine came next.

After the first turn, the road dropped sharply. As they started the descent, everyone was silent. In that silence Manuel imagined that he heard the scream of rubber on asphalt as the wheels of runaway trucks turned faster and faster, hurtling into the horror of end-over-end falls into the canyon. He shook his head to erase the picture in his mind and forced himself to look at the woman seated across from him.

She was brown as cinnamon and shapeless in a faded blue dress from which the sleeves had been torn with an obvious concern for comfort, not form. She dug in her pocket and brought out the black beads of her rosary. Her hands moved along the beads with trembling fingers. Manuel looked away.

"Padilla is a careful man," he whispered to his sons. "He will take no chances." Then, with an enthusiasm he did not feel, he pointed into the ravine. "Look there on the hillside. See the clusters of wild grapes?"

Although the stakes and the sideboards that fenced the truck bed creaked loudly and the tires squealed as they swerved down and around the steep curves, the truck held the road. It seemed to Manuel that the loosening of muscles as they reached the flat land was almost visible, like a ripple.

The woman with the rosary whispered something to the man beside her and he whooped, *"¡Es la verdad!"* And whatever it was that was true was also funny because they both burst into gusts of laughter.

Conchita smiled up at Carlos and he patted her hand. She leaned on his shoulder and within minutes she was asleep, her head slipping along his arm to his lap. He shaded her face with an old grass hat.

Chapter Seven

With The Grapevine left behind, Pablo Padilla's old truck rattled comfortably on the gradual downslope as it headed toward the town of Bakersfield. Continuing north to Delano, State Highway 99 traveled through vineyards that were green and heavy with clusters of grapes. Padilla relaxed at the wheel, his arm stretched loosely across the back of the seat.

In the bed of the truck, most of the workers slept. The young ones, Ricardo, Alberto, and the boy called Lalo, kept up a monotone of conversation. The woman in the blue dress snored contentedly while Manuel dreamed fitfully, half-asleep, half-awake, as he tried to watch a card game going on beside him.

At twilight they made camp under cottonwood trees by a dry stream bed. Padilla settled himself under a tree apart from the others, pulled out a battered pack of Chesterfields from his shirt pocket, and lit one. Manuel and his sons ate from the box of food Dolores and the girls had packed for them. When he was through, Manuel walked over and sat on the ground beside Padilla.

"You have traveled this road many times, eh?" Manuel asked. When Padilla said nothing, he added, "The truck did well today, no?"

"It is good enough." Padilla took a deep pull on his cigarette and exhaled smoke through his nostrils.

"It was a tiring trip," Manuel said.

"You are tired, eh?" Padilla responded.

"Who is not? For myself, I don't mind. But I am sorry for that little Conchita Vasquez."

Padilla thumped him on the back. "Martín, Martín, stop worrying about others. In any case, tomorrow we will be in camp and you will all sleep on mattresses."

"A mattress would be good," Manuel said. "Tonight, however, I could sleep on a plot of rocks."

It was not on rocks that the crop laborers made their beds
that night, but on dry hard earth. Except for awakening once
or twice—his mind's response to his body's discomfort—
Manuel slept soundly, his two sons stretched out at his feet.

They broke camp at dawn and drove on roads which cut
across miles of field crops: first, cotton, then sugar beets.
Later in the day the highway was bordered by orchards of
fruit trees.

"It is as I have told you, my sons. The *norteamericanos* are
skilled. This land, too, has been made rich by irrigation. Some
day I hope to be a part of this." He swung his arm in a broad
arc. Then he told them of his dream. "Sugar beets. They are in
demand, so our farm would be sure to prosper. And if we grew
too fast, I would send for Ramón." With any kind of problem it
would be a good thing to have his old friend near at hand.
Ramón Salgado said of himself that he was a simple man with
little or no understanding of things beyond his trivial experience. But Manuel knew Ramón's simplicity for what it really
was: an ability to look at one thing at a time with all of his
attention committed and focused. "Yes," Manuel said to his
sons, "it will be a good thing to have Ramón with us."

Late that afternoon they pulled into a dusty clearing, a
widening of a dirt road on which they had been traveling for
some time. The road, it seemed, had ended. Before the truck
had come to a complete stop, the men jumped to the ground.
"Here is the camp," Padilla said.

Manuel looked around expectantly. They were in a small
bowl, its sides a series of rock-strewn hills. The open space in
which the truck finally came to a stop was almost filled by two
wood-frame tents made of faded green canvas. A sultry breeze
was blowing, and shreds of the rotting canvas slapped softly
against the torn screening beneath them. Beyond the tents,
several dry trees clustered close to the base of a hill. On the
earth around them was strewn the garbage of other crews:
rusty cans, dank papers, decaying rags. And flies. They glistened over the garbage, humming like honeybees around a
hive.

Manuel strode to the nearest tent and pulled back the
flap. A rancid smell slapped him, filling his nostrils and his

mouth. He felt his stomach knot as he swung around and spat. Then he looked again. Two rusting metal cots were shoved against a wall. Mattresses, lumpy and stained, were scattered on the ground. From a pile of rags in the darkest corner he heard scurrying noises. He whirled around. "Padilla," he called, "*¿qué pasa, hombre?* Surely, this is not our permanent camp?"

"This is it," Padilla said. "It is true that it was left in bad shape. But with a little cleaning..." His words shifted into a shrug.

There was derisive laughter from a couple of men and a nervous giggle from a woman behind Manuel. A hollow-faced man coughed and spat and finally said, "God arranges these things. It could be worse."

Carlos and Conchita appeared from behind the tents and Carlos said, "Water, Padilla? Where is it?"

Manuel made a full circle, his eyes scanning the clearing. No water pipes. And then he heard Padilla's answer to Carlos. The irrigation ditch on the other side of the road, it seemed, was their only source of water.

"Rats! There are rats in there!" Ricardo cried, racing out of a tent. Behind him, Alberto said nothing, but his eyes were dilated, his face flushed.

Manuel understood. He thought of the room that his sons shared at home. He thought of the cots and the clean cotton pads that Dolores covered with muslin sheets bleached to a surprising whiteness and ironed with care. He turned from the boys to Padilla. "*Es imposible, hombre.* This cannot be."

"It could be worse, eh?" someone said to the hollow-cheeked man. "If you still feel that way, you tangle with the rats. Martín is right. We need a better place to live."

"We need a better place to live," Padilla mimicked. "You sound like the sainted ladies of the gringos' church. *¡Basta!* It is enough that you have jobs!" He jumped into the truck and circled in front of them, raising a thick cloud of dust. "Be ready at daylight!" he ordered.

After Padilla left, Manuel moved their bedrolls close to a boulder, then sat beside them. In groups of twos and threes around the clearing, the rest of the men talked in subdued tones. Only Ricardo, Alberto, and Lalo continued to explore the camp. The woman in the blue dress came out of one of the tents, dragging a mattress behind her.

A woman near Manuel looked up. "Ay, Cuca," she said. "you cannot do it all." But she made no move to help.

The woman called Cuca ignored her. She wiped the sweat from under her nose with the back of her hand, then signalled to the boys. "*¡Muchachos!* Come here!"

The boys looked at one another, shrugged and went to her. Manuel got up and joined them. "*Bueno, señora,*" he said, "we will move the heavy things."

The cleaning went on until dark. The mattresses were pulled outside and brushed. The dirt floors were cleared with a shaky iron rake and swept with a stubby broom. When they were through, Manuel laid a small fire. Cuca produced a chipped enamel coffee pot and they drank her strong brew and shared food. Later, Carlos played his guitar and some of them sang. But half-heartedly, Manuel said to himself. Still, that was with half-a-heart more than he was putting into the singing—or had put into the cleaning of the camp. He was certain that no one would sleep in the tents tonight.

Several hours later, Manuel sat up abruptly on the mattress he had pulled near the boulder. He scratched his forearm with disgust. Bedbugs. Nearby the two boys were sleeping, but not he. He would have welcomed sleep, but he was being persecuted by his thoughts. "The camp is well equipped," Padilla had said that day in The Plaza. And he had gone home and assured Dolores that the living arrangements would be fine. From the start, he had tried to cover up his doubts. One thing only was in his favor. He had been right to leave Dolores and the girls at home. "Bedbugs," he grunted, and lay back.

A heaviness had settled on Manuel since their arrival here. Now as he lay there, the night absorbed that heaviness and obscured the stars. But not for long. He stretched and stared into the sky. Ah, there! A faint, flickering light. Another, and another, of course. The night was filled with stars. Now, too, he heard the crickets, and soon their song brought him to the place where sleep begins. As he hung there for an instant, he thought of the rancher Kirk. Why had he not thought of Señor Kirk before? Yes, yes, that was the direction one should take. The crickets' song melted into the glimmering of the stars, and Manuel let go and slept.

Chapter Eight

It was dawn when Manuel opened his eyes. Above the hills to the east the sky was tinged with pink, and below them the trees had a reddish glow. He sat up, puzzled for an instant. Then recollection came.

He scanned the camp. Nothing had changed in the night. Even with all their efforts, it was still the same dirty place it had been yesterday. But today there was hope. There was Señor Kirk. Manuel stood up and stretched, and the air smelled fresh and good.

In the years that he had lived in the United States, his respect for the *norteamericanos* had grown. The dairy had been a good place to work. The machinery that milked and bottled intrigued him; he admired its efficiency. It had been a sore day when he was given his layoff slip, but not a day that had caught him by surprise. He knew that the Depression would not end until changes were made. A great country, he thought, should be led by a restless man, one hungry for new ideas. He let his eyes circle the camp and grinned. *Bueno,* Manuel, let us see what *you* can do about changing things.

He walked down the road to the irrigation ditch. At the edge of the water he stopped. Did he dare to drink it? In Los Angeles he had often heard stories of dysentery and other miseries of those who followed the crops, but he refused to believe them. "A man makes his own conditions," he had argued. Yet here he was, preparing to drink from a trough like an animal. He leaned over the ditch, hesitated, and then quickly splashed water over his head, but he did not drink. He wiped his face on his shirt sleeve and started back to the clearing. Within half an hour Padilla's truck swung into camp, and they climbed into it and headed for the orchards.

As they drove by a gatepost bearing the sign H. A. Kirk & Sons and through rows of peach trees to a shed where the crew was handed canvas sacks, Manuel was having doubts.

After all, he said to himself, I am new to this business. Dolores would be the first to tell me that prudence is required. But on the other hand, what harm in a question or two? I will be sufficiently prudent when I make inquiries about Señor Kirk.

It was the middle of the morning before Manuel saw Padilla alone. He had lost track of the number of sacks he had filled and of the times he emptied them into crates stacked beside the trees. All he knew was that the sacks grew heavier with each trip. Like this one. He watched the green-gold peaches roll into a wooden crate and looked up to find Padilla standing nearby. Manuel mopped the sweat off his face and said, "This Kirk, Padilla, the one who owns the orchards, what kind of a man is he?"

"A man of business," Padilla said, and walked away.

Manuel shrugged. There would be another time to ask. He found the opportunity that afternoon when they were ready to return to camp. Padilla was in the truck behind the wheel as they waited for a few stragglers. Manuel walked up to him, pushed his hat off his brow, and said, "Hot again, eh?"

Padilla grunted.

"Tell me, Padilla, does Señor Kirk ever visit his orchards?"

"When he finds it necessary."

"And that is not too often, I suppose."

Padilla's eyes narrowed. "Why all the questions? Señor Kirk is no concern of yours. Anything bothers you, you go through me. Stay away from him." He bent over the wheel and started the engine.

During the next two days Manuel climbed up and down the orchard ladder, dully measuring the size and ripeness of the peaches, his mind elsewhere. Padilla had called their camp a "good" one and dared to claim rent for it. If he could take money for the camp, he would be sure to invent other charges. Just yesterday he had told them what the trip from Los Angeles cost. Today it would be trips to and from the orchards and the company store. Tomorrow he would add bookkeeping costs. Their pay envelopes would be flatter than tortillas. It could not be, Manuel told himself, that a man of good conscience would allow such things to go on. Señor Kirk must surely know nothing of this. He would not expect his workers to be treated so unfairly.

Still, Manuel cautioned himself, he needed to weigh the business of ignoring Padilla's warning. Walk softly, Manuel. It might be better to leave things as they are. To keep a job, one could put up with a certain amount of unfairness. In the camp a few days later, the problem was still baiting him.

It was dusk as he leaned against a tree and watched a trail of red ants work their way up the base of a rocky hill. A fly landed on his arm and he slapped it angrily. Flies were everywhere. It was only a matter of time until they brought sickness. Ricardo will be the first to fall ill, he told himself. That boy is not strong. Perhaps I should have left him at home.

He spit on the trail of ants. One-hundred dollars! That's what this job would bring, and he needed that money. Should he see Kirk? Or should he put up with things the way they were? He had to make up his mind. His thoughts were interrupted by a rustling sound behind him. He turned to find Carlos and Conchita walking toward him.

When they reached him, Carlos said, "I need your help, Manuel."

"It is yours. Tell me."

"Pués, it is about my wife. And the rats."

"The rats?"

"You know. They come in the night and..."

"And we throw what we can at them," Manuel said.

"Sí, sí," Carlos said, "but there is more. The rats cause my wife great problems. She has monstrous dreams about them."

Conchita nodded.

Manuel said nothing.

"We are afraid," Carlos said in a harsh whisper. "We are afraid for the child."

"Ah-h-h," Manuel said, understanding.

"Those dreams can mark the child," Carlos explained. "And there are more and more rats. It is this place, Manuel. Is there nothing we can do?"

Manuel nodded wearily. "We must talk to the man who owns the orchards," he said. "He cannot know of these conditions."

"He should be told," Carlos said.

"It is six miles to Hansonville," Manuel warned.

"That is not too far," Carlos said, and they agreed to see Kirk on the following night.

It was still hot at seven o'clock the next evening as Manuel and Carlos trudged along the highway to Hansonville. The asphalt was bordered by white oleanders and behind them a windbreak of eucalyptus trees. The two men walked silently on the shaded shoulder, stopping only to signal approaching cars for a ride.

"It cannot be much farther," Manuel said.

"No," Carlos agreed.

"And someone is sure to pick us up soon."

"Yes," Carlos answered, and kept on walking.

Finally an old roadster pulled up beside them. Gratefully, they scrambled into the rumble seat. Within minutes they were in Hansonville, once again on their own.

Finding out where Henry Kirk lived was not difficult. The first person they asked directed them to his address. Mulberry Road was broad and tree-shaded, with large old houses and deep well-watered lawns. The air was sweet with the perfume of jasmine and honeysuckle vines. Henry Kirk's house, white with broad porches, was on a corner.

Manuel and Carlos climbed the steps to the front door and knocked. The door was opened by a small gray-haired woman. Manuel removed his hat and asked to speak to Señor Kirk.

"You are orchard workers?" the woman asked.

"*Sí, señora.*"

"Go to the back door," she said.

"But, señora, we are not beggars," Manuel said. "We are here on business."

"Go to the back," she said, and quickly closed the door.

Carlos cleared his throat and coughed nervously.

Manuel, walking slowly down the steps, said, "The señora does not understand these matters, Carlos. She is a woman. Señor Kirk will treat us differently."

As they turned the corner of the house, the back door swung open and a slightly-built man stepped out. He was wearing a white cotton shirt that hung loosely on his rounded shoulders. His pale blue eyes peered at them questioningly through the lenses of gold-rimmed glasses.

"What do you want?" he asked.

"Only a moment of your time, Señor Kirk," Manuel said.

"Who in hell are you?" Kirk asked.

"I am Manuel Martín. This is my fellow worker, Carlos Vasquez."

"And what do you want from me?"

"It is like this," Manuel said, reaching for the right words. "We were brought here by our crew leader with a promise of a full summer's work, of reasonable pay and a reasonable place to live. But there is a problem and we would like to discuss it with…"

"Whoa, there," Kirk said softly. "Who's your crew leader? Padilla? He's the one to go to."

"We have already tried that, señor," Manuel said. "It is *about* Padilla that we are here. And about conditions at the camp."

"Well now," Kirk said, his voice rising, "my foreman tells me that this Padilla is a good man. As for what he promised you, that's no concern of mine."

"Ah-h, señor, that man Padilla is not what he seems to be."

"You people," Henry Kirk said with a shake of his head. "Always out to make trouble. Can't even get along with your own kind."

"It is because we are not all of one kind," Manuel said quietly.

"That's enough," Kirk said, "Go on! Both of you! Scram!"

"But the camp, señor," Manuel insisted. "The conditions. Just a word. It will not take long."

Kirk looked at Manuel, puzzled. Then with a shrug he turned to the door.

"Señor Kirk!" Manuel called. "The men are troubled. Perhaps there will be sickness. Perhaps they cannot work."

Kirk swung around, his face reddening. "You'll work. That's what you're here for. And remember this: I don't like trouble. Not one bit. Don't go making any trouble or I'll have your asses across the border."

"But I am in this country legally," Manuel said.

"What good will that do you?" Henry Kirk said with a laugh. "Seems you're not only a troublemaker, you're a damned fool, too." He stepped into the house and slammed the door.

Manuel did not move. Behind him he heard Carlos exhale and then felt a tug at his arm.

"I think we had better go," Carlos said.

"Yes," Manuel said, turning slowly, "let us go."

They walked most of the six miles back to the camp.

In the men's tent, Manuel dropped on his bed and watched Carlos pick his way around the sleepers to a lantern-lighted corner where three men were playing cards. He turned stiffly on the hard mattress, feeling shamed and impotent. *¡Esé cabrón!* It was arrogant men like Kirk who pushed workers into despair or into resistance. And when no one would listen, resistance was all that was left...Manuel sat up. He had heard about the fruit pickers in Foley. They had refused to work until they were paid fairly. And they had won. Resistance...If others could do it, well, then?...

For a few minutes Manuel remained motionless, listening to the soft slap of cards and the muffled voices from the lighted corner. Finally, he spoke.

"Amigos, wake up. We need to talk."

The card players looked up. Alberto stirred in his bed. Ricardo groaned and sat up.

"Amigos," Manuel said again. "Wake up. We must talk."

"¿Qué pasa, Martín?" a sleepy voice grumbled.

"Open your eyes and I will tell you."

"Forget it," the same voice muttered.

"No," Carlos called. "Listen. We should listen."

Slowly and grudgingly, the men awakened. When most of them were sitting up, Manuel said, "This is the thing: it occurs to me that for the next few days the fruit will ripen more quickly than it can be picked. The sun is hot."

Lorenzo, a card player, shrugged and his lengthened shadow shot up into the canvas of the roof. "So?"

"So we can let that hot sun work for us," Manuel said gravely. "We can do what others have had the courage to do. We can refuse to work until we are given a better camp."

"You have more nerve than you have sense," Felipe, the hollow-cheeked man, said, and coughed. "You are a dreamer."

"I have been called worse," Manuel said.

"Maybe," Felipe said sourly. "But I was at Foley. I know what went on and it was not all that sweet. Look, in a day or two, maybe things here will get better."

"Or maybe they will get worse."

"Precisamente," Carlos said. "And that Kirk is no friend of ours."

"Be that as it may," Lorenzo said, "we cannot win. They will find others to take our places."

"I think...I think that will not happen," Manuel said, carefully controlling his voice. "The camps in the arroyos are empty. The workers are gone to other fields. Only this morning I heard Padilla muttering that they were after him for more men. Believe me, they will pay attention to us."

"Don't underestimate them, Martín," Lorenzo said. "They will bring other workers. Or they'll try to split our ranks, and if they do..."

"I will be the loser," Manuel said. "So if we are not all in accord, let us forget it."

A long silence followed his words. In that silence Manuel recalled something that Dolores had said to him. She accused him of always trying to change people into thinking as he did, when change for most people, "perhaps not for you, Manuel," was the harshest of punishments. He had laughed and told himself how wrong she was. But what was he attempting here but to persuade Felipe and the others to accept his idea? Still, there was not much that he could do alone. Even the women would have to be told.

He looked around at the men. Some avoided his eyes, making him wonder if he had been a little crazy to propose such a thing. Finally he said, "What do you say? Yes? Or no? Speak up. Then we can either talk more or go back to sleep."

Lorenzo dropped the cards he was holding. *"Bueno.* I am with you."

From the shadows in the far corner another man called, "It is worth a try." Who was it? Manuel peered into the gloom but could not tell. One by one, the others spoke until all had agreed.

It was then that Manuel felt a strange anxiety. Things had moved too fast. In truth, he had not expected to convince them so quickly. But the men had been ripe for this, as ready to be picked as the peaches. And yet...*Basta, basta,* he said to himself. What we have decided to do is good. And a good cause should not be weakened by doubts.

"*Bueno,* Martín," Lorenzo said. "How is this thing to be done?"

An hour later they had completed their plan. "Tomorrow then, when the southbound train goes by," Manuel said, his voice calm and sure, "it will be our signal to meet at the water tower and return to this camp. You will see. They will listen to us."

At mid-morning the next day, from the high rung of his orchard ladder, Manuel looked beyond the trees to the distant road where the heat rose in shimmering waves. Steely glints sprang from the railroad tracks that paralleled the road. For a moment the events of last night seemed to him to be only a dream, but now a glance at the height of the sun brought back reality. It was almost time.

From his vantage point he watched Padilla. The stocky man walked heavily beside the trees, digging his boots into the furrows of loose earth, pausing now and again to have a word with one of the workers. Finally he stopped beside a loading truck, where he smoked and watched Manuel with contrived indifference. Manuel knew that Padilla's casual manner was put on, but that did not surprise him; the man was a practiced deceiver. Still, there was something in the air. A short while back while filling crates, Lorenzo had failed to meet his eyes, and there were none of the good-humored gibes from the others. Everyone was strung as tightly as a fat lady's corset. But why not? It was not an easy thing they were about to do.

Padilla was finishing his second cigarette when Manuel heard the squeal of car brakes and the sound of urgent voices. Almost instantly he heard the train whistle, and in another moment the earth below him rumbled as the train roared past the orchards. Manuel moved quickly down the ladder and plowed head down to the water tower. Ricardo and Alberto, red-faced and breathing hard, were waiting for him.

"They're...not...coming!" Ricardo yelled.

Manuel swung around.

Carlos was a step or two behind him. But he was the only one.

"It is time!" Manuel shouted to the others. But his comrades of last night, those within view, turned their heads. "It is time!" Manuel shouted again, and his eyes swept the orchards. Two men stood at the edge of the road, shotguns cradled loosely in their arms.

So Kirk had been told. In time to bring on his dogs. In time, too, for Padilla to intimidate the others. I should have known, Manuel told himself. I should have been warned by Padilla's manner. I should have guessed it was Kirk's car that screamed into the orchard. Now here was Kirk walking toward him, the sun making gleaming rounds of his glasses. And following Kirk was Padilla.

Manuel whispered, "Go back, Carlos. There is no need for you to stay here."

Carlos' face was drained of color, but he said, "No, I will stay."

"Go!" Manuel ordered, giving him a convincing shove. Carlos scrambled around the water tower.

Kirk stopped to watch Carlos, a slow smile covering his face. The smile was alive, menacing, and then, with the suddenness of a surprise attack, it was gone and he moved toward Manuel.

"You went ahead and did it, huh?" he said. "I asked you nicely not to make trouble, didn't I? But you had to do it anyway. All right, you sonuvabitch, get out!"

"Bueno," Manuel said quietly. "Of course, we will leave." And then to Padilla who stood hesitating a yard or so behind Kirk. "Take care, Pablo. You will come to harm some day." He signalled to his sons and together they strode out of the orchard.

When they reached the roadside, Alberto asked, "Who told?"

"Felipe, I'll bet," Ricardo answered. "Felipe's a snake!"

"Maybe it was Lalo," Alberto said.

"No!" Ricardo shouted. "Lalo's okay!"

"Stop that!" Manuel said tersely. "It does not matter any more."

He looked up at the sky and became aware of billowing white clouds that shimmered and blurred through tears. He pulled at a handkerchief, stumbled, and coughed to cover up a sob that escaped him. Alberto and Ricardo stopped. Manuel mopped his face, straightened his hat and nodded. They moved on again.

At the camp they gathered up their belongings and headed down the dirt road toward the highway. Manuel threw a sidelong glance at his sons. Earlier in Los Angeles, he had promised them a summer of adventure and work. He had not made light of the length of the hours or the heaviness of the labor. Now all that he could promise was uncertainty and hardship.

The next three days were filled with both. Images blurred one into the other in Manuel's mind. The burning shoulders of asphalt roads. The occasional hand that beckoned them to ride for a few miles. Other hands that brought food, food for which Manuel offered to work, only to be told, "No, no," by women in flowered aprons through their locked screen doors, "rest in the shade while you eat, and then go." Dust. Always the dust, either kicked up by their own feet or by the cars that shot by them.

Late in the third day when the sun was starting to lose its strength, Manuel and the boys walked on the edge of the highway, their eyes scanning the countryside for a place to rest and sleep. A truck came to a stop on the shoulder ahead of them.

A man's head, almost concealed by a grass hat, poked out the window of the cab and twisted on narrow shoulders to look at them. "Where you going?"

"Los Angeles, señor," Manuel answered.

"That's where I'm heading with my cabbages," the farmer said, motioning to the rear of the truck. "Hop in. I'll take you there."

"*Gracias.*" But before Manuel called the two boys, he blew his nose and bent over to tighten the strings on his shoes. Now he could speak. They threw their packs into the truck and climbed in after them, making room beside the crates of cabbages.

The farmer pulled into the produce market just after dawn the next day, but it was mid-morning before Manuel and his sons turned the corner of Twenty-eighth Street. Manuel's heart beat fast when he saw the familiar green siding, but he climbed the steps slowly and removed the pack from his back before he turned to the door.

He pulled at the knob. When he found that the screen door was hooked, he felt a surprising anger. "Dolores!" he shouted into the shadows of the entry hall. "Dolores! We are home!"

From deep in the house he heard the sound of a spoon clattering to the floor and then hurrying footsteps. "Manuel!" Dolores cried, opening the screen door. "What is this? Are you all right?"

He put his arms around her. "Yes," he said into her soft hair, "yes, we are all right." He went into the living room, leaving her with the boys. He heard them reassuring her, and soon Alberto came in and sprawled out on an overstuffed chair. When Ricardo and Dolores followed, Manuel stared at them, wondering where to begin.

It was Dolores who spoke. "There was trouble, no? And you could not leave it alone, could you? Manuel, Manuel, will you never change?"

The screen door slammed and Angela and Bonita raced into the house. When they saw their father, their dark eyes widened and filled with questions. Manuel kissed them and pinched their cheeks. And Dolores, ignoring their complaints, rushed them out of the room.

"Bueno, Manuel," she said from the doorway. "What happened?"

Now all the doubts that had tormented him for days had to be faced. "Can you not see that we are about to drop?" he said crossly. "You shall have the whole story later. For now, what is there to eat?"

Chapter Nine

She was glad to see the sign: SAN CLEMENTE NEXT FIVE EXITS. Angela Raine relaxed a bit behind the wheel as she continued her journey to San Diego and the Mexican border. Soon she would have her first glimpse of the water. From that point on to San Diego, the ocean would parallel the freeway. Like her leisurely and somewhat ritualistic baths, being close to the water not only refreshed her, its nearness seemed to give her strength. She was enjoying that prospect.

Suddenly, red taillights glowed in the sunlight. Her tires squealed as she pushed on the brake pedal; she came to a complete stop. When the cars started to move again, it was at a slow and halting pace. She turned off the air conditioner and lowered the window. Ahead of her brake lights formed a glittering ribbon that wound blinking through the hills. What was going on up there? A stalled car? Someone being ticketed? She eased into the lane to her right, squeezing between a dusty green Datsun and a silver Mercedes, ending up beside a panel truck.

SAN CLEMENTE NEXT FIVE EXITS. Two lane changes would put her where she could leave the freeway if she wished. But not yet. She still had time to think about it. At least she was protected from the sun by the small truck beside her. She glanced idly at the driver, a shaggy-haired young man who at that moment raised the mouthpiece of a CB radio to his face. He's calling his place of business or maybe his wife, she thought. Honey, he'd be saying, I'm caught in a lousy mess on the freeway, nowhere to go but up, expect me when you see me.

She glanced at the clock on the dash. Walt would be trying to reach her too. In the last couple of weeks he had made a habit of calling her two or three times a day. She understood his anxiety. None of this had been easy for him, either.

❧

On the fifteenth floor of a glass-walled building on the Avenue of the Stars in Century City, Walt dropped the phone on its cradle. No answer again. He stretched his arms out over the papers on his desk and looked east across the city to the snowy top of Mount Baldy. He felt a strange numbness as he turned his head and stared out the window. Angela, don't do it.

The snow on Mount Baldy glistened. A crown, he thought. That's how Angela would see it. "They *are* purple majesties," she had said years before on one of their walks on Olympic Boulevard. "Look how they tower over the tallest buildings. Look how the snow makes a crown at the top." It was one of her rare fanciful moments, those moments that warmed him, and he had grinned broadly at her smile.

We were happy those first years, Angela. I'm sure of it. Walt frowned, looking for justification in remembering. He had carried Angela across the threshold of their garage apartment when they returned from their short beach honeymoon. It was in what they called their "bird cage" that Ken was conceived and lived his first years. They bought and hung their first oil painting there. They celebrated there when Angela brought home her B.A. and when he got his advanced degree. Champagne both times, cheap, but bubbly. They toasted with orange juice, sitting side by side in the breakfast nook, when they knew for certain that Gloria was on her way.

When Gloria was born, he bought Angela a diamond. "Time we were engaged," he said and she blushed. A month or two after that they moved into a larger place, one that could accommodate a new baby and her preschool brother.

Sure, there'd been diapers and colds and chicken pox, too. And there was the night when Ken grumbled, "Damn bastard," on stubbing his toe, and they had looked at one another accusingly over his head. There was the spider that bit Gloria when she was still crawling that, hours and the emergency hospital later, proved not to be a black widow. But there had also been those crazy birthday parties and Tinker Toys and the nightly ritual with "The Little Engine That Could." There were picnics at the beach. A weekend trip to Santa Barbara without the kids. Promotions. And then they bought The House.

Yes, Angela, I know you were happy then, and later, too. After all, we had two pretty special, healthy kids, and I knocked myself out to make enough money for the kind of life you wanted. But then things changed. The frown on Walt's face deepened as he thought of the disquieting distance that had grown between them.

When Ken left for college, when he moved in with the girl he eventually married, when Gloria left and they had come full circle back to being two, they talked, yes, but on the surface. It wasn't just Angela. He, too, found it hard to communicate with her. It was as though she had changed abruptly into a woman he no longer knew. Well, no doubt she could say the same about him. And yet the change, though gradual, couldn't have been unannounced. He should have seen it coming and acted. What could I have done? he asked himself. Was it something I did? Or was it... But this is crazy! Why try to lay blame now?

He looked around his office: at the comfortable cushioned chairs and couch in the corner, at the paintings on the wall above them. They were water colors of a lagoon on Molakai and an open boat on a beach at Hanalei. Angela and he had bought them when he was on a business trip to Hawaii. It was the first time Angela had seen the islands. She was like a kid, not knowing which cove or waterfall to love the best.

Angela was two different people: a happy child, a disaffected woman. Why? Why? Maybe if she had stayed close to her family... Maybe. Could I have done something about that?

With a slam, Walt flattened his hands on the papers before him. The large walnut desk felt solid and sturdy beneath them. That's what he was: solid, reliable, someone you could count on to produce results. And yet he'd gotten nowhere with Angela. She should be home from the psychiatrist's by now. Where was she? He jumped up and paced the room, rubbing the back of his neck. He stopped at the window and stared at the mountain, seeing nothing, then seeing nothing but the mountain until it seemed to him that he was standing alone on a plain with only the mountain above him.

"Your Majesty," he said. "Your Majesty, let me keep her near me." He looked down to the floor and then once again up to Mount Baldy, and it occurred to him that he was praying. "Grant me that, I beg you," he whispered. Then the tightness in his throat broke into a sob, and another.

❦

Seventy miles southeast of Century City, her car barely moving, Angela's fingers drummed impatiently on the seat beside her. Behind her was the familiar sign of the old San Clemente Inn, and ahead of that, hidden behind greenery, was Richard Nixon's Western White House. She had traveled the length of San Clemente, all four or five miles of it, and it had taken close to an hour.

All right, so she had made the wrong gamble. She should have left the freeway. And if she had, then what? A crawl on surface streets? You're here for a while, she told herself, so just grin and bear it. But maybe...maybe I don't have to. Bear it, that is. She dug in her purse and brought out a brown plastic cylinder.

"For those moments," Doctor Eichar had said earlier, "when you hit a low, just as we all do. You don't have to worry about these pills, Angela. I say they're okay. Don't hesitate to use them."

But she had hesitated, not filling the prescription until that morning. Now she slipped the pink capsule between her lips and with a backward toss of her head swallowed it. Uppers. Downers. Is that what she was into now?

Angela twisted restlessly about to see how the traffic was behind her. A large gray truck had replaced the Mercedes. The same truck. Yes, the one she had passed twice before. She turned back and thought, maybe Walt's home by now. And if he is, then he knows I meant it. Up to now, she hadn't been able to convince him.

"It's too late for us anyway," she had told him.

"Too late, Angela? Cut that out! Who says it's too late? Things will get better."

She hadn't been surprised to hear him say that. She knew that their relationship had become anchored in the hope that things would get better. But when? In the last few years, their discontent had become magnified. Little incidents became crises. And there was no longer that old closeness to help them out of tight places. Their lovemaking had become mannered. A peck on the cheek by Walt to test her mood; a cool acceptance or a denial from her. So different from the old Walt, who would claim her with a boisterous embrace. "Come here, woman! I hunger for you!"

Their lovemaking then was passionate and deeply felt, filled with the comfort of familiarity and trust. She trusted Walt, never asking about the nights he spent away on business or making too much over the mild flirtations he often engaged in at home. She felt no threat. His happiness, she had known, was with her and the kids.

But a year and a half ago, Julia Canby *had* posed a threat. One day Julia was nothing more than the subject of a casual conversation with Maggie; the next she was a reality, flying in from New York, arriving by cab at her Cousin Maggie's home, and passively disrupting the already fragile pattern of Angela's life. It started late one afternoon...

ॐ

The telephone rang.

"Come meet Julia," Maggie said. "We're having drinks on the patio."

Walt, already settled with his newspaper and a Scotch and water, said, "Do we have to?"

"I think so," Angela answered. "What excuse can we give Maggie? She knows our every move. Besides, do we have anything better to do?"

"I guess not," he said with resignation.

When they walked in through the Pauls' back gate, Julia Canby put down her drink, got up gracefully from a deep lounge, and walked toward them. She was of medium height with striking blonde hair, blue eyes, and a lightly freckled skin.

"Hey," she said, and her smile revealed straight white teeth and a whisper of lemon-scented vodka. "So you're the Raines. Glad to meet you." She turned to Walt and extended her hand.

Angela and Walt were persuaded to stay for supper. During the meal, Angela left the table to find a Kleenex. When she returned, Julia was saying, "Actually, I'm not a native New Yorker. I come from an unbelievably small town in Maine called Gorham."

"Gorham?" Walt said. "I know it well. Not far from there, there's a river where my dad and I used..."

"Trout!" Julia interrupted. "Big, beautiful trout, right?"

That was the beginning of a laugh-filled dialogue between them that seemed to exclude everyone else. It lasted all evening. Angela fought feelings of resentment when Walt arranged to meet Julia on the following day, even though the arrangements occurred innocently enough.

Julia was in Los Angeles to confer on some TV scripts she had written, and she had appointments in Century City. One of them turned out to be in Walt's office building.

"The *same* building?" Julia said. "Really? Well, that'll make me feel more at home, won't it?"

"Tell you what," Walt said. "Drop in when you're through. I'll take you to lunch."

That first lunch led to a second. Although he had hardly mentioned his first meeting with Julia, Walt described the second to Angela in detail. "We ate in that little French place across the boulevard...the food was great...we had a pretty good bottle of Grey Reisling..." Walt seemed to be taking care to leave nothing out. Almost too much care, Angela thought.

She studied his face as he talked, trying to see him with fresh eyes, Julia's eyes. Walt, with the quarter-inch scar on his cheek where Ken's dog had bitten him, with eyebrows so unruly they needed trimming, with a five-o'clock shadow that was beginning to glisten with gray. But he had white-streaked temples that evoked a September song and a hairline that refused to recede. If his waist had thickened, only a wife would know it. Walt, at his age, was attractive. And, damn it, so was Julia.

Julia was the girl next door grown into sleek maturity, a maturity glowing with self-confidence. Of course, Angela made comparisons. No one else had ever prompted her to look in the mirror with such dissatisfaction. For the first time she had seen that her hair, which had only a gray strand or two, had lost its youthful luster, and that her features were less sharp. True, she was slim and still shapely, but looking at Julia she became acutely aware of the beginning flaccidity of her own body, a softness that no amount of workout could circumvent.

Around Julia too, her self image shrank. She became again the little girl with the hand-me-down nationality, caught between two selves, trying to make one fit.

More than that, she discovered a cauldron of jealousy that she had to handle alone. It had simmered during the week of Julia's stay, but it came to a full boil on the night of her farewell dinner.

There were a dozen or so people at the Pauls'; Maggie was using Julia's visit as an excuse to repay social obligations. They were people Angela knew and liked, and under other circumstances she would have enjoyed the evening. After eating, they moved out on to the terrace. It was a warm September twilight, with the remnants of an ocean breeze moving lightly as they enjoyed coffee and a panoramic view of the glittering South Bay lights.

All evening Don had hovered around Angela like a concerned parent, and that made her feel miserable. She wanted him to hover around Julia. Once outside, though, Don disappeared. Julia, looking as smooth and creamy as her pale yellow dress, hooked her arm through Walt's and pulled him over to a bench in a far corner.

At the other end of the patio, Angela frowned and moved restlessly in her chair. She looked up as Maggie sat down beside her. "Your cousin's quite beautiful," she said stiffly. Maggie nodded, and there was a look of such dismay on her face that Angela felt compelled to add, "And she's monopolizing Walt."

"I know, I know. Do you mind terribly?"

"Yes. I'm starting to think I do."

"She'll be gone tomorrow," Maggie said with a regretful shake of her head. "There'll be a whole continent between you."

"What good will that do if Walt's fallen for her?"

"Oh, Angie, what can I say?"

Maggie was called away then, leaving Angela to her uncomfortable thoughts. Walt might not be hers "until death" after all. And if he were to leave her now, the whole structure of her life would shatter. For an instant she felt crumpled, and then she stiffened. That wasn't true, that wasn't true. Whatever Walt did now wouldn't change things for her. *She* had built her world; she didn't need him to keep it intact. Besides, she told herself, even without Walt she had almost everything she wanted. Except for blonde hair, blue eyes, and freckles on her nose. She stood up.

In the house she found Maggie refilling a coffee server. "I'm going home, Maggie," she said. "I'm sure I left something burning on the stove."

"You did? I thought maybe you were going to say you had a stinking headache."

"I have a stinking headache too."

At the door Maggie said, "I'm sorry," and Angela read several layers of meaning into her words and was afraid to reply.

Outside, she fought back tears and an urge to run. She looked over her shoulder and, realizing how foolish her hope was, ran across the lawn to her own front door. But once there, she turned away. This was not where she wanted to be. Circling her house slowly, she pushed open the gate to the garden and sat beneath the elm tree. This was not where she wanted to be either. Angela rose and went into the house.

When Walt came in later, she was already in bed. Without turning on the light, he walked into the bedroom quietly and sat on the edge of the bed. "Is something the matter? Why did you leave?"

"I was tired. Besides, you didn't need me. You were getting lots of attention and really lapping it up."

"That's a dumb thing to say."

"Not so dumb. I saw how much you liked it. So did everyone else, for that matter."

After a moment's thought, Walt said, "You're right. I did like the attention. I don't get much from you."

"Well, fine. I really don't want to talk anymore."

"That's the trouble, Angela. We ought to talk. We ought to talk about what's happening to us."

"Alone?" she said sharply. "Or with a lawyer?"

"Oh, for Christ's sake," he said and got up and left.

Regretting her tone, Angela raised up on one elbow, waiting for him to return. But he didn't. Walt slept in the guest room that night, and the next day Julia left for New York. All that remained of her was the scent of a lemon twist in vodka and a glimpse here and there of a special shade of yellow...

꩜

Looking back on it later, Angela could see that she had made a big thing out of nothing. All that had happened was that Julia had touched a vulnerable spot in Walt and a wounded one in her. In a day or two the exposed feelings were almost covered over, and life returned to normal. But that night she had lain awake, twisting uncomfortably, calling herself a fool for her mistrust of Walt. Her jealousy, she realized, had stemmed from her longing for their old intimacy. But if they had become routine and uninspired lovers, they were still husband and wife and remained loyal. Together, she had thought then, they would muddle through and set things straight. But when?

Walt seemed as uncertain as she. His face was pleasant when at rest, but whenever he looked at her, his eyes and mouth formed a stiff shield of renunciation that she found hard to take. Angela sensed that it had started with her. She felt that all she needed to do was reach out, take Walt's hand if words wouldn't come, and that he would respond. But a growing reserve stopped her. This was no longer the easygoing young man she had married. This man was a stranger. Something's gone very wrong, she would say to herself. Why can't we talk? But there was no easy answer. So she ignored the question and went on with her life.

In the last few months there had been the usual back and forth of dinner and theater parties, the practiced pleasantness of business entertaining, and then the crazy circus that Christmas had become. Instead of pleasure, her days were filled with what now seemed a monotonous routine.

Just over five months ago she had been busy making out guest lists for a holiday open house, conferring with Walt and his secretary with Maggie, even with Ken and Gloria.

"I've got to beg off, Mom," Ken had said. "Those teeming, stand-up things leave me cold."

Gloria begged off too.

It wasn't that Walt and she hadn't raised them to appreciate success and to do the things that success required of them. They had. But they had taught them other values, too. Ken and Gloria knew that their father could have moved even higher in his company, but that he had refused to uproot them and move to the east. They knew, too, that their mother loved spontaneous get-togethers, that to her "entertaining" was a dutiful chore, one she insisted on doing in an extraordinary way.

Everything Angela served at her parties was prepared at home. No caterers, not even the best, would do. Months before this last open house, she had ordered hams from Virginia and began pouring over cookbooks and recipe files. In the weeks that followed she stocked the pantry with non-perishable ingredients. Then, two days before the party, Jessie, her daily household helper, and she prepared miniature puffs to be filled with crabmeat, concocted cheese balls, whipped-up spreads and dips, and stuffed and marinated mushrooms. They cleaned pound after pound of prawns and roasted a tremendous turkey, which they glazed and stored in the auxiliary refrigerator. The bite-sized fruit cakes and other holiday sweets had been baked the previous month and frozen.

They carried the last of the trays to the refrigerator in the laundry room. "Well, that's it, Jessie," Angela said. "We're just about ready for tomorrow."

Jessie, a stocky gray-haired woman with a slight mid-European accent, shook her head. "I don't know how you do it,

Mrs. Raine. None of the ladies I was with before I came to you ever worked as hard as you do."

"Oh, well," Angela said, "it's just that I want things especially nice." And then, with a long weary sigh and a shrug that dismissed a troubling subject, "I wouldn't feel comfortable otherwise."

Jessie said, "Well, you needn't worry. Your parties are always fine, very fine. You know that. Everyone tells you so."

The next day Angela gave final instructions to Jessie and Jessie's daughter and retreated into her bedroom to dress. In this room with its white antiqued furniture, sheer lace curtains, and Chagall prints, Angela always felt a sense of peace. This was her sanctuary, as the den was Walt's. Whenever she closed the door to this room, with that one motion she shut out the world. When she soaked in her tub in the adjoining bathroom, with the mirrors veiled with mist, the scented steam rising slowly, and the water moving over her skin in gentle undulations, she luxuriated in the illusion that she was isolated from trouble, protected forever from pain or discomfort. She emerged from her peaceful fantasy refreshed, somehow purified and ready to face the world.

But on this day, there was not enough time to lie back in the water and be cradled. Reluctantly, Angela stepped out of the tub and reached for her towel. In her dressing room she looked appreciatively at the dress she was about to slip into. Red. Because she loved the color and because it was a young color. And because she was never going to be any younger. The lines were simple, to provide an unobtrusive frame for her dark eyes and hair. She was sliding a gold chain over her head when Walt came into the room.

He whistled. "You look great. I'd watch out for Schacter if I were you. He'll have his mitts all over you."

She shook her head, dismissing his praise and said, "This color isn't too much, is it?"

"It's perfect." He came to stand behind her at the mirror, the composed look of resignation once more on his face. "Everything is."

"Good. Does the table look all right? Is the food fancy enough?"

"Angela, why do you ask? You always knock yourself out to make it perfect...and it's a stupid thing to do. It'll be a fine party."

It was. The white and gold living room provided a perfect background for holiday decorations, and Angela had made the most of it. A mass of poinsettias in white pots flanked the black-framed fireplace, in which a fire roared. The white-flocked tree, trimmed in gold and green, was, as always, recessed in the bay window, and pungent pine boughs in gleaming bowls accented the stairs and doorways. It took only one look in the dining room to make mouths water and only one stop at the bar or punch bowl to make hearts warm. Yes, it was a fine party.

The young members of Walt's department were impressed. They came and went from four to six o'clock in smiling groups, treading lightly, the young wives looking to their husbands to be sure they were saying the right things to the right people. Angela, moving from one to the other, found the young women eager to be proper but entirely secure. Years before, in similar circumstances, she had appeared equally poised and proper, while underneath that facade she had been suffering a painful inadequacy.

At six o'clock, with proper thank you's and goodbye's, the young crew left and friends and neighbors and business equals began to arrive. These were the people with whom Angela shared holiday hugs and kisses and whose news about weddings and babies and college degrees made up a part of her life. They arrived, gold chains glistening on velvets and polyester silks, and when they left the air stayed warm with a sultry commingling of after-shave and perfume. By nine o'clock, all of the guests except Maggie and Don were gone, and Jessie and her daughter were setting the house in order.

In the den, Walt and Angela and their two neighbors sat with their shoes off having coffee. Angela picked up the coffee pot on the table before her and poured the steaming liquid into their mugs.

Don, who was overweight and relaxed about it, reached for the cream and said, "This bash beats all your others, Angie. You knocked 'em dead."

Angela looked at Don affectionately and then turned to Walt, wanting his approval, too. But Walt was lying back in his chair, staring at the ceiling.

He's far away again, she thought. The way he's been all afternoon and evening. Mechanical. Well, maybe nobody else noticed it, but I certainly did. He could at least say something nice now that it's over, even if he did think it was stupid that I knocked myself out. She felt a sharp pang of loneliness, an emptiness that seemed intolerable, and she looked at Walt with anger. Why had he drawn away?

Within minutes she was blaming her ill humor on her tiredness. And later that night while getting ready for bed, she blamed her irritable mood on hormones because she was spotting again. This damned menopause, she thought as her head hit the pillow, it goes on forever.

In the bright sun of a clear December morning, it was easy to put aside the prickly irritations of the night before. On that day and those that followed, life went on pretty much as usual.

One evening in mid-January, as if in accord, Walt and she both sent out feelers, reaching to one another. They had shared an almost silent meal and were settled in their places in the den, each waiting for the other to make the opening move, to set the tone.

She studied Walt's face from across the room. "You look tired," she said, putting to one side the need to talk about the ill-defined despair she felt; whatever she might say would be inadequate. "Have you been working too hard?"

Walt looked above his usual retreat, the newspaper, and shrugged. "You seem weary, too. Maybe what we both need is a vacation."

The next night Walt brought home travel folders. They looked through them together and decided on a Caribbean cruise. "You'll love it, Gypsy," he said, the old bouyancy back in his words.

And because he had called her Gypsy again, and because she really wanted to love the trip, she went to see her internist. She didn't want a niggling worry on her mind. It was in the doctor's office that things had started to change.

"We want some further tests, Angela," her doctor said. "Things aren't entirely clear yet."

She hadn't allowed herself to panic. She reasoned that he had to run every test available to protect himself. Malpractice suits. But she didn't like it. The cruise had to be cancelled. And as if that wasn't enough, a week later she had run into Ricardo at that ill-fated fund raiser and an old guilt, disguised and imprisoned, had broken both its bonds.

Chapter Ten

It was a week after Manuel, Alberto, and Ricardo returned from the fruit picking. To Angela it seemed that the house that had been full of friendly feelings those first days—even with the crowding in the kitchen and the pushing for the bathroom—was once more the same as always. Each day was a part of an unexciting routine. Each day was sleepy with sameness.

Then two things happened that jolted Angela and everyone else in the house on Twenty-eighth Street out of their comfortable boredom. Three things, maybe. Because, first, there was Sara.

The day that Angela met Sara was especially quiet. Her father and Alberto were out looking for work. Mamá was in the kitchen ironing, stacking the folded sheets and shirts into neat piles on the kitchen table. Bonita was at Maple Park with a girl friend and, if Angela's guess was right, a boy or two. Angela was in her usual place, the rocker on the front porch, looking longingly toward Rosa's.

At Rosa's house there was candy in a round glass dish in the living room and soda pops surrounding the square of ice in the ice box. There were tablets of paper to write on and a telephone on the kitchen wall. Best of all, thought Angela, there was the Victrola and the records that Rosa sometimes let her play. As much as she wished she was over there, she could see that the shades were drawn at Rosa's, and she had been told that drawn shades meant that Rosa was busy or sleeping. But why would anyone want to work in the dark or sleep in the daytime? Angela gave the rocker one last push and got up. There had to be something better to do inside.

She stopped at the door and turned. A moving truck was coming to a stop at the curb across the street. Angela reasoned that if the FOR SALE sign had been gone from in front of the apartment house for a couple of weeks, this could be somebody moving in. In a matter of minutes, she found she was right. At last! Something interesting to do. She sat on the steps and watched as two men in overalls began to move furniture from the truck.

The first thing the men carried into the house was a pair of long metal lamps, their shades carefully wrapped. Then came a heavy overstuffed couch that had green and gold flowers on it. Next, the men lifted out of the truck a large quilt-wrapped piece of furniture. They placed it carefully on the sidewalk. Unwrapped, it proved to be a dark-wood Victrola. Angela shifted around on the step and sighed.

In a little while, a girl in a green dress ran out of the building and chased after the workmen, talking and laughing until a woman called to her to stay on the lawn and just watch. The girl in green sat in the small square of grass until she discovered Angela. Then she ran to the curb and yelled, "Hey, you!"

"What?" Angela said.

"What's your name?"

Angela walked to the curb. "What's *your* name?" she said.

"Sara Ann Feldman," the other girl answered. "I can talk Yiddish."

"So what?"

"What d'ya mean, so what? I'll bet you don't even know what Yiddish is. It's a language. I can talk two languages."

"Well, that's not so great. I've been talking Spanish since before I was born."

Sara opened her mouth to say something, seemed to think better of it, and sat down on the curb. "I'm from Miami," she called.

"*Where?*"

"Miami," Sara repeated impatiently. "That's in Florida. Don't you know anything?"

Angela shrugged, slid down to the curb, and studied a torn gum wrapper and a piece of cellophane in the gutter by her feet.

Sara went on talking. Her poppa, she said, had bought the apartment house and they were going to live there. Anyway, for a while. They were going to live downstairs and rent all

the other places. "I can play the piano," she said, and started
an interrogation of Angela. What was *her* name? Did she have
a sister? What was she called? Where did they go to school?
And was that her cat?

A man's head pushed out of a downstairs' window. "Saralah," he called, and Sara said, "Coming, Poppa," and jumped
up and ran inside.

Darn it, Angela thought, why didn't I ask her questions? I
wonder if she has any brothers or sisters? If she does, I wonder if they all get to play their records on the Victrola?

One hour later, Manuel came home. After he changed his
clothes, he said, "Come, Angelita, come help me in the garden."

Dolores looked up from the ironing. "If she must be in the
sun, Manuel, she has to wear a hat. Her skin is pale like mine,
not that anyone would know it. She's already shamelessly
brown."

"Do as your mother asks," Manuel said. "Get your hat."

Later that afternoon, it was Rosa who brought the next bit
of excitement. "Dolores!" she called at the screen door.
"Dolores, I have some news for you!"

Angela came running. When she saw Rosa, she stopped
and stared. Rosa was wearing one of her party dresses, bright
blue with a ruffle of pleats at the bottom. Her face was pow-
dered. Her lips were red with little pointed peaks. And on her
cheeks, there were rounds of rouge.

"Dolores!" Rosa called again. "I have a message from
Alberto." And then, "Hey, kiddo, aren't you going to let me in?
I only have a minute."

Angela opened the door and followed Rosa into the kitchen
where her mother and father were seated having coffee.

"What did you say about Alberto?" Dolores asked. "Is he
all right?"

"Better than that," Rosa said as she slid into a chair. "He
telephoned that he's found a job. He'll be home at six."

"My prayers to San Antonio have been answered," Dolores
said. "You see, Manuel, the saints *are* looking out for us."

"So they are," Manuel answered evenly as he rose and
went outside.

During the rest of the afternoon Dolores hummed as she worked in the kitchen. She dumped flour into her biggest bowl. When a handful of lard followed, and then another, Angela knew that her mother was making "Sonora" tortillas. They were the ones everyone liked best: thin, thin tortillas that were as big as the black iron griddle on which they were baked. On the stove was a kettle of *albondiga* soup. The wonderful smell of the little meatballs with cilantro made Angela's mouth water all afternoon.

Just before six o'clock, Bonita was told to set the table in the dining room, not the kitchen, so that they could all eat together. At five after six, Alberto walked into the house. Manuel clasped Alberto to him and patted him on the back, and they walked into the dining room together.

Alberto did most of the talking at supper. This was how he had found the job: a friend of Gordo Ramos' told him that somebody had told the friend that there was a man who had told...

Angela stopped listening when she lost track of who told what man what and started listening again when Alberto said that he was an apprentice presser in a men's suit factory. "What's a prentiss presser?" she asked. But no one answered.

Alberto said, "Maybe later, I can get a job for Rico."

"Isn't that a fine thing, Ricardo?" Dolores said.

"I already have a job," Ricardo said. "Besides, I'm getting a better corner."

Alberto laughed. "Selling papers isn't real work."

"It's real!" Ricardo said. "It's hard! I work as hard as you do!" He turned to Angela. "Hey, leave the tortillas alone!"

Angela dropped the towel that covered the tortillas and drew her hand away. She finished her supper silently, her mind busy. Why was Alberto's job causing so many happy and unhappy feelings? There was her mother. So glad because there was a worker in the family, and yet sounding hard underneath the soft words with her father. And her father. She was sure he meant it when he smiled at Alberto, and she was sure he was proud of him. But there was something in his eyes that looked like sadness. And how could that be? Ricardo, too. Acting as if he couldn't wait to leave the table.

When they were through eating, Manuel jumped up and patted Alberto's shoulder. He smiled broadly at his wife. "Dolores," he said, "this is the time we have been waiting for. Bring out your guitar!"

Angela was the first one out on the front porch. They all sat on the steps and Dolores played their favorite songs. They sang until it must have been very late, but Angela really didn't know because it was still twilight when she fell asleep.

❧

"*Hola*, kiddo!" Rosa called over the fence to Angela the next afternoon. "I heard you singing last night. You had fun, eh?"

Angela nodded. "We sang and sang. I was up pretty late."

"Late enough to see the sun set, eh, little chicken?"

"I'm not a chicken!"

"You're not a rooster," Rosa said. "But don't let that bother you. Sometimes I think it's better to cackle than to crow." She smiled. "Come see me later. I have a nice new box of..."

"Chocolates! In the little brown papers?"

"You guessed it. But hold your horses. Come over in an hour or so."

Angela ran to the front porch. As always, Ricardo and his books were half-hidden behind the blue rocker, so she sat on the steps to wait for the hour to pass. Soft music drifted out from Rosa's house. In the distance, on Maple, streetcars whirred and clanged as they went by. Across the street a woman pushed a baby carriage past the apartment house, pausing to bend over the carriage and murmur softly. An ice truck rumbled around the corner from Main Street and stopped abruptly at Jake's junkyard. There was a blast of a horn as a black automobile that had been following swerved around the truck. The iceman waved his pick at the driver and yelled. The men in the black car ignored him as they drove slowly down the street, finally coming to a stop in front of Rosa's house. Both men got out and went up to the door.

When she opened it, Rosa said, "No, no, this is not where he lives," and the men marched down the steps.

Angela watched them curiously. They were plain-looking men, each wearing a dark suit and a felt hat. They might have been hard to tell apart, except that they walked differently, one with a stride that was young and brisk, the other with a heavy, dragging step. They made their uneven way along the sidewalk and turned at Angela's house.

"Say, little girl," the man with the young walk said, "does Manuel Martín live here?"

Ricardo's books thumped heavily on the wood floor as he dropped them and jumped up. "Who wants to know? Who are you?"

"Say, Bascomb," the other man said, "I think we've got a smart aleck here."

"No, the boy's right. We shouldn't ask the kids any questions." The man called Bascomb turned to Angela. "Just tell your father we want to see him."

Angela pulled herself up, but looked hesitantly at her brother.

Ricardo said, "It's okay. Go ahead."

She found her mother in the kitchen. "Somebody wants to see Papá," she said. "Two men."

"¿Americanos?" her mother asked and Angela nodded.

Dolores hurried to the front door and held it open. "Come in, come in, señores," she said. "I will call my husband. Tell them in English, Angela."

Angela did what her mother asked, and the man named Bascomb smiled at her and said, "Thanks."

The two men walked in to the living room. Angela followed as far as the hall.

"Ven, Angela," her mother said, gesturing her to come in the room. "Tell them to sit down while I call your father."

Bascomb understood because he said, "No, gracias. We will stand."

When Dolores returned, instead of sitting down she stood by the wall. Angela knew she was nervous because she kept digging into the pocket of her apron. Then her father came into the room, his hair damp and freshly combed. He stretched his hand out to Bascomb's partner.

The man nodded but did not take Manuel's hand. Instead he reached into his coat and brought out a white envelope. He shoved it under his arm while he peeled the wrapper off a stick of gum.

Bascomb dug in an inside coat pocket and produced a leather identification folder. He held it out for Manuel. "I'm John Bascomb. My partner, David Pyle. We're from Immigration."

The man called Pyle said, "Are you Manuel Martín?" When Manuel replied yes, he said, "You have to come with us."

"Why? What is this about?"

Dolores caught her breath. "¿Qué dicen?" She pressed Angela's shoulder and repeated, "What do they say?"

Angela shrugged her mother's hand away. "I don't know yet," she whispered crossly. "I don't know what's happening."

The man named Pyle wadded up the gum wrapper and crammed it in his pocket. "Do you hear, Bascomb? The man wants to know what this is about. He's funny." He turned to Manuel. "It's about Hansonville. It's about inciting to riot. You don't know anything about that, do you?"

"Riot?" Manuel said. "No, I know nothing about that. Please tell me what this is about."

Pyle grinned. "I never seen a Mex that didn't talk too much," he said. "Or one that didn't have a rotten memory." He tapped Manuel's chest. "This one's forgotten everything."

"Please keep your hands off me," Manuel said in a cold flat voice.

"He's right," Bascomb said. "Now, let's do this thing right." He grabbed the envelope from Pyle. "We have papers signed by a Henry Kirk that..."

Manuel slammed his fist into the palm of his hand. There was a sharp, cracking sound.

Angela stared at her father. What was happening? Why didn't he tell these men to go away? Why didn't somebody do something? She looked up at her mother. Dolores' eyes were closed as she muttered a prayer. Angela looked around the room. Where was Ricardo? And Alberto. He should be here. Bonita, too.

Bascomb said, "The complaints are legal, Señor Martín."

"What're you wasting time for?" Pyle said, glancing at his partner.

John Bascomb shook his head. "Look, Martín. There've been several charges made against you. We have affidavits."

"What charges?" Manuel said angrily. "*What!?*"

Pyle was chewing gum loudly. "Look at him," he said between chews. "He knows the answer, all right. There's nothing to tell, Martín. Let's get going." He pulled a pair of handcuffs from his coat.

Ricardo was suddenly in the room. "*Stop that!* You can't take him! You don't have the right papers!"

"I can't, huh?" Pyle said. "Just watch me, kid." He took a step toward Manuel.

"Goddam you, leave him alone!" Ricardo growled, running across the room. "Goddam you," he said again, and jerked his knee hard against Pyle.

The handcuffs fell to the floor. Pyle bent over, moaning.

Bascomb grabbed Ricardo's shoulder and whirled him around. Ricardo swung a fist at Bascomb. Then there was a loud thud and a groan, and Ricardo staggered backwards, a stupid look on his face.

The sound sent chills over Angela. Her stomach began to twist and turn. Everything in the room except her brother seemed to be floating. Ricardo, upright, tottered for a moment and then began to fall, all the while looking right at her. "Mamá-a-a-!" Angela screamed and pushed her face into her mother's apron.

Ricardo wasn't floating. He was falling hard and he knew it. It was Angela's scream that was pushing him to the floor. The sound of her voice seemed to encircle the nightmare that was going on around him. This wasn't his living room. Nor was that his father being pushed around by two men in suits and white shirts. That wasn't his mother huddled in a corner calling "*¡Madre de Dios, auxilio!*" as she clung to a little girl who wasn't his sister. A mist covered him with cool soft grayness and then drew away, allowing bits of the scene through. Mostly he saw his father's eyes, furious at first and then blank as he lunged at one of the men. Ricardo knew that he had to get up, but the mist covered him and he gave up. He closed his eyes and raised his hands, and the mist circled his wrists and pulled him like a kite far, far into the sky.

When Angela dared to look again, her brother was lying on the floor on his back and it was her father who was fighting. Bascomb was trying to get hold of her father's arms. Pyle was hitting him in the stomach and face. Her father hit back, but most of the time he missed. His face was covered with blood. "Mamá!" she screamed, "they're killing him! Do something!"

When her mother didn't move, Angela grabbed the hem of Bascomb's coat and yanked it. "Stoppit! Stoppit! You're hurting my father!"

Bascomb yelled, "Pyle, you fucking fool! You'll kill him. Stop!" He whirled around, grasped Pyle's arm, and shoved him into an overstuffed chair.

At Bascomb's sudden change of direction, Angela lost her grip on his coat. She took two or three quick steps backwards, tripped over Ricardo, and fell to the floor.

"*¡Madre de Dios, Angela!*" Dolores shrieked. She scooped Angela up and pulled her back against the wall.

Manuel was standing in the center of the room, his arms hanging limply, when Bascomb shouted, "You, Martín, up against the wall with your hands flat and high!" Manuel stumbled to the wall, streaking it with the blood and sweat from his hands.

Dolores had been holding Angela tight. Now she gave her a little push. "Go bring wet rags."

Angela shook her head. She thought she should be standing by her father with her hands high, and that she too would smear blood on the wall. She stared at her hands and began to cry, but her mother turned her toward the kitchen and said, "Go."

When Angela came back with wet towels, her mother was kneeling on the floor beside Ricardo and her father had handcuffs on his wrists. Angela dropped the towels and stared at the handcuffs. They can't do that, she told herself. That's only for criminals in gangster movies. She ran to her father and pulled at his hands. "Tell them to take them off!" she shrieked.

"Dolores," Manuel said, pushing Angela away, "get this girl out of here."

"Go to your room, Angela!" Dolores said.

Angela raced into the front hall. What was happening? Had her father done something wrong? *What*?

Bascomb and Pyle came out of the living room, her father between them. She followed them as far as the front porch. There she watched the two officers shove her father into the back seat of the waiting automobile.

"Papá!" she cried, "stay with me! Don't go! Don't let them take you!"

Her father hid his blood-streaked face and slumped farther down in the seat. The car pulled away from the curb.

Angela hugged the porch pillar. It was hot against her cheek and wet with tears. When the car disappeared around the corner of Twenty-eighth Street, she slid down to the porch step. There was blood on her hands. Papá's blood. She wiped her hands hard on the hem of her dress. The stains wouldn't come off.

Chapter Eleven

When Angela awakened the day after the Immigration men came, it was almost dawn. It was Sunday. Outside the house on Twenty-eighth Street there were muted morning sounds: a car door being closed with unaccustomed quiet, suppressed footsteps on the night-cooled sidewalk. And then the sudden whirr of a lone bird's wings. Inside, the house was deeply silent.

Soft, shadowless light sifted through Angela's window. She shuddered and pulled the blankets over her face. There was something from which she needed to hide. She could not yet place what it was, but she knew that it was something frightening and hateful. And then she remembered. It wasn't a dream. It had happened. They had taken her father. Abruptly, she pushed the blankets aside. Maybe he'd come back!

She rushed to the door of her parents' room and looked in. Mamá was sleeping on one side of the bed; the other side was empty. Nothing had changed since last night. He was still gone.

In the kitchen, she put her head down on the table and cried. Who were those men? What would they do to her father? And there was another more nagging question: Why? Why? What had her father done? She needed to know. She wiped the tears from her face with the flat of her hand and went into the hall. The hinge on her brothers' bedroom door squeaked when she opened it a crack. They were both asleep.

Alberto was sprawled on his stomach, breathing heavily. She knew why he was tired. She had heard Tía Lupe and Mamá talking with him until very late. Carefully, she pushed the bedroom door open wider. Ricardo was lying on his back. One side of his face was swollen, his eye almost hidden under puffy, purple skin. But he was going to be all right. Rosa had said so.

Yesterday afternoon Rosa had come over and helped her mother get Ricardo off the living room floor and into his bed. Then Rosa brought ice from her house and they made cold packs for his face. When Ricardo opened his eyes, Angela was so glad that he wasn't dead that she shouted, "He really fought those men, Rosa! And they were bigger than he was!" Rosa said, "There's something you should know, kiddo. In a dog fight, it's not the size of the dog that counts, it's the size of the fight in the dog." And even though it must have hurt, Ricardo smiled then and Angela had liked him very, very much.

Now, Angela closed the door quietly and went into her own room. Bonita was sleeping, her face toward the wall. Angela sat on top of the rumpled blankets on her bed and, feeling remote, stared at the huge pink roses on the fading wallpaper. Somewhere near her window a bird called hesitantly, waited, called again. On some nearby street, a paper boy sang out, "Sun-n-nday mor-r-rning paypur-r-r! Get your Sun-n-nday mor-r-rning paypur-r-r!" Ordinary sounds. But today she was a stranger hearing them from a far-off lonely place.

❦

It was dawn, too, on the east side of Los Angeles, and Pablo Padilla's brothers, Inocencio and Julio, walked cautiously down the hall of their house near Evergreen Cemetery. Their mother was still asleep. And even though it had been she who demanded that they make this trip, they did not want to disturb her rest.

They had told the sheriff in the north that they would be up on Sunday to discuss Pablo's disappearance, but it would be late in the night before they got to Hansonville. They had had business last night on Fifth Street. Saturday was their best night on the street, and, brother or no, business was business. Still, there *were* family obligations. Besides, Pablo was a sly one; they needed to find out what he was up to.

They had decided to drive the old Ford. The new Studebaker might arouse suspicion. This sheriff who wanted to ask them questions was better left in the north, not brought to Los Angeles to sneak around. Up there, he could not know about the stuff they carried back from Tijuana packed inside the statue of the Sacred Heart of Jesus.

Julio crossed himself as he climbed behind the steering wheel. He would be forgiven the sacrilege. Next Saturday, as a certainty, he would be in the confessional preparing for communion. He would clear his conscience of his sins and receive absolution. *¡Qué pendejos!* Those gringo customs' cops. They might as well be blind. Julio laughed and signaled Inocencio to hurry.

Inocencio jumped into the car beside his brother. As they turned the corner, he twisted around and lifted the heavy back seat to look under it. He nodded. Lying reassuringly on the folded gray Army blanket were the blue steel and brown mahogany of the .45 automatic and the Smith and Wesson. The guns were there, well-oiled and waiting. They never went anywhere without their guns.

At the same moment, miles away in the camp near Henry Kirk's peach orchards, Lalo mumbled as he tossed on his narrow cot. He scratched his chest and arms furiously, and, remembering that it was Sunday, returned to an uncomfortable sleep. The night had been hot and humid; the mosquitoes and bedbugs active; the hours dream-filled and restless. In a few minutes Lalo awakened again.

He sat up and glanced at the sleeping men. He missed Ricardo and Alberto. Everyone here now was older than he was. Outside, a bird trilled a brief morning song. Lalo pulled on his pants and left the tent. Better to be cool, he thought, than to fight for sleep in the sour-smelling closeness inside. He walked to the irrigation ditch and splashed water on his face, then tramped past the end of the road into a cluster of trees beyond the camp.

He had never walked this way before. When he came to a grove of elms and sycamores tucked into the cleavage of the two rounded hills, he cried, *"Bueno, bueno,"* and laughed. A blue jay, high on the branch of an elm, awakened and scolded, and he laughed again.

The ground was piled with a thick mattress of last year's leaves. Lalo ran and jumped and kicked at them. Dropping to his knees, he scooped up a handful. Then he raised his head and the leaves fell unnoticed from his hands. What was that smell? He shuddered as he stood up. Calm down, man, he told himself. Almost embarrassed, he kicked at the leaves, uncovering a patch of white. A crushed, unopened pack of Chesterfields. He picked it up, turned it over, and shrugged as he stuffed it into his shirt pocket. He walked a few more yards into the grove. The shade was deeper. The coolness was more comforting. But the smell was stronger here.

He gasped as he heard scurryings in the leaves and saw rats scratching on the wooded slope beside him. Now the smell made him sick. He buried his nose and mouth into his arm and was glad for the warm odor of his armpit. He wanted to run, but he could not because he had seen something. Something he recognized. A boot. There was an icy lump in his stomach that touched his spine. The chill crawled into his eyes and froze the picture there.

The devil has touched me, he thought, and stared in fascination. There were more rats now, squeaking and scuffling, digging into the body above the boot. Lalo tried to scream, but a hoarse retching sound left his throat. He knew those boots, and the pants above them. They belonged to Pablo Padilla. Lalo ran, his hand over his mouth. He reached the tent, pulled open the flap, and without uttering a word dropped to his knees and vomited.

❧

In a three-room apartment above Johnson's Hardware on Post Avenue in Hansonville, Deputy Sheriff Cyril Stoner awakened in his darkened bedroom to a cheap whiskey hangover that blasted like a raucous trumpet in his head. Outside there was only the indolent stillness of a Sunday dawn in a town that would soon awaken to the prospect of a pew in church, fried chicken and biscuits, and a rocker on the porch.

No sense to hurry the day. There was plenty of time on Sunday.

Stoner turned on the bed and groaned. Damn Saturday nights! Nothing to do in this town but drink. He sat up slowly and stumbled to the kitchenette where he filled an ice bag from the built-in refrigerator. Back at his bed he fumbled with the pillows. Jesus Christ, what a hangover! And even though it was Sunday, because Henry Kirk had told him to, he had to show up at the office to wait for Padilla's brothers. This Padilla business. For some reason Kirk was making a stink about it. So Padilla left all his things, so what? That was just one more reason he'd be back. Stoner groaned again. He'd give his right arm to stay in bed, but, damn it, he couldn't.

Henry Kirk always fixed it so that he could tighten the screws on the people he needed to deal with. He, Stoner, was no exception, and they both knew it. Kirk had him where the hair was short. That business with Immigration and the fruit picker, Martín, for instance. He sure hadn't wanted any part of that. That poor dumb Mexican had taken on too much when he decided to tangle with Henry Kirk. With all the charges they'd thrown at Martín, legal alien or not, he would be deported for sure. He hoped the poor bastard didn't have a family living here.

The telephone rang. The ice bag flopped on the pillows as Stoner sat up. The sudden movement plunged him into blackness, and he reeled across the floor to the wall phone. "Stoner here," he said hoarsely.

"Cyril? That you?"

"Sure, Henry. I'm just leaving for the station."

"That can wait. Get down to my camp at Rust Hill. They've found Padilla." There was a pause and he heard Kirk sigh. "Bring Doc Follick with you. Padilla's dead." Another pause, another sigh. "Not that it's such a loss. Tell you, Cyril, they're a bad lot."

❦

At about the same time that Henry Kirk called Cyril Stoner in Hansonville, Manuel sat up on his cot in the county jail in Los Angeles. Far in some distant chamber there were hollow echoing voices and the muffled din of an institutional kitchen. He thought he smelled coffee. There were small barred windows high on the cement wall of his cell. For the last hour he had watched them change from rectangles of dense dark to rectangles of light-touched gray. Sunday was dawning.

Manuel had slept but little. He had spent most of the night staring at the ceiling. Why? Why? He had never tried to be a hero. Still, he had always been led by a strange sense that seemed to be outside himself to where there was a stand to be taken. Dolores claimed that he was addicted to trouble, searching it out like a drunkard searches out a shot of tequila. But he denied that; he always expected to better the situation, not cause trouble.

Yet it had been the failure of such a stand—some called it a revolution—that had brought him to the sanctuary of this country. In all the years he had lived here, he had been grateful for his new home and respectful of its law. Yet the voice of Henry Kirk had been heard, and he, Manuel Martín, was sentenced without a hearing. Where was the fairness of that law? He looked around at the other men in the cell. It was no comfort to him that he was not alone.

Before the sun had risen, they were herded down dark corridors to a bleak hall for a breakfast of oatmeal and coffee. Then they were marched out of the building and crowded into a bus that waited for them in the shadow of a stone wall. Manuel sat silently, unable to lift his spirits, staring out of the bus window.

The glass, darkened by the wall, mirrored his face. A large red welt rose from a purple mass that was his right cheek. On his cheekbone a two-inch scratch was covered with dried blood. He stared at his swollen face, remembering how he had been dragged out of his home, remembering that his wife and children had witnessed the whole thing. He sighed a long, sad sigh and dropped his head on his arms. Immediately, he heard a voice behind him.

"*¿Qué pasa, hombre?*" Manuel raised his head and turned. A boy, walnut-brown with lank black hair, leaned toward him. "You all right?"

Manuel nodded. "*Sí, sí,*" he said, trying to smile. A child, this one. About the same age as Alberto, but with eyes that showed a youthful innocence. A child was offering him solace. This should not be. Manuel nodded again, and with his good eye winked. "It is only a matter of time, no? In a day or two we will return."

Chapter Twelve

Sunday was a hot day in Los Angeles, even into the afternoon. The ocean breeze had deserted. The hot weather continued into Monday, adding thunderstorms in the deserts and mountains and damp wilting air in the city. In the house on Twenty-eighth Street, the painful memory of Manuel's departure dimmed the discomfort of the heat.

Early on Monday, Tía Lupe arrived. "I awakened knowing that there was trouble," she said. "It was clear that you needed me." And no one questioned her uncanny awareness. It had been part of her for too long.

Late in the morning, Tía Lupe waved down the ice man. She counted out the exact change for the twenty-five pound block, all the time explaining to Angela that they were buying ice because of Dolores. "Your poor mother," she said, "is lying in her darkened room suffering. She needs ice to calm her headache."

But in the middle of the afternoon, Tía broke off a chunk of the treasured ice and filled a large pitcher with lemonade. She brought it to the front porch where Ricardo was reading, Angela was rocking, and Bonita was mumbling complaints as she fanned herself.

Tía put the tray down on the porch railing. "This is for you," she said somberly. "You children will die of heat in this weather."

Angela and Bonita giggled, more embarrassed by their aunt's kindness than amused at her exaggeration. When the lemonade was gone, Bonita decided that she too needed to lie down in a dark room. Only Ricardo and Angela were left on the porch.

Angela said, "What's 'inside to write'?"

"What's *what?*"

"'Inside to write'. What the man said Papá did. You know, at the fruit picking."

"You mean *incite* to *riot*. Well, it's not true, so just forget it."

"Is it bad?"

"Must be. It's against the law."

Angela stole a glance at Ricardo. His disfigured face was made uglier by a frown. "Did he do it?" she asked.

"Don't be a sap!"

"I'm not!"

"Well, don't ask any more questions."

At suppertime it was still so hot that Tía Lupe, contrary to all she deemed proper, allowed them to eat sandwiches under the pepper tree in the back yard.

Night brought no relief. When Angela and Bonita went to bed, Tía Lupe called, "Open your window wide." Later, she came in and whispered, "Diego's come for me. Good night, girls." She walked to the window and pulled the curtains back. "Leave your bedroom door open," she said, "so that the air can move."

It was that open door that allowed the midnight conversation in the kitchen to reach the two girls. The sounds were muffled. Angela heard only the rumble of Alberto's voice and the threadlike curls of her mother's. She wondered who else was there. Because there *was* someone else, a man with a voice that was jagged and fast.

Bonita sat up. "What's going on?"

"I don't know."

"Well, let's find out."

They slid out of their beds and stood for a moment at their doorsill. The light at the bottom of the kitchen door showed like a stripe of gold in the dark hall. They stole toward it.

Bonita looked like a ghost trailing down the hall in one of their mother's old nightgowns. Angela was so intent on avoiding the nightgown's dragging hem that she forgot to step over the loose board by the bathroom. When it squeaked, she pushed herself against the wall, sure that they were caught, that someone would open the kitchen door and frame them in its light. But the door stayed closed. In a moment they moved nearer to it. They heard their mother talking.

"I don't understand what this is about, señor," she was saying. "Why must you warn Manuel?"

"He's already told you," Alberto said. "Padilla disappeared the night we left, but they didn't find his body until yesterday. They think...they're saying..."

The stranger spoke. "Señora, they believe that Manuel killed him."

"Ai-e-e-ey," their mother moaned.

"How can they think that?" Ricardo asked. "Carlos, *how can they?*"

"But they do," the man called Carlos said. "When I learned of that, I told my señora, 'We must warn Manuel'. So we took a bus and here I am. She is waiting for me at her sister's."

There was a long silence, broken only by the sound of a chair being moved. Their mother spoke. "*Al fin,*" she said, her voice flat and weary. "At last, Manuel has killed a man. For years I have been dreading that he would."

Angela shook her head. "No," she muttered and stared at the kitchen door. Her father wouldn't kill anyone. Why had her mother said that?

On the other side of the door, Ricardo was struggling with the same question. How could his mother say that? He stared at her. Her face was glistening with moisture under the single electric light. Her eyes were dark and radiant. He had never seen her more beautiful. He knew that his face was red, for he was filled with something that he couldn't name, but that was deeper than anger. "Mamá! He didn't! He couldn't!"

"Sh-h, sh-h, Ricardo," she said softly. "There are things you do not know."

A knot in Ricardo's stomach tightened. He moved away from the table, pushing his shoulders sharply into the back of his chair. Sh-h, sh-h, Ricardo. How *dare* she treat him like a child! How *dare* she think that of their father? He clenched his hands and stared past his mother to the gray enamel coffee pot on the stove. They had put it on to heat, but it was immediately forgotten. The scent of coffee rose from the simmering pot. He got up and turned off the burner. When he returned, he gripped the back of the chair and spoke to Carlos.

"Padilla was alive when we left, and we three were together every minute. We know everything our father did."

"That's true," Alberto said firmly. "What Rico says is true."

A flush deepened Carlos' mahogany face. He looked away from Alberto. The excitement that had shone in his eyes just an instant before was gone. He looked tired and plainly unhappy. *"Bueno,"* he said. "You both know that I am your father's friend. Why else am I here?"

"We know," Alberto said. "Thank God, he's gone. They'll never find him now."

"Warn him, anyway." Carlos shifted uncomfortably in his chair. "They say that Padilla's brothers are mean ones. And the sheriff and that Kirk have decided that Manuel did it. They will all be looking for him."

"What have *you* decided, Carlos?" Ricardo asked.

Carlos cleared his throat. "Your father is a good man, but anyone can be pushed..."

"Sure!" Ricardo said. "Anyone could have killed Padilla. Everybody hated him."

"Manuel was very angry," Carlos said flatly.

"But he wouldn't kill anybody," Ricardo said, and shook his head. What was going on here? First, Mamá, and now Carlos think that... He left the thought unfinished. What was going on?

Carlos got up. "There is no point in arguing. I have done what I came to do."

While the others pulled their chairs out and stood up, Ricardo sat down. He watched them walk to the door and then dropped his head on his arms on the table.

In the hallway Angela heard the scraping of the chairs and the mumbled goodbyes. She turned to Bonita, but her sister was gone. She picked her way back to bed, fighting her confusion and wishing that things could be as they had been... was it only two days ago?

❧

August was half-gone, and like the ivy that covered the garage roof, Tía Lupe had attached herself to the house on Twenty-eighth Street. Tía lived with her daughter Teresa and her son-in-law Diego. Teresa was a bland, round-faced woman who put up with the antics of her roguish husband with all the patience of a mother. Diego, a small thin man, had, along with softness, a glint of mischief in his dark eyes. A lighted cigarette and a steaming cup of black coffee almost always filled his hands.

Angela was sure that Cousin Teresa and Diego were happy to send Tía to them. She came early each morning, plodding down the street with two shopping bags hanging heavily from her hands. When she reached the front steps, she called loudly, "Girls, hurry! I am waiting for you!" Bonita and Angela came running and struggled up the stairs, each carrying a sack.

In one of the bags were Tía's house shoes, old and flattened; a large butcher's apron; a prayer book; and a worn black rosary. The other held bowls of food from Teresa's house. Each bowl was covered carefully with waxed paper that was kept in place with rubber bands. Once the bags were emptied, Tía took charge.

The days repeated over and over again. In the morning Dolores made coffee and hot cereal. Alberto ate and then left for work. The two girls had their breakfast. Then Ricardo. Ricardo was allowed to sleep late, so long as he got up before Tía Lupe arrived. By lunch time, under Tía's supervision, the house was swept and dusted and the kitchen floor scrubbed. When that was done, Angela and Bonita were allowed to play. But quietly. Because every day now Dolores rested in a darkened room. In the late afternoon Ricardo left to sell papers, and after supper Diego came for Tía. Diego was never in a hurry. Each night he sat at the kitchen table with his coffee and his cigarette. Angela and Bonita hovered around him. Diego was a bright spot in their day; if he didn't have a riddle for them, he had a joke and always gum or candy.

Each day, too, the mailman came, but there were no letters from Manuel. After the frantic telephone call that had relayed Carlos' warning to Manuel, no one really expected them. But one day a letter came from a distant cousin of Dolores. "I ran into an old friend today," the letter said. "He is well, but misses his family and wishes he were with them." When she finished reading, Dolores looked up at her children and said, "Your father is all right."

August ended. There was a hint of autumn in the air. The late sun now had the comfortable feel of a light sweater and there was crisp coolness in shadowed places. One night after Tía Lupe had been coming to them for a few weeks, Teresa invited Dolores and her children to celebrate Diego's birthday.

At the party, Teresa's round face was covered with smiles as she placed platters of steaming tamales and refried beans on the table. When the coffee had been served, she brought out a cake covered with lighted candles, and they all shouted *"¡Felíz cumpleaño, Diego!"* Diego, his eyes shining with pleasure, made a wish and blew out the candles. Once they had their fill of cake, he snuffed out his cigarette on the edge of his saucer and jumped up.

"Bonita! Angela!" he called. "Come dance with me!"

Facing Diego with hands on their hips, they kicked their feet in time to the singing and clapping of hands of the others. *La Raspa!* Ta-rá! Ta-rá! Ta-rá! Ta-ra-ra-ra-ra-ra-rá! When the rhythm changed, Diego hooked his hands through their bent arms and swung them around and around the room. And then Ta-rá! Ta-rá! Ta-rá! Faster and faster until Bonita and Angela fell on the floor, laughing and breathless.

On the way home from Teresa's, Angela leaned against her mother in the back seat of the Ford and slept. She had a dream. It was a half-awake, half-asleep dream, so that the strange stillness of the familiar streets seemed to be a part of it. In the dream, her father and she were once again walking by the surf in Ocean Park. Her father's footprints, broad and deep in the wet sand, began to fade. Then he, too, disappeared. And suddenly the sound of the ocean was gone!

When her mother shook her awake, Angela stumbled into the dark house. Instead of getting into bed like Bonita, she dug in her dresser drawer, fumbling through her clothes. At last she had what she was looking for. She held the curled-up shell tightly, fighting down the fear that was rising in her.

Then she did what she had planned to do. She put the shell to her ear and listened intently. Her shoulders loosened and she sighed. It was all right. The ocean sounds were still there. Just like the day her father and she had found it.

Bonita grumbled, "What's going on?"

"Nothing," Angela said. "Nothing. Go back to sleep."

Chapter Thirteen

Six weeks before, on the day of his deportation, Manuel had tired of weighing the fairness of his situation. Left in Tijuana by the sheriff's bus, he made hurried arrangements for moving on, and in the middle of that same week found himself in the town of Guaymas in Sonora.

As he embraced the familiar sights, Manuel thought, too bad that Ramón is no longer here. Still, there are others I must see. First, he visited his mother's grave and sat by her marker in the stark cemetery for longer than an hour. Finally he rose to go. "I must leave now," he said softly. "But being near you has comforted me." He walked back to town then and looked up old friends.

His friends understood that he was waiting for Padilla's murderer to be uncovered before he could safely attempt to return to his family. They sympathized with his situation so heartily that in the night his sleep was often troubled or irretrievably interrupted by too much self-concern. It was in the middle of one of these restless nights that he knew he must go to Ramón Salgado. Ramón, who had left Guaymas for an even simpler life in Punta de Cruces, would have slapped him across the back and challenged him, "*¿Qué pasa, Manuel?* Feeling sorry for yourself? That will do no good, eh?" The next day Manuel pushed a handful of borrowed pesos across a wooden counter in return for bus passage to Punta de Cruces.

Two days later it was Ramón Salgado who watched him jump down from a northbound bus, disbelief giving way to gladness on his face. "Manuel! *Hombre, ¿qué va?* What are you doing here?"

They embraced in the hot sun by the door of Ramón's small store. They talked and drank cold beer and even had a laugh or two. Manuel went to bed that night knowing that his coming to Punta de Cruces had been the right thing to do.

It was in the morning when he stepped outside that Manuel saw the dusty Studebaker and the two men in it and the gun pointed at him. There was an instant, a fraction not measurable in time or space, when his face showed terror. And then a shot rang out and Manuel fell heavily to the ground.

❧

The weather in Los Angeles had been moving steadily toward fall, but in the third week of September it reversed itself. It was summertime again. The cool pleasant hush of the evenings was gone. Along with the renewed hot weather, created in the canyons by Santa Ana winds, there was a return of the crickets' song and the nights were filled with sound. The days were setting records for heat. Native Californians were explaining away the "unusual weather." On drying devil-grass lawns, flocks of blackbirds pecked and strutted.

The blackbirds scattered from the grass in front of the house on Twenty-eighth Street as Sara Ann Feldman raced down the steps and across the street. "It's gonna rain, kid!" she called to Angela from the curb and then turned and disappeared into the apartment house.

As Angela started up the porch steps, a bright flash zigzagged in the sky above Sara's building. When thunder crashed around Angela, she slapped her hands over her ears and ran into the house.

After supper, with another crash of thunder, the rain began. It pelted the roof steadily and its sound filled the house, almost drowning out the ringing of the doorbell. Alberto opened the front door. A man in a yellow slicker, his visored cap dripping water from its edge, was standing on the porch. He asked if this was where Dolores Martín lived and then handed Alberto a telegram.

Dolores came into the living room, hurriedly wiping her hands on her apron. "Who is it?" she asked, and Alberto held out the envelope.

She took the damp yellow rectangle and turned it over and over in her hands while Angela, Bonita, and Alberto waited. Finally, she tore it open. Her face paled as she read. The line of her chin grew slack as she spoke, "Your father is dead. He has been killed." She held out the telegram, pushing the air with it, and Alberto took it from her and sank into a chair.

Angela heard what her mother said, but it didn't make sense so she waited to hear what her mother really meant. Dolores looked around the room, then took a hesitant step or two towards the sofa. There she stood staring at the wall, her back to the others, and then, with a sharp little shake of her head, sat down. "Your father is dead," she said to Angela and Bonita. "He died in Punta de Cruces. Ramón Salgado says so." She bent her head.

Angela thought that her mother was praying, but she was crying, making harsh whimpering sounds. When Alberto got up and put his arm around her, Angela ran into her room and flung herself on the bed. Through the wall beside her she heard the whimpers turn to wails. She pushed up on one elbow, listening, and the wails sifted through the wall like agonizing ghosts. At last they stopped. In a little while she heard indistinct talking, and then only the dripping of the rain.

Bonita walked slowly into the room. "I can't believe it," she said. "Papá's never coming back."

"You're wrong!" Angela cried. "You're wrong. He's gotta come back."

"He's dead, Angela. You heard Mamá. I guess you're too little to understand."

Angela pushed her face into her pillow. Bonita was wrong. Somewhere somebody had made a mistake. Her father would come back. He always did.

Bonita said, "There's no one to take care of us now."

"Yes, there is! Papá will!"

Bonita sat on the bed beside Angela. "He *can't*," she said softly. And then with a long drawn-out sigh, "We'll just have to go to the poorhouse."

"Stop that!" Angela cried. "You don't know that! You don't know everything!"

"More than you. You're not just little, you're dumb!"

"I *am not!*" Angela shoved Bonita. "Get off my bed!"

"Make me!"

Angela bounced up and yanked at the hair at the back of Bonita's head.

"Stop it!" Bonita swung around and grabbed a handful of Angela's hair and pulled hard.

"Ow-w-w!" Angela caught hold of Bonita's arm.

They grappled, trying to escape the other's hold, but neither girl could do it. Finally they slid off the bed to the floor, the bedding sliding with them.

There was a shocked silence, and then Bonita muttered, "Hey, where are you?"

"Under your smelly foot. Take it off."

"If I can find it," Bonita said, laughing.

Angela giggled. They lay on the floor, wrestling with the bedding and laughing until it hurt to breathe. When they disentangled themselves and sat up, they were in a square of light coming from the hall. Tía Lupe stood in the doorway.

"You girls are making the angels weep," she said, shaking her head. "Quickly, now, straighten up this room." Tía disappeared behind the firmly closed door.

Later, when Angela heard Alberto in the hall, she followed him into the kitchen. "Where you going?" she asked, watching him push into his jacket.

"To get Ricardo. He should be here."

At the stove, Tía nodded. "Go, Alberto. Yes, go. The family should be together at a time like this."

Angela said, "Can I go with you?"

"No. You stay here." To Tía he said, "I'll be right back." He closed the back door with unusual care and stepped out into the wet night.

"Where is Mamá?" Angela asked her aunt.

Tía let out a long tired breath. "She is resting. Do not disturb her."

Angela tiptoed to her mother's door and opened it carefully. She wanted to be close to her mother, to press her head into her shoulder and breathe the sweet smell of face powder that was as much a part of her as her long waving hair. But she stood stiffly in the doorway, staring at the little hills and valleys that the woven bedspread made around her mother's body.

She leaned against the door frame, holding back a sob. She sensed that to make a sound right now would be unkind, that her mother needed to be alone, maybe as much as she needed to be *with* somebody. And that somebody was her father. She wanted her father, but he was somewhere far away and a man named Ramón Salgado said that he was dead. She whispered the word, "Dead," and then shook her head with a little shudder.

Papá is dead, she thought, and tried to absorb the immensity of that knowledge. He has been dead since before we got the telegram. He died after the Immigration men took him away, and now he won't come home anymore. When we heard from Mamá's cousin, he was alive. But now he's dead. She closed her mother's door.

In a few minutes she was outside, ignoring the rain as she knocked at Rosa's back door. Her heart beat fast as she waited. Her mother had told her never to bother Rosa when the shades were drawn, but tonight was different. Tía had said, "We should be together at a time like this." Angela knocked once more. There was no answer. She knocked again and finally turned away. She had reached the pepper tree when she heard the squeaky hinges on Rosa's screen door.

"Oh, Rosa, you're here!" she called, and ran back.

Rosa was wearing a red satin robe and her hair was mussed up as if she had been sleeping. "What is it?" she said. "What is it? What are you doing here?"

Angela threw herself against Rosa. "It's...something's happened...Papá's...my father's..." She couldn't say it. "I need you, Rosa."

Rosa glanced hurriedly over her shoulder and stepped outside. "Whatever it is, kiddo," she said close to Angela's ear, "it will have to wait until tomorrow."

"No, please, I have to tell you..."

From somewhere in the house, a man's gruff voice shouted, "Jesus, Rosie, this is one helluva note!"

Rosa straightened up.

"I'll go," Angela said, her face burning. She had done something terribly wrong.

"Yes, you'd better go."

Angela couldn't see Rosa's face because of the light behind her, but she was sure that tonight Rosa would not look the same. Even her perfume seemed different. Only the touch of her hand was familiar.

"I'm sorry, kiddo," Rosa said. She went into the house and closed the door.

Angela, already walking away, heard it shut, a dull heavy sound in the dank night. The scent of Rosa's perfume followed her. She thought of the feel of the red satin robe and of Rosa's body beneath it, and she kicked at a puddle, splattering drops of mud on her legs. She went to the front of the house and sat in the rocker. Rosa had turned her away. And she hadn't even asked what the matter was. Angela pulled her legs under her and twisted uncomfortably.

Nothing would have happened, she thought, if they hadn't taken my father away. Or, if he hadn't gone to the fruit picking. Because that's where he did something wrong. But what? Somebody said something about a crime, and right after they all came back from the fruit picking, Mamá said Mexicans were treated like criminals here. Was that why they took him away? Angela frowned deeply as she swung her feet to the floor. And if they hadn't taken him away, she told herself, he wouldn't be dead. She watched the rain fall from the roof's edge onto the porch railing and felt the drops splash against her legs. "He's dead," she whispered, and shook her head.

When she heard her brothers' voices in the back yard, she went into the house.

Bonita said, "Where've you been all this time? Why are you so muddy?"

"I was outside," Angela said, and went into the bathroom to wipe the mud spatters off her legs. Then she went into the living room to look for Ricardo.

He was slumped in a corner of the couch, his hair and clothes still wet. Damp spots were spreading on the rug by his feet. His eyes, always heavy from his reading, looked even

more tired. They had blotchy red circles around them. Angela
felt a new sadness as she looked at him.

"You're all wet," she said, swallowing hard, and he nodded. "Do you want a towel?" He shook his head.

"Leave him alone," Alberto said.

Angela sat down in a chair across from her brothers. She
waited patiently, glancing at Ricardo now and then, hoping he
would say something. He didn't, not even to Alberto. Ricardo
still had not spoken when Tía Lupe came in the room.

"Here you are, Angela. We have been looking for you." Tía
Lupe took a moment to settle herself on a straight chair that
creaked and groaned at her weight. "Your mother and I have
been talking, and it is decided that you are to go to Punta de
Cruces with her."

Punta de Cruces? Where was that? And then Angela
remembered her mother's voice, hollow and distant as she
said, "He died in Punta de Cruces." Angela said, "Me, Tía?
Why?"

There was a droop to the corners of her aunt's mouth, but
as she looked up at Angela she raised her lips into a small,
weary smile. "Because your mother needs someone to speak
English for her on the bus. Because it won't hurt you to miss
school. And because your passage costs very little." Her eyes
went to Ricardo as she added, "It is all we have to spend."

Ricardo nodded. "It's all right, Tía. I understand."

Alberto stood up. "Guess we'd all better get some sleep."

When Angela and Bonita were ready for bed, Dolores
came in to see them. She paused in the doorway. Angela
thought, how old she looks. Her skin is looser and more pale
and her eyes are swollen, not pretty like before.

When Dolores finally spoke, her words seemed pulled
from a deep place. "Angela and I are leaving for Punta de
Cruces at midnight." She glanced at Angela. "Your aunt says
you are all packed." Angela nodded.

Dolores spoke to Bonita. "Remember, Bonita, you are to
help Lupe in every way."

"I know," Bonita said with a sigh. For a moment Angela
thought she had seen Mamá's crying look on her sister's face.

Angela got into bed and asked, "What are we going to do in Punta de Cruces?"

"Only what we can. The rest is in God's hands."

Yes, but *what?* Angela said to herself, and slid under the blankets.

Dolores bent over and kissed them. "Sleep now. I will wake you in a few hours."

When her mother awakened them, Angela thought that only a few minutes had gone by. But it was almost midnight. It seemed all right to be talking and drinking hot milk in the kitchen even though it was so late. It seemed all right that everyone was up and moving around as if it was daytime. But the ride with Alberto at the wheel of her father's car was strange, and the large gray bus traveling through dark wet streets was strange too, and not all right at all.

Chapter Fourteen

For nine-year-old Angela the all-night bus ride from Los Angeles to the border town of Calexico on the way to her father's funeral had been a long, miserable journey. During those dark hours she had slept, awakening often to the slow and unwelcome realization of where she was. And why. Now, it was late morning and Angela was in the U.S. Immigration office at Calexico, waiting impatiently for her mother.

The man in the gray uniform had said "Stay right there, little girl" when he called Dolores to the other side of the counter. Angela, cramped and tired from the night's bus ride and from sitting so long on the hard bench the man had pointed to, still did not dare to move. Her mother had warned her that they would have to make a stop in Immigration on the American side before they crossed the border into Mexicali. Her papers, she said, had to be stamped so that she would not have trouble returning to the United States. But her mother hadn't warned her that it would take so long.

The office was crowded with layers of heat that pushed in through the open doors and windows; with lines of sweating people and their warm, leathery smell; with the noise of typewriters and telephones and voices talking in both Spanish and English. Except for new people coming in and others going out, nothing changed. Outside, however, the shadows cast by the sun were now shorter and sharper, as if cut carefully with scissors, and Angela realized that it must be near noon. She looked longingly over the counter to where she could see her mother's head in the back of the room. She squirmed uncomfortably. No matter what the man said, she *had* to stand up. And just as she did, her mother did too, nodding to the official across from her as she put papers back into her purse.

Somewhere in the distance a church bell was sounding the hour as Angela and Dolores walked out of the building to a narrow sidewalk and past a gate that was as wide as the road.

Even before Angela had finished counting the clangs of the bell—seven, eight, nine—they had crossed the border between Calexico and Mexicali. Ten, eleven, twelve! It was noon, and she was in another country. This was Mexico.

The building they walked by had an arched doorway and windows covered with iron grillwork. There were brilliant posters on its walls advertising a dance, *Gran Baile,* on the following Saturday. And, of course, everyone here talked in Spanish. When her mother stopped to ask directions, Angela kicked at the dry earth, watching the dust rise and settle again. She decided that it looked just like American dust. And the posters. They weren't really that different from the ones in the Plaza at home. If that was so, then why did she feel so strange, as if she was in a place across the world from Los Angeles?

Her mother tapped her shoulder. "Here, Angela. Carry our bag for a while and follow me."

Angela took the large mesh bag that held their clothes and hurried after her. They paused by a restaurant. A woman standing in the doorway nodded and smiled as Angela peered inside. The place was filled with the wonderful aroma of onions and chile and oregano. Angela's mouth watered; she was very hungry. But they didn't go in. Instead, her mother went into the shop next door and asked something about Punta de Cruces. A heavyset man came out of the shop with them and, talking rapidly and waving his arms about, pointed out directions to her mother.

When the man went back into his store, Dolores turned to Angela. "There is time," she said. "We will have something to eat." They went into the restaurant and ate beans with chopped meat and chili, and, because it was so hot, her mother let Angela have a glass of iced tea with lemon and sugar.

Outside once more, they walked briskly toward the street that had been pointed out. Angela carried their bag again. It seemed heavier now and she lagged behind. When her mother turned a corner, Angela followed and bumped into her. Her mother was standing absolutely still, staring at two men who were tying a canvas cover over the top of a small yellow bus.

"*Madre de Dios,*" Dolores whispered.

One of the men yanked at a knotted rope near the top of the bus. *"Bueno*, Luis," he said, "that will do it."

From behind the bus, another man showed his head above the canvas. He gave a tug to the ropes and nodded. "It will hold." He came around from the other side, wiping his face on his shirt sleeve. "Punta de Cruces?" he asked. Dolores nodded and he moved quickly to open the bus door. "As soon as I pick up the mail, we will be ready to leave. Meanwhile, señora, you must get out of the sun."

The man called Luis took the bag from Angela and held it as he helped her mother into the bus. Once Dolores was seated, Luis put their sack on a seat across the aisle from her. Angela hesitated, wondering where to sit, and her mother motioned her to the place beside their things. Spread out on the other seats were boxes and bags and bolts of bright fabric, but they were the only passengers. Luis returned, climbed into the driver's seat, and started the motor. They began to move.

Through the rear window and the cloud of dust following them, Angela saw the low crowded buildings of Mexicali shrinking behind them. Ahead, a dirt road stretched in a thin straight line across a rocky plain.

The desert was tan and gray and sometimes gray-green, and it went on—maybe, forever, Angela thought—without really changing. Once in a while she caught sight of the ocean beyond the desert to her right, and she pushed her head out the window, hoping to feel a cool breeze. But there was none. Every now and then, far ahead, it appeared that another ocean or a large lake sprang up, shallow and quivering in the hot sun. But when they came near, it disappeared. Sometimes, too, it seemed to her that the land was moving, not the bus. Hours passed as they bumped along the lonely narrow road.

❧

Once Angela fell asleep, but the bus ran into a chuckhole, jerking her head and hurting her neck. She wished that she could sit near her mother. She wished that she could say, "I'm

scared, Mamá. I don't know what's going to happen to us
now." But she couldn't. There was something on her mother's
face that stopped her—something that made her mother seem
not grown-up at all. And that new something was much sad-
der than the crying look. She needs Papá too, Angela thought.
She closed her eyes and imagined that he was there saying,
"Patience, patience, Dolores. It is not all that bad, eh?"

At last ahead of them and near the ocean, a cluster of
boulders rose against the sky. As they neared them, Angela
saw that they were actually buildings bleached by the sun to
desert colors. Beyond the buildings a point of land pushed out
into a smooth blue bay. Below the point there was a long
wooden pier and at its end a shed roofed in corrugated aluminum rose. Several small ships hovered close by.

The brakes of the bus squealed and the floorboards quiv-
ered as they came to a standstill. The motor shuddered and
was silent as Luis twisted around and smiled at them.
"Bueno, señora," he said, "we are here. This is the Salgados'
store." They were stopped alongside a long low building.
Above its faded green door and its one window, peeling white
letters proclaimed *Tienda La Reina*.

Luis stepped down to the bus door, paused to stretch, and
then pushed it open and jumped to the ground. He strode
through the entry of the building shouting, "Ramón! Ramón
Salgado!" The green door closed behind him, but not before
Angela heard the jingling of a bell and a deep voice calling,
"*Ven, hombre*, I am in back."

Dolores got up. "Come," she said to Angela, and walked to
the bus door.

Angela wiped the perspiration off her face and followed
her. Taking her mother's hand, which felt clammy and cold
against hers, she stepped down from the bus into the late
afternoon strangeness of Punta de Cruces.

Her mother paused in the sun, and Angela followed her
look down the deserted street. There were four or five other
buildings on either side of the road and a single gasoline
pump at the end. Beyond the gasoline pump there was a scattering of white wooden crosses on the promontory by the sea.
The sun was low in the sky above the water, coloring every-

thing with a subdued rosy glow. Dolores turned and opened the green door, and the bell jingled as they walked into the store.

They were in a crowded low-ceilinged room that smelled of cinnamon and drying chili peppers and of stale, smoking lard. Shelves with canned goods lined the back wall. Below the shelves, a wooden counter ran the width of the room. Sacks of dried beans and rice leaned against it, and on the wall at the end of the counter there was a large electric icebox. Rows of beer bottles and soda pops showed through its glass doors. Angela turned to look at it as it started up with a squeaky, whirring sound.

Her mouth was dry and hot. Her words cracked as she said, "Mamá, there are sodas!"

Dolores nodded. "So I see. I think you may have one."

At that moment the curtains in an opening behind the counter parted. A tall thin man hurried through them. A strand of graying hair fell on his forehead above eyes that were circled darkly.

"Dolores," he said, "Dolores, *linda*." He put his arms around her. "After all these years, to see you under such a cloud."

Dolores sighed deeply. "It is the way with life, Ramón."

"But not the way it should be." The tall man turned to Angela. "And this must be Bonita, or is it Angela?"

"I'm Angela," Angela said, and put out her hand. Then, embarrassed, she drew it back, but Ramón Salgado took it and held it in both of his. "I am glad to meet you, Angelita." He strode behind the counter and brought out two grass chairs. "Sit down, sit down. Carmen will be here in just one moment. Meanwhile, a cold drink? What will it be?"

Dolores said, "A lemonade will do. Thank you."

Ramón Salgado winked at Angela as he opened the icebox door. "For you, Angelita," he said, "not lemonade. I know what young girls like. Hidden behind these others, I have a bottle of strawberry soda."

Angela's knees were suddenly rubbery and her eyes filled with tears. She sat down quickly and took the cold slippery bottle he handed her. By the time she had finished the soda,

Carmen Salgado, a small woman with green eyes, had come in and met them, and Luis had brought in the bag with their clothes.

Carmen Salgado said, "You must be very, very tired. Would you like to rest?"

"Not I," Dolores said. "We have a lot of talking to do."

"No, thank you," Angela said, straightening up in her chair. The grown-ups were going to talk; she needed to listen. "I am too old to take a nap."

Carmen smiled and Ramón Salgado said, "Yes. Angelita is almost a grown lady."

"You need to sleep, Angela," Dolores said firmly. "You have been up all night."

Angela knew the finality of her mother's tone. It would do no good to argue, so she rose and followed the two women into the back of the store. The little room to which Carmen led them had one small window. Carmen unfolded a canvas cot and placed it at the foot of a large iron bed. "Leave the door open," she said, "and there will be some movement of the air."

After the women left, Angela tossed uncomfortably on the cot. If the air was moving, it certainly wasn't here. She looked across the room at the window. Light filtered through worn spots on the lowered green shade, but there was no indication of air sifting through. She stared at the patterns the light made on the scratched-up shade and imagined that one of them was an old man resting on a cane. Were there others? She raised her head slightly and dimmed her eyes. Her heart hammered in her chest. There. There, ever so clearly, was her father's face. But when she pushed up on one elbow, his face disappeared. Disappointed, she lay back and the canvas cot creaked. Almost immediately she heard a creaking sound outside followed by men's voices.

"*¡Qué infierno, hombre!*" Is it always this hot in September?"

"*No, amigo.*" She recognized Ramón Salgado's voice. "But this year *has* been hell." There was a pause, and then he added, "We must bury Manuel early tomorrow. Fernando, at the shrimp shed, has been making extra ice for us, but we cannot wait another day."

The creaking sounds began again, and then there was a thud. The other voice exploded, *"¡Cabrón!"*

"Sh-h, Luis. The girl is sleeping. Hurry."

Angela slid off the cot and ran to the window. She pulled the edge of the shade back in time to see Ramón Salgado and Luis trudging by, carrying between them a long wooden box. Transfixed, she watched them pass the window and as she understood what she was seeing, a confused anger swelled in her.

Now she knew what had been covered by the canvas on top of the bus. She had wondered about Mamá's white face when they had first seen the bus. Now she knew. It was a coffin for Papá. She flung herself on the cot and cried. Now she knew. Her father was dead. They were going to bury him tomorrow and nothing would ever be right again.

Angela lay spent from her tears and her tiredness. Within minutes, the droning voices of Dolores and Carmen in the next room lulled her into a half-sleep. Once in a while she heard the jingling of the bell in the store and the scraping of a chair as Carmen hurried to a customer, and those sounds became a part of her daydreaming. Then new sounds awakened her completely.

At first there was a sharp clang. Then thu-h, thu-h, thu-h followed by a burst, hee-ic, hee-ic, hee-ic, hic, hic, hic. And silence. The pattern was repeated. Only this time the metallic hiccuping became a hum that was almost covered up by shouting. *"¡Adiós, compadre! ¡Hasta mañana!"*

She sat up, her heart hammering again. Slowly, she lay back. Someone had started a car with a crank the way her father always had. That was all it was. She turned her face away from the window, and the cot creaked and sighed once more.

Angela was sure she couldn't sleep now, not with hearing the car and seeing the coffin and wondering where her father was. But the hum of the women's voices, the jingling of the bell, and the soft scraping of the chair blended into swells of sound that flowed over her. And for a little while before she fell asleep, she forgot about tomorrow.

Chapter Fifteen

It was later in that same day. Far from Punta de Cruces in the house on Twenty-eighth Street, supper was over. But the gloom that had accompanied it was not. Alberto, Tía Lupe, and Bonita had eaten their meal silently. Now, as the back door slammed, they raised their heads eagerly, welcoming a break in the mood that had settled over the kitchen like a gray fog.

Ricardo came into the room. "That's a long streetcar ride," he said, and slumped heavily into a chair. "What smells so good, Tía?"

Tía Lupe's face flushed with pleasure as she rose and served him a large bowl of soup. Bonita, already at the doorway, said, "I'll be back to help when everyone is through," and disappeared. In a few minutes, Tía Lupe left too.

Alberto got up and poured himself a cup of coffee. "Well, they're in Punta de Cruces by now."

"And they'll bury him tomorrow." Ricardo fought back a desperate urge to cry. He wanted to cry because it was good to be home. Good to be away from the frantic downtown corner where he sold his evening papers. Good to sit in this well-known, creaking chair. He wanted to cry because his father would never feel these things again. He rubbed the back of his neck. "Was it Padilla's brothers, do you think?"

Alberto shrugged then held up the coffee pot, a question on his face. Ricardo nodded and pushed his cup forward. Alberto filled it then brought the small enamel pan with hot milk back to the table. "Too bad you couldn't go instead of Angela," he said, sitting down. "You might have found out if Ramón saw the killers."

"Maybe. But what if he did?"

"*What if he did?* Shit, what a question! When are you going to grow up? To go after them, of course. I know where I can get a gun, and I'd go after them."

127

"To do what?" Ricardo said evenly.

"Kill them. What else?"

"Maybe they'd kill you first."

"I'm not afraid. I'd take that chance."

"Hey, Alberto, maybe I'm not grown up, but you're the one talking like a kid. More killing isn't going to bring him back. What would be the use?"

Alberto threw out his arms in an angry gesture. "We ought to do *something* about it!"

"Sure. But what?

Alberto's shoulders drooped. "Something," he said hoarsely. "Something."

Ricardo felt choked, as if the knot he had been carrying around all day in his stomach had abruptly moved to his throat. He swallowed hard. "Maybe when they get back, maybe then we'll figure what."

The two brothers said nothing for several minutes, sitting silently across from one another. Finally Alberto pushed his chair back and rose. "It's going to be up to us now to take care of them," he said, looking into his coffee cup. He picked it up, took one big gulp and left the room, wiping his mouth on the back of his hand.

Ricardo stared at the doorway and nodded. There were a lot of things they would have to take care of now. He was glad Alberto had been thinking about that too.

❦

Supper was being readied in the Salgados' kitchen in Punta de Cruces. At the stove, Carmen Salgado looked up from a steaming iron pot she was tending and smiled as her two sons walked in the building's rear door.

In the room where Angela was sleeping, a candle burned unsteadily as Dolores bent over her daughter's cot and shook her gently. Angela opened her eyes and looked into the wavering flame. She groaned and turned her back to the light.

"Angela," Dolores whispered, "hurry. Supper is almost ready."

Angela sat up abruptly, rubbing her eyes. The candlelight threw jagged shadows on the ceiling and on the walls, making the room look strange, but she knew exactly where she was. And she knew exactly why she was here. She had been dreaming about the coffin.

Dolores put the candleholder on the floor. "Here," she said, handing her a dampened washcloth, "wipe your hands and face while I find you another dress." She emptied the mesh bag on the end of the cot and rummaged through the clothes. "You will wear the pink one. At least it is clean." And then, reaching into the pocket of the dress, "What is this? A seashell?"

The candle sputtered and shadows danced wildly as Angela thrust out her hand and seized the shell. "It's mine!" she shouted, then quickly lowered her voice. "Don't take it away, please." If she spoke too loudly or said too much, the desolate nightmare held fast within her might break through its bonds. "Please."

"Keep it, keep it," her mother said wearily. "There is no time to worry about such things."

Angela was fully awake now. Quickly, she slid the shell under her pillow and pushed her arms into the sleeves of the dress. She brushed her hair and followed her mother into the kitchen. In the light of a single flickering light bulb, Angela saw two boys in white shirts and black ties at an oilcloth-covered table.

Dolores said, "Angela, these are the sons of Señor Salgado, Juan and Salvador." The boys rose and mumbled that they were glad to meet her.

Remembering that her dress was wrinkled, Angela rubbed her hands across it in a useless effort to smooth it. The boy called Juan watched her and smiled. He was eleven, maybe, and dark like his father. Salvador's face was angular, his hair a light brown color. He looked about Alberto's age.

Carmen Salgado pointed to the chair beside Juan. "Sit there, Angela," she said.

Angela sat down and Juan leaned over and whispered, "It's too bad your brothers aren't here."

"Yes," she said. "But Alberto has a new job and he couldn't leave it. Ricardo wanted to come, but I got to because I didn't cost as much."

Juan nodded seriously. "What bad luck."

"Why?"

"*La vela,*" he said. "You know, the vigil with your father. They must have wanted to do it."

"I guess so." Angela was not at all sure that she knew what he was talking about.

Juan moved uneasily in his chair. His face was getting red. "Don't think we don't want to do it," he said. "We do. And that's the truth. Besides, it's only for one more night. Your father was a good friend and we know he shouldn't be left alone."

"Oh." They were guarding her father. But from what? She looked up as Carmen put a plate in front of her. "Thank you," she mumbled, but her mind was not on food.

Juan nudged her. "Please eat. You're company, and Mamá says we can't eat until you do."

Angela nodded, picked up her fork, and discovered that she was hungry. Before she had finished eating, Juan left the table and returned with a bottle of strawberry soda. "My father said this was for you," he said.

A frown darkened Salvador's face as he looked at his brother. "We don't have much time, Juan. You'd better eat." In a matter of minutes Salvador stood up. Juan gulped down his food and did the same.

"Where are you going?" Angela whispered.

"*A la vela,*" Juan answered, as quietly as she. "To keep the vigil."

When the two boys were gone, Angela rose and carefully pushed her chair against the table. "May I be excused?"

Dolores looked at Carmen who said, "Yes, you may be excused, but there are no lights in that back room." As Angela hurried out of the kitchen, she heard Carmen say, "There is only enough electricity for the store and the kitchen."

Without the candle, it was dark in the bedroom. Angela felt her way by the cot and the bed to the window. Just as she got there, the bell in the store jingled. In a few seconds she heard the grind of footsteps on the gravel by the side of the building, and then voices.

"You'd better stay awake tonight, Juan," Salvador said crossly. "I don't like sitting there alone." There was a grunt for an answer and the footsteps went by the window and receded into the night.

Salvador and Juan were on their way to guard her father. But he was *her* father; she should be there too. She pulled open the window, jumped out, and raced to the rear of the building. In the light of a fading moon she saw a bench by the kitchen door and a large boulder a few yards away. But where were Juan and Salvador? How could they have disappeared so quickly?

The ground sloped up from the back of the store into a small hill. At its highest point she could make out a tall, narrow building. A cross pushed up from its roof. A church. Was that where her father was? Even as she wondered, Juan and Salvador appeared on the incline beyond the boulder. She started after them, but the loose rocky earth made the going difficult. She had only covered a few yards when she saw that the two brothers were already at the church. A door opened in a smaller structure beside it, and Ramón Salgado stood framed in a rectangle of light. He said something to the boys as he stepped outside, and they nodded and closed the door.

Angela turned around and ran back down the hill. When Ramón circled the boulder and headed for the front of the store, she raced on the opposite side to meet him. She knew what she was going to say. "Señor, I want to be with my father. I am old enough and I will stay awake. Please take me there." She rounded the corner of the building and ran toward him. "Señor," she called.

"Angelita. What are you doing out here?"

"Nothing. Just...just looking."

"And are you coming inside now?" He held his hand out to her.

Angela went to him and slipped her hand into his. "Señor," she whispered. Her mouth was dry and hot. "Señor, I want to...I am old enough...I think I should..." Her words refused to go anywhere.

"What is it?" he asked gently, and his fingers closed tightly over hers.

"Nothing," she said. For now the warmth of Señor Salgado's hand was enough.

The next morning after breakfast, Carmen brought a galvanized tub into the back bedroom. "For your bath," she said to Angela. "You can help me carry in the water."

Dolores laid out Angela's clothes on the bed. Clean white socks and panties and her blue dress, the one with the white flowers, freshly ironed.

"It should be black," Dolores said with a sigh.

"But it's my best dress. Won't it be all right?"

"Yes, yes, it will have to do." Dolores picked up a black lace square that lay on the bed beside her. "This is for you. Tuck it in your pocket now, but wear it on your head in church and at the funeral."

Angela took the scarf and went outside to wait. The bench she had seen in the moonlight was there by the kitchen door. She sat on it for a few minutes and then stood on it to look out toward the sea. The water was steel-gray and glassy and as still as the air. There was a boat far in the distance that seemed as motionless as the water.

The back door slammed and Juan stepped outside. His eyelids were heavy. He seemed to be fighting to keep his eyes open. "My father wants to know if you're ready," he said in a tired voice.

She shook her head. "I don't want to go at all." Seeing the shock on Juan's face, she added, "But I will. I'll come inside soon."

He shrugged indifferently and went back into the house. Within a few moments, the door opened once more and Ramón Salgado came out.

Last night, like his sons, he had worn only a shirt and dark tie above his trousers, but this morning he was wearing an old suit coat too. His hair was slicked back so that the stubborn lock remained in place. Smoke from a half-burned cigarette curled ahead of him as he came and sat on the bench by Angela. "Juan tells me you aren't ready. *Bueno,* there is no

hurry. I could use a little more time, too." He drew on the cigarette and exhaled slowly.

"It's not that I don't want to go," Angela said. "It's that...
I'm...I'm afraid."

Ramón shifted his weight on the bench and his dark eyes
softened as he said, "*¿Cómo no?* Of course, you are." After
that, he smoked silently.

The quiet was long and heavy and real. It was there, like
the rocks and the hot sun, and Angela wanted it to go away.
She was beginning to regret having confided in him when he
flipped his cigarette to the ground.

"It is not easy to lose a man like your father," he said. "I
will miss him too." Then with a touch of a smile on his mouth,
he added, "The day he was here he talked of many things. One
of them was you."

"Me? What did he say?"

"How much he liked to be with you. That you are a young
lady with much understanding. That you brought him great
joy. He made me wish for the daughters I do not have."
Ramón raised his head, and Angela saw a little light dancing
in his eyes. "Manuel sometimes 'counted money in front of
beggars.'"

She smiled. That was a saying her father liked to use. It
made her almost happy to hear it. She sat quietly for a
moment and then reached in her pocket and dug out the black
scarf. "Look, señor," she said, holding it up before him, "do I
have to wear this?"

"You don't like it?"

"No. It's black and ugly."

"Then why are you carrying it around?"

"Mamá told me to wear it later," she whispered almost
inaudibly.

Ramón straightened up and said, "*Bueno.* That is different. If it will please your mother for you to wear it, I think you
should."

She nodded, glaring at the lace scarf that she held loosely
on her lap and feeling deeply ashamed. She stole a glance at
him, and he held open an arm. She slid across the bench to
him. He patted her shoulder and said, "It would be a kindness

to your mother. It has not been easy for her, knowing that
your father was killed."

"Who killed him? Do you know?"

He shook his head.

"Why was he killed, señor?"

"We don't know that either."

There was a silence in which Angela felt something growing, something that would become clear in a moment, something dark and ugly like the scarf. She pushed away from him
on the bench and said, "Only bad men get killed, señor."

Ramón Salgado shook his head. He stood up, removed his
suit coat, and laid it on the bench, carefully creasing the collar
at its fold. "Listen to me, Angelita," he said. "It doesn't matter
how your father died. What matters is that he was a good
man. Nothing can change that."

Angela stared at her feet. She kicked at the dirt with the
toe of her shoe. That man Pyle had said, "What were you
doing up in Hansonville, Martín?" And her father hadn't
answered. Why? Why? "Only bad men get killed," she muttered again.

Ramón said, "I wish that were true, but it is only that way
in stories." He took a few steps up the slope and stared across
the bay. In a moment he turned. "There never was a better
man than your father. I knew him as a boy and as a man. He
was brave and kind and generous. Whatever he did, his intent
was always for good. Your father was a good man. I want you
to remember that."

She wanted to believe him. But why had those men taken
her father away?

Unexpectedly, Ramón closed his eyes and turned to face
the bay again. He sighed a long shuddering sigh and remained
with his back to her for a moment. Then he walked to the
bench. "Come," he said, putting on his coat. "It is time to say
our last goodbye."

Angela laid the square of lace out on the bench and tried
to smooth it.

Ramón held out his hand and took the scarf from her. He
put it on her head and tied it carefully under her chin. "What
do you say, Angelita? I think we are ready, no?"

Chapter Sixteen

The church of Santa Marta, on its hill above Ramón Salgado's store, waited passively in the late morning heat. It had a worn, beaten look, having given in to the corrosive attacks of the sun and the sea. Its paint was peeling, and the large wooden cross that rose from the roof above the arched front door was dry and faded and leaned slightly to one side. To the people of Punta de Cruces, it did not matter that the cross was not straight. What mattered was that it faced the water, and those who sailed on the shrimp boats were comforted by its outline even when they were many miles out into the gulf.

This morning the small church shaded the men and women waiting together for Manuel's funeral service. The mass was delayed because the priest, Father Abelardo, had driven out into the desert earlier that morning to administer last rites and had not yet returned. It was a small group: six or seven men and Carmen, Dolores, and Angela. The women stood on a raised square of cement in front of the doorway, Dolores' face almost hidden by a thick black veil.

Angela, standing beside her mother, felt sweat beading at the edges of her hair and brushed the scarf back from her forehead. When she heard a voice say, "Angela, come down here with me," she turned to find Juan standing on the ground below her. He was wearing a fresh white shirt and his hair was wet and plastered against his head. Even from this distance he smelled like soap.

"Come on," he said again, "come talk with me."

Dolores said, "Go ahead," and Angela went with Juan toward a shaded corner of the churchyard. The men were gathered a few yards away.

"That's Fernando," Juan said, pointing to a short heavyset man who was talking with Salvador. "He works at the shrimp shed."

Behind Fernando, huddled against the wall of the church, four men talked intently.

"Who are they?" Angela asked.

"Your father's friends from Guaymas. My father telephoned them."

Looking at them, Angela was touched by a vague sense of wonder. They had known her father. They had talked to him, maybe since she had. It was all right that *she* didn't know *them*. *They* had known her father.

One of the strangers said, "Let's go after them! I didn't come here just to stand and..."

"*No, hombre,*" another broke in. "We came because Manuel is our friend. Leave the others to God."

The first man shook his head and muttered something Angela couldn't hear. The speaker shrugged.

"*¡Cuidado!*" a third voice said. "Careful. Here comes Father Abelardo."

A man in a black robe strode with Ramón Salgado to the raised platform, his black skirts sweeping the ground and raising little swirls of dust. He talked briefly to Dolores. Then Carmen beckoned to Angela, and Angela left Juan and followed her mother into the church.

They sat on rough wooden benches. In the front, candles flickered on a table that held a statue of Mary with the baby Jesus. The priest walked in from a side door, his head bent, his hands pressed together. He began to pray in Latin, and in the back row two old ladies who had been there when they entered began to cry loudly. Angela twisted on the bench to look at them, but her mother took her arm firmly. For the rest of the service Angela sat looking straight ahead, wondering where her father was.

Once they were outside, Ramón Salgado motioned to Juan and Salvador and to her father's friends. They all hurried to the back of the church, returning in a few minutes. They were carrying the coffin she had seen the day before. A pickup truck backed around from the side of the church and the men lifted the coffin into it. When the truck began to move down the hill to a broad dirt street below, her mother took her hand and they followed it.

The air was hot and still and dust-colored. Here and there sunlight glinted off a rock, and Angela blinked as she watched the coffin bumping in the back of the truck.

Her father was in that box. Killed.

The pickup made rattling noises. It moved very slowly, zig-zagging to avoid large rocks and raising a great cloud of dust behind it. Angela licked her lips and coughed.

Killed. But it doesn't matter. He was a good man.

They passed the gasoline pump and turned onto a road that led in the direction of the bay. Suddenly, the road ended and a hill began. The truck stopped. There was even more dust. She had to spit, but she knew she shouldn't. She swallowed instead.

Killed. By two men. But it didn't matter how he died. He was good and kind and brave.

The men slid the coffin off the truck and carried it up the slope. Father Abelardo stood at the top and pointed to his left. The men carrying the casket went that way.

He was good and kind and brave. Señor Salgado said so.

Along with her mother and the Salgados, Angela climbed to the top of the incline.

Killed. He had been killed. But no matter what, her father was good.

This was the point of land with the white crosses. This was the cemetery. This hot, rocky place was where they were going to bury her father. She followed her mother around the crosses and the mounds of rocks that marked each grave. The men put her father's coffin down beside a freshly dug hole in the ground. Then the priest began to pray.

Angela shut out his voice and listened to the sound of the surf beating against the rocks below them. She shut her eyes, and in her mind her father and she were once again walking along the surf in Ocean Park. He bent over and scooped up a shell from the sand. "Look what I've found," he said, holding out a shell. He pressed it to his ear for a moment, then handed it to her. "Listen carefully. It has music in it, no?" She shook her head. "I can't hear anything." Her father told her to try once more. She held the shell tight against her ear, and he said, "Can you hear it this time?" She had cried, "I can! Yes, I can! It sounds just like the waves."

Now, standing by her father's grave, she dug into her pocket and curled her fingers around the same shell. She opened her eyes. Across from her, Father Abelardo raised his face to the sky.

"We entrust to You, oh, Lord, a sinner," he said in a scratchy, grating voice. "We commend to You his soul that it may be cleansed of evil."

There was a rustle as her mother and Carmen Salgado crossed themselves and some of the men from Guaymas shuffled their feet. Angela pulled at her mother's skirt. "Why is he saying those things?" she whispered.

"Shush, Angela."

The priest said a few words in Latin. "Save him from the everlasting fires of hell," he added loudly.

"Tell him to stop, Mamá," Angela whispered. "Don't let him talk like that. Tell him to stop."

"*Be quiet*, Angela," her mother whispered urgently.

Angela closed her eyes tightly, but that didn't shut out Father Abelardo's raspy voice. "We are born in sin and we die in sin," he said. His words seemed to burn holes in the scarf covering her ears. She tore it off.

"I won't listen anymore!" she cried.

"Angela!" Her mother's fingers dug into Angela's shoulder.

Angela flung the scarf to the ground and ran away from the grave. After a few steps she whirled around. "You can't say those things!" she yelled at the open-mouthed priest. "My father was good!" She ran again, the image of her mother's ashen face floating in the sky before her.

She stumbled and fell. The sharp-toothed rocks scraped her knees, but she got up, brushed them, and kept on running. There was something she had to get away from, something dreadful that gave a bitter taste to the tears that rolled down the side of her nose and into her mouth. She looked over her shoulder and found Juan racing after her.

"Wait, Angela, wait! My father wants you!"

"No! Go away!" But when she reached the edge of the promontory, Juan was by her side.

"Why...did you...do that?" he panted. "You shouldn't have."

"And he shouldn't say bad things about my father!"

"But he's the priest. You shouldn't run away from him."

"I don't care. I'm not going back. I'm going to stay right here."

"You can't. It's a cemetery. You can't stay here all alone."

"Why not? Nobody cares. Not even my father. He said he would never leave me."

Juan's face paled. "But he was killed, Angela."

Angela turned away from him. "You think I'm bad," she said. "Well, I'm not. Just go away." A few yards away from her she saw a large boulder with a flat top. She fought back tears as she ran and climbed on it.

A distant voice called, "Juan!" Angela turned. The people by the grave were walking away, including her mother. She was leaning on Carmen as they made their way down the slope. Angela watched, hoping, but her mother didn't look back.

The only one remaining was Ramón Salgado. He waved his arms high above him. "Juan!" he called again. "If she does-n't want to come, leave her alone. She'll be all right."

Juan said, "Your mother won't like it. Come back with me."

Angela shook her head and Juan left, walking reluctantly, making several stops to look back. Finally his head disappeared below the slope that led to the road and she was alone.

From where she sat, she could see the bay and, if she turned, the crosses and the mound of earth that was her father's grave. She felt a strange uneasiness. She had done something wrong...not shouting at the priest, somehow she felt that that wasn't it, but something—and she didn't know what it was. She slid off the boulder and walked carefully to the edge of the cliff.

Jagged rocks were piled high against the bluff below her and all the way around the curve of the bay to the pier. There was no way to walk along the water here, but it didn't matter because there was no one to walk with anymore. She turned back and her eyes fixed on two men with shovels who were filling her father's grave, scooping earth from the mound beside it. They had put him in the ground. Now she was really alone.

Aloneness, she became convinced as the day wore on, was the never-ending sound of the water slapping against the rocks and the almost unseen movement of hundreds of puffy clouds in the sky.

Several times during the early afternoon she started toward the grave, but each time she stopped, returning to the shade of the big rock. Later, she leaned her head against the boulder and fell asleep. How long she slept she didn't know, but when she awakened she felt rested and strong and not quite so afraid until she saw something scuttling from rock to rock a few feet from her. A rat! She scrambled up on the boulder. The rat sniffed and nibbled as it searched the ground. When a pebble slid down the face of the rock, the rat turned bead-like eyes in her direction, stayed immobile for a second, then scurried away. Well, it was gone, she thought. And if a little stone could scare it, she wasn't going to be chased away. But she stayed up on the boulder until the unsparing sun drove her down into the shade.

Then, almost before she knew it, the sun was going down and she realized that she was extremely hungry. She could see the town and the sign that said *Tienda La Reina*, and knew she could find her way there. But she also knew that no matter how scary it was here, she wouldn't go back. Her mother had let the priest say terrible things; she wouldn't go back. It's as if I didn't care about anything anymore, she thought, and gave a tortured little sigh.

The first star had appeared in the sky when she saw headlights on the road below the cemetery. Then she heard footsteps walking toward her. She was lying on the ground, pressed close to the boulder and more scared than she had ever known she could be, when the footsteps stopped and a match was struck. In its glow she saw the face of Ramón Salgado. She didn't know what she had expected, but her teeth were chattering from fear. She dug her hands into the earth and little by little stopped shaking.

Ramón Salgado must have known how frightened she was because, although he had seen her, he stayed where he was.

In a little while he said, "Angela? Angelita? It is I, Ramón. I have come for you."

"I'm glad it's you, *señor*," she said. She pushed herself up, brushed herself off, and climbed up on the boulder.

"Are you all right?" he asked as he sat beside her.

"I'm all right," she said, at once embarrassed and pleased.

"The boys have never been too far away. They have been looking out for you."

"I'm sorry if I was trouble, *señor*. I had to stay here though."

"Your father would be unhappy if he knew."

"Would he?" Then hungry to share the thoughts that had built up during the day, she said, "Papá said he loved me, señor, and then he left, and then those men killed him. I wanted to see him, but the coffin was closed. I wanted to tell him about Carlos from the fruit picking and about what Ricardo said and about the letter I wrote him. I wanted to tell him that Mamá thinks he did something bad..." She clapped her hand against her mouth. Slowly, she dropped it. "More than anything, I wanted to tell him I was sorry."

"Sorry, Angelita? For what?"

"For...for not...for... That's what I don't know," she finished lamely. "But my father would have known."

Ramón Salgado coughed. Then she heard him fumbling in his pockets. Soon she heard the crinkle of paper and rustling sounds, and then the smell of tobacco. He lit a cigarette, and in the burst of match light she saw that he looked deeply tired. "Yes, your father was a wise man," he said, exhaling smoke. "He would have been able to help you."

"I know, I know." She nodded vigorously. "That's why I had to stay here."

He put his hand over hers. "Your father is no longer here, Angelita. You must believe that. Your mother and you are the ones who matter now, and we must not worry your mother anymore."

Ramón Salgado talked for a long time, but Angela did not want to listen. Still, some of the things that he said comforted her, and after a while some of the things he said even made her want to laugh so that finally she was willing to take his hand and go with him past her father's grave and down to the road. The small truck that waited there smelled richly of gasoline. As she climbed on the front seat, she thought she couldn't bear being alone ever again. She edged close to Ramón Salgado as they drove back to the store, the truck's dim headlamps barely lighting the way.

Chapter Seventeen

A helicopter was circling above the freeway. Its whirring, sputtering clatter swelled whenever it was overhead and diminished as it curved to the south. As if at a signal, several heads pushed through open car windows and twisted to peer upwards. Angela's was one of them. She pulled her head back into the car, and through the windshield watched the helicopter disappear over the hills ahead of her. She wondered if it had something to do with the hangup on the highway, then quickly dismissed the thought—not because it made no sense, but because it didn't matter.

She dropped her head on the steering wheel for a fraction of a second, quickly raised it, and sighed. She was feeling strange. Her head buzzed and her fingers, now on the seat, now on the wheel, were limp and slightly shaky.

In front of her, a battered Oldsmobile had replaced the Datsun. Big cars, little cars. She felt a comradeship for them. They were all in this funereal march together. Even the gray monster with the flashing eyes that was, as usual, behind her. A camper slipped between her and the Olds, and she decided that the sticker on its rear door would be an epitaph: Don't Follow Me, I'm Lost.

But I'm not! I have somewhere to go, some thinking to do. Find out what kind of a mess they were in here. She had to figure how to get out of here. But how could she think clearly when she was so tired? Besides, her mind had been taken over by an army of confusing thoughts, leaving no room for planning. And she hurt, all the way down her right leg. The on-and-off braking of the car was pulling something and, damn it, she hurt. No matter what Doctor Eichar said.

"Look at that scar," he had pointed out pridefully last week. "Clean, clean. And only eight weeks since your surgery. You mend beautifully, Angela." She had mended, yes. But what was *under* the clean scar? Doctor Eichar had held forth reassuringly."...You're a lucky lady...everything is fine. The therapy? That's to put *my* mind at ease..." But how much of what he said could she believe?

Leaning back against the headrest, she concentrated on not braking the car, letting it roll with its own momentum. About half a mile ahead, the four lanes of cars slithered like a great snake around an uphill curve. When the road straightened out on the crest of the hill, she saw a large sign by the shoulder that said "Road Construction Ahead." So that was it. Well, she'd get off the freeway at Oceanside.

To her right, beyond the fields and cliffs that edged it, the ocean was beginning to reflect a bronzed path of light from the declining sun, and on the road, brake lights were beginning to flash again. She came to a halt behind the camper. Keep calm, she told herself wearily, we'll soon start up again. But long minutes passed and the cars didn't move. She turned off the ignition. Beside the freeway a dirt road led to a distant rise where yellow bulldozers, trucks, and other road-building vehicles were clustered, their outlines sharp against the sky. Above them masses of white and gray clouds were fired with coral, reminding her that the sun would soon be setting.

Not long until dark and she was nowhere near San Diego. Much less Punta de Cruces...

❧

When Angela and her mother returned to Los Angeles from Punta de Cruces and her father's funeral, it was early afternoon. From the bus station they had taken the Maple streetcar to Twenty-eighth and, even though they were both worn physically and emotionally, they walked quickly up their street. To Angela their return seemed a miracle, and for a moment tears blurred her eyes. They were half-a-block away from their house when she saw her new neighbor, Sara Ann Feldman, sitting on the front steps.

The day was clear and warm, a mild benevolent warmth, not like the harsh heat of Punta de Cruces, and Angela was so glad to be home that she dropped the bag she was carrying and ran to meet Sara.

Sara jumped up. "Hey! Hey, kid! Where've you been?"

"To Mexico," Angela said as she reached her. "To my father's funeral."

"Your *fa*-ther? He's dead? How'd he die?"

They killed him! But he wasn't a bad man! He wasn't! Angela didn't want to answer. On the way home from Punta de Cruces she had made up stories about her father's death. He was on a fishing boat and was lost in a storm. He had had a strange sickness with a fever that was so high that a thermometer couldn't measure it. He had slipped and fallen off a high cliff into the sea. And more. But her fabrications crumbled and slid into an unreachable place when Sara repeated, "How'd he die?"

Angela's shoulders stiffened. It was no use. She'd have to tell Sara. She parted her lips to speak, but her mouth was so dry that the words she formed stuck on its roof. She tried again. "He...he was...some men..."

Sara couldn't wait. "Dying's no good," she said matter-of-factly. "I sure don't want Poppa to die."

By that time Dolores had reached the girls. Angela said, "See you later," and followed her mother into the house.

The next day Sara wanted to know about Mexico. "What did you eat?" she asked. "Did you ride donkeys? How come everybody wears those big hats?" Angela made up answers where she didn't have any. So long as the questions asked were not about her father.

One late September morning when their teacher was putting a lesson on the blackboard, Sara leaned across the aisle that separated their desks and pulled at Angela's skirt. "Hey, kid," she whispered. "I've been wondering. Are you some kind of Jewish, too?"

"Me? Uh-uh."

"Well, what are you then?"

Angela thought for a while, remembering her teacher last semester and the boys who had chased her after school. "I'm American," she said. "It's my family that's Mexican."

"*Huh?*"

Their teacher whirled around and slammed a ruler on the back of her chair, and Angela and Sara quickly busied themselves with their books. After school, Sara, in a green flowered dress with its sashes untied and hanging limply, caught up with Angela. They said nothing for the first few steps, but when they were nearing a street corner, Sara threw Angela a sidelong glance.

"Kid," she said, "I've been thinking. "

"What about?"

"About how come you're one thing and your momma and poppa are something else. I never heard of that."

"So?" Angela said, running down the cement steps of the crossing tunnel, racing through the tunnel itself and, with a catch in her breath, climbing up the steps at the other end as fast as she could. At the top, she turned and looked below her into the dimly lit darkness from which Sara would soon emerge. "WELL, NOW YOU HAVE!" she yelled, and the echo of her words bounced back and forth against the gray cement walls.

She waited for Sara at the top of the tunnel steps, feeling a little bit proud—she'd told her all right—and a little bit shaky. What would Sara say now?

When Sara reached the street, she pulled at her sashes and said, "Tie these for me, will you?"

"Huh?"

"Tie them. And hurry. So we can go to my house. I want you to meet my Poppa."

"Sure," Angela said, "but I don't tie so good and I've got to get permission." In the house on Twenty-eighth Street, Angela's mother, lying on the living room couch, gave her a weak nod and said, "Yes, yes, go." But Tía Lupe followed Angela to the front steps and watched the two girls cross the street.

In the apartment building, Sara paused by a door which had an oblong metal ornament attached to it. She blew a kiss at the metal tube. "That's our new mezuzah," she said.

"It's nice. But what is it?"

"A mezuzah, like I said. You can touch it for good luck."

Angela touched it hesitantly and Sara opened the door. The room they entered had shiny tables and several lamps, and in one corner, the Victrola. At the far end, by a small bookcase, a man with gold-rimmed glasses sat at a desk reading a newspaper. When Sara cried, "Poppa, hey Poppa, this is my new friend Angela," he rose.

"So?" he said. "A friend of my Saralah's. That's very good." He returned to his newspaper as Sara's mother walked into the room.

Mrs. Feldman, like Sara, asked a lot of questions. "Have you lived in your house a long time?" And then, "I see you have a sister. Do you have brothers too? And that nice plump lady, the one who comes to your house early each morning, is she your grandmother?" Before all the questions were answered, Mrs. Feldman herded them into the kitchen where they drank cold, cold milk and ate great airy chunks of sponge cake with bits of orange peel scattered through it.

Nearly every day from then on, Angela spent the after-school hours at Sara's. Her own house seemed empty without her father, with Bonita so suddenly distant, with Alberto at work, and with Ricardo at his corner selling papers. Tía Lupe and Dolores were there as usual, but they sat and drank coffee and discussed sad things.

"Things you should not be listening to," Tía would say, a note of soft concern in her voice. "Go. Go play with your chatterbox friend, *la israelita.*"

One day when Angela had stayed at the Feldmans too long, Bonita was sent to get her. She knocked on the Feldmans' door and when Sara opened it, she said, "Where's Angela? Doesn't she know the time?" She waited by the open door, looking around curiously.

As they crossed the street, she complained to Angela. "They don't have any crosses, and not even one picture of the Sacred Heart of Jesus." Angela didn't answer but ran quickly up her own front steps. Bonita shrugged and walked contemptuously into the house.

The September days disappeared. October came, and November. Behind Angela's house, the vegetable garden was dead. After Manuel left, it had flowered briefly, the spreading vines of the yellow squash being the last to bear any fruit. In the garage, the gardening tools leaned idly against the wall. They were beginning to rust. Then December arrived, wet and cold. And the cold rain spilled over into January.

The Feldmans had lived on Twenty-eighth Street for six months. They filled a vast, empty place in Angela's life and she clung to them, making her afternoon visits as long as possible. Bonita didn't like it.

"Why do I always have to come get you?" she whined one afternoon as they left the apartment house. "You might as well live there."

Angela ignored her, racing across the street in the soft twilight. On the front porch she fell into the old blue rocker.

Bonita walked leisurely up the steps and sat on the porch railing. "Seems to me," she said, "that you don't like your own family anymore."

Angela blinked furiously as she rocked. It wasn't just that Bonita was acting grown-up and superior. It was more than that. She felt trapped, as if she had been caught without her clothes on. She jumped up, ready to race into the back yard. But when she saw Rosa walking down the street, her beaded purse swinging at her side, her heels making sharp clicking sounds on the sidewalk, she changed direction. Rosa liked her just the way she was. With a great sigh she ran to meet her.

In the next few years Angela learned to ignore Bonita's mocking comments, and her friendship with Sara grew. Sara and she became inseparable, fighting for the use of the Victrola at one house, a spot in the blue rocker at the other. Periodically, Alberto repaired the porch rocker, even painting it, and Angela guessed that her brother did that to keep close to the memory of their father. The heavy rocking chair had been Manuel's purchase and a place he too had loved to sit. Except for Dolores and Ricardo, all of the family used the rocker. Tía Lupe was sitting in it when Angela returned from school one day in her fourteenth year.

Her aunt had bad news. Rosa was leaving Twenty-eighth Street. When Angela heard that, she ran over and pounded on Rosa's back door. "Is it true?" At Rosa's nod, she added, "Why? Why?"

"Because I'm getting married, kiddo," Rosa answered. "One of my gentlemen has the crazy idea that he wants me around all the time."

"Oh." Angela sat down slowly on the steps. Rosa sat beside her and Angela said, "Do you love him?"

Rosa threw her head back and laughed. Angela straightened up quickly, her eyes on Rosa's face. "No, kiddo," Rosa said, "I'm not laughing at you. It's just that when you get to be my age, you don't worry about finding love. You worry about corns and backaches and bulges in the wrong places. He'll be good to me and I'll be good to him. You want to call that love? Okay."

It was to Sara that Angela spilled her sadness at losing Rosa.

Sara listened, quiet for a change, and then said, "Hey, it's not all that bad. You've still got me, haven't you?"

"I know," Angela said. She wanted to say more. At that moment she wanted to tell Sara that she loved her more than anyone else in the world. And she knew she couldn't because they would have laughed and giggled, making silly remarks to cover up their embarrassment. She also wanted to tell Sara how important she was and how lucky she, Angela, was to have a friend to whom she could tell anything, anything at all. But all she said was "I know" once more.

A couple of years later Angela discovered that there were some things she could not talk about even to Sara. And that was only one of the truths she learned about herself because Armando came along.

❦

Angela was fifteen when Ricardo brought Armando, a slim dark-eyed fellow of seventeen, to the house on Twenty-eighth Street.

They were at supper in the kitchen when the back door opened, letting in a crisp fall breeze and the sound of Ricardo's voice saying, "Come on, come on in."

At the kitchen door, Ricardo said, "Hey, everybody, this is Armando. He's got my old corner. Armando, these are my folks."

Armando held back at the door. "I'm glad to know you," he said. "But I'll wait outside. I don't want to butt into your supper."

Angela stopped eating and stared. She had never seen such long eyelashes. "You're not," she said, and blushed.

Ricardo nudged his friend into the kitchen and they dragged a couple of chairs up to the crowded table. Tía, at the stove spooning rice and beans onto individual plates, nodded at the newcomer. "Sit down, sit down. There is plenty for everyone."

"You don't know how much I can eat," Armando said, grinning.

Tía smiled. "Show me."

Armando turned to Dolores. "With your permission, señora, I will." Dolores, shaken out of a revery, smiled and nodded.

Along with his steaming plate, it was obvious that Armando had received Tiá Lupe's heart and Dolores' approval. He made himself at home as Ricardo had suggested, immediately becoming a part of the household, spending as many hours under the old Model T as Ricardo and Alberto did, and sharing about as many meals.

Everyone liked him, including Dolores, who usually responded negatively to even little changes. Tía Lupe bloomed when he was there. She smiled a lot and actually hummed under her breath and, whether anyone else wanted it or not, served *salsa fresca* because Armando liked it. When he wasn't around and was mentioned, she would say, *"Ay, qué simpático,"* brushing her hair away from her face and sighing.

Simpático. Armando was truly *simpático.* He had all the requirements. He was as easy as the old blue rocker, with a well-disposed and unexpected sense of humor that lit up his face and his surroundings like a burst of sunlight. And he had a light-hearted empathy that was as honest as it was rare.

Of course, Bonita liked him. He was a male. Besides, he was handsome. A little too thin maybe. Bonita, who at sixteen spent a great deal of time contemplating marriage, said, "If he had a wife, I'll bet he'd put on weight. Can you picture what his shoulders would look like then?"

The first time Sara caught a glimpse of Armando, she drew in her breath in a low whistle. "*Who* is that?" she asked Angela.

It was late afternoon and the two girls were doing homework at a table by Sara's living-room window. Sara had been looking out the window, daydreaming, when she straightened up, pulled back a corner of the curtain, and leaned forward. Angela pushed her books aside and looked out the window too. Across the street, Armando was walking around the front end of a battered green Chevy parked at the curb.

"Well, who is he?" Sara asked again.

"Rico's friend," Angela said. "He's...he's okay."

"Okay? Who're you kidding? He's cute. Does he like you?"

Angela felt her face grow hot. "Gosh, Sara, how would I know?"

"You mean you don't want to tell your very best friend." Sara's round blue eyes sparkled with mischief. "You ought to watch out, though. If I weren't so in love with Rico, I'd go after him myself."

"Cut that out, Sara! You're not in love with Rico, *or* Henry Greer, *or* Nathan Goldsmith. You just like to flirt with them all." Angela picked up a pencil and put it down again. Her voice softened as she said, "If you want to know the truth, I hope he does like me."

"Well, kid, if that's the case, you'd better go after him. You'll have all sorts of competition, beginning with Bonita." Angela nodded and thought sadly of her pretty sister.

She need not have worried. Armando treated Bonita pleasantly, but when he got a job ushering in the local movie house, it was Angela he smuggled into the theatre a couple of times a week. She would sit in the back row and, whenever he could, Armando came and sat with her.

There was a night when he found her hand and held it, brushing his fingertips across hers, squeezing it lightly. To Angela, breathless as she stared mechanically at the figures flickering across the screen, that light touch was electric, charged with wonder. When after a moment he went back to ushering, she was filled with a loneliness that took her by surprise. When he returned, an equally surprising gladness took its place.

"Angela," he whispered, "know something? It's raining outside. Hard."

"No kidding?"

"No kidding. Will anyone worry if you stay till the last show? I've got my brother's jalopy and I can take you home then."

She didn't know if anyone would worry, and for that moment she didn't care. "I can stay."

Later, they waited by the darkened box office for the rain to let up, and when it seemed that it had, they dashed down a side street to Armando's borrowed Chevy. They were drenched and filled with laughter as they sat in the rain-curtained car catching their breaths and steaming up the windows. Instead of starting up the car, Armando slid his arm around her shoulders, and she looked up at him and counted her heartbeats until he kissed her.

They wore their feelings like sandwich boards, but only Tía Lupe teased her. "I don't know what you see in him," she would say each time Armando left. "He is so ugly."

"Yes, isn't he?" Angela answered her with a smile. "And he hates your cooking."

The others in the family said nothing. They hung back, treating the pairing as something too delicate to be disturbed. They obviously loved the match. But their eager approval frightened Angela. Even though she preferred Armando, she began looking for other boys to date, sneaking out of the house to meet them. One of those dates had been to the Old Plaza and Olvera Street.

She found that Olvera Street had changed, growing more crowded and more gaudy, but the Old Church was the same and the walkways and the benches were the same too. Walking through the Plaza, a dry November breeze had rustled the leaves of the trees and memories assailed her. "Remember, remember," they whispered. "In that little shop you're passing, your father bought you a painted clay cup in which the water always tasted sweet and cool." She pushed the haunting voices away, refusing to remember.

A day or two later, Armando asked her to be his "steady." "You're my girl, Angela," he said. "I don't want you seeing other guys." His eyes and his words held so much hurt that Angela's own eyes filled with tears.

"I don't want to see them either," she said, and vowed that she would never cause him pain again. But in just a few weeks she forced herself to forget her vow.

It was New Year's Eve, and there was a great enamel pot of *menudo* on the stove. The steamy, rich aroma of the broth had tantalized them all day. Early that morning, Tía Lupe and Dolores had washed the tripe carefully and, along with onion and garlic and large kernels of white corn, set it to simmering. Then in the evening they chopped green onions and fresh cilantro to float in the *menudo*, which was to be served at midnight.

The house on Twenty-eighth Street was full that night. Cousin Teresa and Diego were there; Alberto's girl, Raquela, and her sister; the new neighbors and their three sons, around whom Bonita hovered happily; and Armando, of course. Armando, carrying chairs for Tía, listening to Diego's jokes, talking seriously with Ricardo about the possibility of war. And always returning to be with Angela.

Just before midnight Diego hurried to fill wine glasses for all, and when their old console radio blared with horns and bells and shouts of "Happy New Year," they all drank to Diego's toast of "Peace in 1941." Then came the usual commotion of hugs and kisses for everyone. When Diego squeezed her tightly, he whispered, "I like your young man, Angelita."

"Armando's my boy friend, Diego, that's all."

"But he soon will be more than a boy friend, no?"

"No, Diego, no," she said, her face turning hot with an emotion that was more like anger than embarrassment. Diego, she knew, meant well. He had said what he thought would make her happy, but it didn't. It didn't! She edged away from him and stood in a doorway. This was bound to happen, she thought. Somebody was going to do it sometime. Diego had made her look, and she didn't want to. She didn't want to look at her life without Armando—but that was how it had to be.

Someone had brought out Dolores' guitar and most of the people were gathered around her, crowding the floor at her feet to sing. From across the room, Armando waved to Angela. She nodded and waved back, and in a moment he was by her side. They sat on the floor together, leaning against the wall in a darkened corner, joining in the singing at times, at times quietly looking into one another's eyes.

"I'm glad you're my girl," Armando whispered, brushing her ear with a kiss. She nodded because she was afraid to talk.

It was then that Diego found them. "There you are, Angelita," he said with a wink. "Will you lend us Armando for a moment? We're moving tables into the dining room."

Armando squeezed her hand as he helped her up and then went with Diego. For a few minutes she stood in the doorway listening to the songs. Then she turned abruptly and rushed into her bedroom. Tears streamed down her cheeks.

I don't belong here! But Armando will always be content to live in a *barrio*, to sing songs just like those they're singing in the living room, to…to stay Mexican. And that's one thing I won't do. But I love him. How can I live without him?

How long she stood at the window staring at a pale moon that glinted above the pepper tree and searching for a way out of her pain, she wasn't sure. She was brought out of her thoughts by a loud knocking at the door.

"Angela! Are you in there?" It was Alberto. "Angela! Everyone's looking for you."

She didn't answer.

Alberto rattled the doorknob. "Angela! Lupe needs you. And you can't leave Armando out here all alone. What's wrong with you?"

Angela slipped into the closet and closed the door.

"Angela?" Alberto had opened the bedroom door. "Where the heck did she go?" he muttered. There was the sound of the door closing. Angela came back into the room and, later, when she heard goodbyes being said, pulled on her nightgown and slid into bed.

When she got up the next morning, everyone except Tía Lupe was still sleeping. Angela dressed quickly and quietly and went into the kitchen.

Her aunt was mixing masa for tamales in a large bowl. Angela placed a quick little kiss on her aunt's cheek and said, "I'll help with the tamales and the house in just a minute, Tía. I have to see Sara first."

Her aunt gave her a long look. "Yes," she said, "go talk to your friend. But remember, Angela, this is the first day of a new year. What you do today is important. It becomes a pattern."

"Yes, Tía, I know. I'll remember."

Angela pulled on a sweater and ran across the street. Instead of going inside the apartment house, she slid between the side wall of the building and some shrubbery and walked quietly toward Sara's bedroom window. "Sara," she called, tapping on the window screen. "Get up. I have to talk with you."

There was no answer. "Sara," she called again. She raised her hand to tap at the screen once more, but stopped, inhaling deeply the cold morning air. *What am I doing here? Sara won't understand. No one will. I can't talk to Sara about this. I can't, even though I'm right.* She looked again at Sara's window and then turned slowly and walked away.

That afternoon she sat in the porch rocker, telling herself over and over again that sometimes you had to give up one thing to get another. It was in that mood that Armando found her.

"Hey, Angela," he said, taking the steps two at a time. "Where'd you go last night?"

She moved toward him, the usual glow of welcome spreading warmly through her body. And then she caught herself. "To my room," she said. "I had to think."

He sat on the floor near her and leaned against the wall. "Well, I missed you." Patting the floor next to him, he grinned and said, "Come sit by me."

She bit her lip, then shook her head. "No, Mando, I'm not going to sit by you anymore."

"That's silly. Sure you are." He turned toward the screen door and sniffed the air. "Tamales. I'll bet your Tía Lupe is making tamales."

She nodded impatiently. "Yes, she is. But didn't you *hear* me? I'm not going to sit by you anymore."

"Silly."

"Stop that! I'm serious. I've decided that I'm not your girl anymore."

He turned and looked up at her, a puzzled look in his eyes. "Hey, don't say that."

"I'm not your girl anymore," she said.

"Aw, man, you don't mean that."

She told herself that, of course, she didn't, that, of course, she *couldn't*. But she nodded briskly. "I do, I do! Oh, Mando, please go away. *Please!*"

"You want me to? Really?"

"I want you to. Yes."

He got up slowly and stood looking down at her, a pained look on his face. "See you tomorrow, huh?"

"Maybe. But it won't be the same between us."

Armando ran his fingers through his hair in a pathetic gesture of puzzlement. "Okay," he said, "okay. We'll just wait and see."

She avoided Armando all the next day, but in the evening he cornered her in the kitchen while she was doing dishes.

"How come you're mad at me?" he said. "What'd I do?"

"Nothing."

"Well, then everything's okay." He moved quickly, placing a kiss on her cheek.

Soapsuds fell on the floor as she wiped her face. "Don't do that."

Armando took a step or two away and leaned against the wall. "What's happened? I thought it was all fixed. I thought we'd get married someday. Maybe soon even, and now... What's happened?"

"I can't explain. I don't know how to explain. It's just that I don't want to anymore."

"But why?"

"Go away, please."

Armando straightened up, pushed his hands into his pockets and went out of the room. Watching him walk through the back porch and into the back yard, Angela's heart felt swollen with a terrible sense of loss.

Armando hung around the house for another few months, looking at her with hungry eyes. But even though guilt prodded her, she didn't relent. Then the draft got him and he was whisked away into a world war from which he never returned.

🦌

It was after Armando's death that Ricardo volunteered for the Army.

His face was flushed and his eyes as brilliant as patent leather when he rushed into the house late one afternoon. "I've done it!" he shouted at Tía Lupe and Dolores. "I'm going into the Army!" He didn't wait for their reaction, but raced out of the kitchen and into his bedroom.

That night everyone had something to say about his decision. Alberto asked if Ricardo was out of his mind. Wasn't it enough that hundreds of Chicanos from L.A. had been killed in France or Italy or some damned island in the Pacific? Why did he think he needed to go? Besides, he wasn't an American citizen yet. Dolores sighed and shook her head and said that, of course, Alberto was right. Tía Lupe said nothing directly to Ricardo, but studied him thoughtfully and periodically said, "Humph!" Diego took Ricardo aside and counseled him quietly. "Your father," he began, "if he were here..." Ricardo listened respectfully, grinned, and slapped Diego on the shoulder. "*Gracias*, Diego," he said, and ignored him along with the others. Angela watched her brother speculatively. Ricardo, she figured, was going out to tackle the Germans and Japs singlehandedly for killing his friend. She knew, if no one else did, that nothing would stop him. She was wrong.

The medical examination stopped him. There was an old healed tubercular lesion on one lung, and he was disqualified. For weeks after that rejection, Ricardo was angry. He cursed the Army for being short-sighted, the doctors for being dull-witted, the lesion for being apparent, the members of his family for being relieved, and life for being generally illogical, unfair, and lousy. In time he calmed down. He returned to his work-and-study schedule, becoming his old self again.

Ricardo was not the only one who was shaken by Armando's death. Angela was seventeen and a half when they got the news that Armando had been killed, and she thought that she would never get over it. But then Walt came along and she learned to love him. And loving Walt had eased a sadness that never quite disappeared.

Chapter Eighteen

Angela met Walt at Los Angeles City College. She was a student there only because Ricardo had argued on her behalf. Alberto could not see the need for more than a high school education, if that, for a woman.

The day she met Walt was bright, clear, hot—one of summer's leftovers. When her one o'clock class was dismissed, Angela found a shady spot under a tree. The grass felt cool against her bare legs; the tree trunk, sturdy. She settled back for a quiet hour between classes. That was when Walt came along.

"Is there enough shade for two here?"

Angela looked up at a sandy-haired fellow wearing cotton twill pants and a short-sleeved white shirt. He was just under six feet, too thin, and not exactly handsome. But his angular face was somehow nice to look at. "Why here, Walt?" she asked, reading the name machine-embroidered across the pocket of his shirt.

He grinned and dropped his books on the grass by his feet. "It looked like a good spot," he said, and sat down. "You don't mind, do you? I wanted to meet you."

"I guess not," she said with a smile, aware that his shoulders loosened.

Once Walt relaxed, he talked...and talked. His name was Walter Henderson Raine and he worked in a gas station (he patted the name on his shirt) when he wasn't in classes. "For eats," he said. "Not much money, but steady and plenty of time to study." He was an engineering student, deferred from military service for the time being.

From that day on Walter Henderson Raine kept showing up where she couldn't miss him, and it soon became evident to her that when he was late in appearing, she had begun to look for him.

Each time she saw him, she liked him more. Each time she saw him, she told herself he was wrong for her. She was attacked by doubts that she couldn't explain. Still, she kept accepting his invitations for rides on streetcars across the city and back; for coffee at corner stands where everyone seemed to know him; for walks in the park. Each time, he offered to pick her up. Each time she put him off, arranging to meet him away from home. She told herself that she was avoiding a confrontation with her family, that they would want her to date a Mexican boy. But she knew there was another reason, too.

She wasn't ready to let Walt into her "other" life: a life with a mother who had taken to her room as if to hide from shame; a sister married abruptly at seventeen, living in Mexico, and about to give birth to her second child; a brother who had left high school and who was content to earn a skimpy living in a factory. And she was especially not ready to let Walt meet Ricardo. Ricardo, whose searching looks and thirty-second sermons frayed her confidence. No, she wasn't ready. Maybe it was because Walt wasn't important enough to her. Maybe it was because in these short seven weeks he had become too important. It didn't matter. In either case the decision was the same. She would keep him away from Twenty-eighth Street.

But she hadn't counted on Walt.

On a cold blustery day during the Christmas holidays, Angela ran from the streetcar line down Twenty-eighth Street and into her house. She pushed the front door closed behind her, removed her jacket, and was reaching out to a coat hook when she became aware of voices in the living room. One was Tía Lupe's and the other...the other was Walt's.

"*El*," Walt said loudly, "*el pescado*. But that makes all the lady fishes masculine too, doesn't it? It's like calling a pretty girl 'mister'."

Tía Lupe chuckled and said, "That is how it is with our language. Perhaps the fish give such a struggle that the fishermen assume they must all be machos."

Angela heard Walt's laugh and shook her head. So now he knows. And I don't care what he thinks. She leaned against the wall and closed her eyes. In the dark screen of her mind she saw a scowl of disapproval on Walt's face and saw him hurrying out of the house and disappearing down Twenty-eighth Street. She imagined that months and years went by and that she never saw him again. An old ache, a heaviness, crept over her and, unexpectedly, tears filled her eyes and spilled over. She brushed them from her cheeks and stepped into the living room.

Walt was sitting back easily in a corner of the couch. Tía Lupe, her large apron rolled into a loose ball on her lap, was seated on her favorite straight-backed chair. Angela nodded at her aunt and then turned to Walt.

"Hi! What're you doing here? Looking for me?"

"Sure," Walt said, jumping up. "And getting a Spanish lesson to boot."

Walt stayed for another hour, an hour during which Tía Lupe clucked and said, "Angela, where are your manners? Offer this young man something to eat."

"Walt? Are you hungry?"

"Angela!" Tía said disapprovingly. And then, "Stay, stay. I will bring coffee." She brought in a tray with cups filled with thick black coffee and a plate of Mexican egg bread, and Walt ate as if they were his favorite things.

Finally, he said a reluctant goodbye.

Angela went with him as far as the front porch. "Well," she said, "so now you know."

"What?" And then, "Oh, sure. All fish are masculine."

"Not that," she said with an impatient little smile. "That I'm Mexican."

"Oh, that. I'm mostly English, with a bit of Irish thrown in for luck." He looked at her quizzically for a moment and then bent over and kissed her. "We sure have a lot to learn about each other."

"I guess so," she said, wanting to say more but knowing her words would be stumbling and inadequate.

One day she asked him, "Are you going to be a success, Walt?" They were sitting on a bench in the park eating hot dogs and watching storm clouds gather.

"Why do you ask?"

"Because I think it's important."

He watched the traffic for a while and finally shrugged and turned to her. "Success is relative, isn't it, Gypsy? But I *am* going to get an engineering degree and damn well make a living at it, this crazy war willing." He stuffed the remainder of his hot dog in his mouth, crumpled up the wax paper and arched it into a nearby trash barrel. When he had swallowed his last bite, he said, "I'll do whatever it takes to make you happy."

The rain started falling then and they ran for the cover of a doorway. Angela put her hands on his face and kissed him hard.

During the next few weeks, Angela managed to keep Walt away from Twenty-eighth Street. Her mother was ill, she said, it might be better to meet elsewhere. Whether he believed her or not, Walt complied.

Tía Lupe never failed to ask about him. "*El americano*, the one with the large smile, you see him sometimes?" Those were her words, but in her face Angela read "I know you are seeing him, so why does he not come to your home as a proper young man should?"

Angela shrugged vaguely. "I see him sometimes." She was grateful to her aunt for not mentioning Walt to the others, but she resented the reprimand in her eyes. "Yes, sometimes," she repeated, and thought, but that won't be so much longer.

It was February of 1945 and Walt's deferment was cancelled. He had received his greetings from the President of the United States, had passed his physical, and had been ordered to report to his induction center in one week.

"Marry me," he said as they walked through the park on one of those last days.

"I want to, Walt, really I do. But we can't." She wanted to be close to him, to sleep with him, to let her feelings express themselves totally, but her practical mind said no. No. What if he doesn't return? That would shatter you in any case, but if you were married, it would be worse. And what if you were pregnant? She dropped to the grass, reached her hands up to Walt and pulled him down beside her. "We shouldn't get married," she said. "There are all sorts of reasons. For one, you'll have enough on your mind without the worry of a wife."

He scooped up a handful of grass and sent it flying. "Maybe you're right. I guess it wouldn't be fair to you. But after the war…"

She tilted her head and they kissed, slowly, timidly, as if it were the first time. "After the war," she said. "After the war we'll talk more about it." Walt jumped up then and brushed the grass off his pants. She straightened her skirt and they continued their walk.

The first few days after Walt's departure for boot camp, Angela was lonelier than she had ever been in her life. She was alone with a confusion that was hard to bear. She needed to talk; she needed Sara. But Sara was attending an eastern university. They still wrote, but a letter wasn't going to help. She needed to talk, and there was no one here to listen. Except for Tía Lupe, the others in her family were busy with their own concerns.

Besides his job and law school, Ricardo now had a third preoccupation: a storefront legal station where he explained the ins and outs of selective service and the consequences of draft evasion to anyone who wandered in. Alberto had met a girl and was in L-O-V-E again! Being in love for Alberto was in the order of an explosion. He attacked the household with loud happy songs, bombarded Tía Lupe with riddles and jokes, and ambushed Angela in the living room, pulling her to her feet for a few quick steps of a fox trot. One evening he announced that he was going to be married and persuaded their mother to come out of her room and play the guitar. But Dolores' songs were melancholy. Angela, unable to express her longing for Walt and unable to think of anything else, cried herself to sleep that night.

Eighteen long months later, Walt came back into her life. He had been drafted into the Army, the Quartermaster Corps, and ended up in Banner, Texas. To begin with, he had been somewhere on the East coast and, later, somewhere on the South coast—she never knew where he really was. And then Japan surrendered.

Most of Walt's stint was served in peacetime. The war was over, but getting out of the Army had not been easy. Walt kept writing frustrated letters. "Still fighting the battle of Banner, Texas," he would sign himself. Finally, he was discharged.

One week after Walt's return, he bought a car. The next day they drove to Santa Monica to take a look at the ocean and he said, "The war's over. It's been over for a long time. *Now* will you marry me?"

She knew the answer, but she wasn't ready to say what had to go with it. "I think so," she said. "But give me another little while, will you?"

"I love you. You love me. So what's to think?"

"Just another few minutes," she said. He shrugged in defeat and parked the car.

They walked to Ocean Avenue and across it to the grassy strip along the edge of the eroding cliffs. They leaned on a fence and looked down on the Pacific Coast Highway and out across the ocean. The water was sparkling, each undulation frosted with tiny crystals. In the distance below them a group of young people ran across the sand, their laughter echoing lightly. The world was letting out its breath slowly, learning to live again.

She glanced at Walt. She was going to marry him. What did she know about him? A little, a little. He had been born in Maine. He had worked in a paper mill when he was fourteen. Later, he had gone to Oregon with his mother. There had been a divorce. And then, when he was just out of high school, his mother died. "When everything was over, I got the hell out of Oregon," Walt had told her, his eyes wet. "And here I am." She knew other things about him too. He was honest and direct; Ricardo would like him. She knew his grin and his touch, and the loneliness she'd felt those months without him. She looked away from Walt to the beach, following the spots of color running along the surf that were the boys and girls she had seen before.

In a few minutes, mounds of wispy, ragged clouds started to roll in from the sea. Suddenly, it was cold. When she felt Walt's arm circle her waist, she turned and they walked to the car. He sat quietly beside her for a while. Then he kissed her. "Okay, Gypsy, what's the answer?"

"You know what it is. It's yes."

"Sure, I knew. How could you resist me?"

She smiled and then instantly turned serious. "And our kids, if we have any, will be Americans."

He laughed. "What else would they be?"

"I mean just American. I don't want them to have even the vaguest idea that their mother was born a Mexican."

"But you weren't. Not legally." He looked at her with troubled eyes. "Anyway, what difference does it make?"

"What *difference* does it make? Oh, Walt, what a question."She moved uncomfortably on the seat. "A great difference. But then you have no way of knowing that, do you? That's what makes it hard. Because I have to ask this of you anyway. Promise," she said firmly. "Promise that when we have children, you'll never tell them that their mother was Mexican."

"Oh, come on, Gypsy, you don't mean that. Anyway, you'd never get away with it." There was a hint of a smile on his face. "Our kids are going to be too smart."

"I'm serious," she said evenly. "That's the way it has to be."

Walt grasped the steering wheel in a sharp gesture of frustration. "You can't do that, Gypsy. You'd have to erase your family, and you can't do that. They'll be there. And if they weren't, you'd miss them."

"Maybe. But I'll manage."

"This is absurd. Why is it necessary? *Why?*"

Angela's chin came up and she spoke with conviction. "Because there's no other way for me. I decided that long ago."

Walt let out his breath slowly, then took her hand in both of his. "It's all nonsense. Some day soon you're going to see that. But, okay, I promise. Now, let's forget it, shall we, and be happy like we're supposed to be?"

She nodded but remained thoughtful all the way home. Talking to Walt had been difficult, but it was over. She didn't look forward to the next step. Talking to her mother. Before the thought was out in the open, she had changed her mind. Not her mother. The next step should be to talk to her brothers. But she would have to be careful. It would have to be the right time.

It was a cold January night when she found the right moment. Only Alberto, Ricardo, and she were at the kitchen table. Bonita, of course, was living in Mexico with her husband and two children. Alberto's wife Raquela was nursing their baby, and Dolores had left the table immediately, the old crying look now permanent on her face. While Alberto and Ricardo finished a second pot of coffee and discussed the aftermath of the war, she waited silently, staring around at the kitchen that had subtley changed its character.

Three thriving geraniums in new clay pots were on the window sill and a framed print of Mary and The Child had replaced Franklin Delano Roosevelt. There was no bean pot on the drainboard anymore; the boiled beans were now kept in the icebox until they were refried. And the gray enamel coffee pot was gone. An aluminum one that was undented and was burnished from hard scrubbing sat on the stove. Yes, in the last year the kitchen had yielded—as they all had—to the soft, quiet presence of Raquela.

When Angela brought her mind back to the conversation at the kitchen table, it was Ricardo who was speaking.

"Say, brother," he said with exasperation, "you never could see two sides of anything! Maybe Allied lives were saved, but what a cost. I wouldn't have wanted to be in Truman's shoes. Dropping the A-Bomb on Hiroshima and Nagasaki was a damned heavy decision to make."

"They were the enemy."

"Right. We were at war. But maybe we could have done something else. Maybe we could have avoided roasting the populations of two cities." Ricardo took a long drink of coffee and wiped his mouth on the back of his hand. "'For nonviolent people,'" he said, "'the whole world is one family'. That's Ghandi paraphrased. There are other ways. First we have to find them and then we have to make them work." He pushed his chair back. "But I'll never pass the bar this way. Thought I'd study in the house tonight if it's all right with you and Raquela. My garage room is okay for sleeping in cold weather, but not for concentration."

Angela reached across the table and touched Ricardo's arm. "Don't go, please. I have something to tell you. Both of you."

Ricardo pulled his chair back and said, "Shoot."

Alberto said, "What's it about?"

"Me. I'm going to get married. I wanted you both to know."

"You're *what?*" Alberto said roughly. "I'm the head of the family now. You haven't asked my permission."

"I don't need your permission," Angela said.

"Who's the man?" Ricardo asked, stepping into the breach.

"Where did you meet him?" Alberto said.

"At school, but he's been in the Army. He just got back."

"No job, eh?"

"Yes, Alberto, he has a job."

"What's his name?" Ricardo asked.

"Walt. Walter Raine."

"He's not Mexican," Alberto said, shaking his head. "You've turned your nose up at all the Latinos who've paid attention to you, beginning with Armando..."

They were suddenly silent, the three of them, each with his own thoughts. In a moment she said, "Walt's not a Latino, no, but what difference does that make?"

"A lot," Ricardo said. "You'll never reconcile your differences. You'll be living in another kind of a world."

"That's just what I want," she said, and there was a sharp ring to her voice. "Another kind of a world. Look what happened to our father because he was a Mexican."

Ricardo leaned across the table and pressed her hand. "That doesn't matter. The fact is, he was. And so are you. And you can't run away from that." He sat back. "Anyway, why would you want to?"

Angela stared at Ricardo with awakened understanding. He was proud, actually proud, of who he was. And there was something more than pride. It was something held in the hard, determined set of his mouth. Something that was permanent now. When had that happened? She knew, of course. She remembered Ricardo's bruised and swollen face and the discolorations that in the early light of a Sunday dawn had made him look so grotesque. After that day, while she had wandered around feeling lost and aimless, Ricardo had started learning the law.

"He's right, Angela," Alberto said crossly. "You and your wild ideas. You were born a Mexican and baptized a Catholic. You can't change that."

"Oh, for heaven's sake, Alberto, of course I can!" She straightened up and added in a clear, hard voice. "Maybe I can't change the past, but I *can* change things in the future. You've both been good to me, and it will hurt. But if it means giving you up, I will. I know what I want."

Ricardo studied her face for a moment. "You may have to pay a price," he said.

"I know, and I'm willing."

"It may be high," Ricardo cautioned her thoughtfully.

"I've thought of that," she admitted. "I'm willing."

Alberto's face sagged in confused disbelief.

Ricardo shook his head slowly. "You may be willing, but it can't be done. You can run away from us all right, but not from yourself. This Walter may be a fine guy, but he can't change that for you."

❦

...And he hadn't. My God, he hadn't. Everything had worked out for her just as she had wanted it to, except that something had been missing. And now, here she was, shackled by trucks and cars on this stalled freeway while pinpoints of regret jabbed her.

For long minutes Angela stared unhappily at the line of cars ahead of her. She tried to separate herself from her feelings and a curious light-headedness took over. I'm not here, she told herself. I'm not here at all. She thought that she was floating above the cars and that she could, with a snap of her fingers, set them to moving. And then she was back in her car, and the fantasy and the light-headedness terrified her. Tears filled her eyes and blurred her vision. She fumbled with the buttons on the radio, but almost immediately gave up and sat back.

The road ahead now was filled with multi-colored smears. She squinted, trying to shape them into cars. Instead, what she saw was Alberto jeering at her, his teeth shining brightly as he threw his head back and laughed. And Tía. Tía Lupe, grunting as she pushed herself along the highway, twisting her head over her shoulder to mutter soundless accusations. Angela shuddered, patted her face with a tissue, and switched the air conditioning on to high.

Why did I imagine that I saw Alberto and Tía? Why not Ricardo? Almost before the thought was completed, she had the answer. Ricardo would not jeer or accuse. He might disagree, might argue with intensity, but he would be reasonable and fair. Hadn't he always been? She shuddered, thinking of the last time she had seen him, the mime rolling out a red carpet for him as he had walked away. Strange that she had run into him at this crucial time in her life. Especially since she hadn't seen him for over a quarter of a century. And that had been a crucial time too...

❦

Walt and she were still living in the garage apartment they called The Bird Cage. She was relaxing after dinner, glad that the first three months of her first pregnancy were over. Glad, too, that she could now cook dinner without holding her nose and that she could even enjoy eating some of it.

"Throw me a cushion, will you, Walt?" she said from the couch. As he tossed it, the telephone rang on a table beside her. She picked it up.

"Angela?"

"Yes. Who is this? Oh...oh, Rico!"

"Yes, Angela." A slight pause. "I have some sad news. Is your husband with you?"

"Yes, he is. What is it?"

"Alberto called from Mexico. It's Mamá. She died this afternoon."

"Oh, that's...that's awful." She glanced at Walt who was now sitting beside her on the couch. "My mother," she whispered. Back into the phone she said, "Was it...was it..."

"She died in her sleep," Ricardo said. "She'll be buried in Los Palos. Where she's been living with Alberto and Raquela."

Her mother was dead. And although she had not seen her since the day they had said goodbye beside Alberto's car, an old Buick sedan packed and ready for their trip to Mexico, she felt a fierce sense of loss. "Is there something I can do?"

"I don't know," Ricardo said evenly. "I'm going to call Pan American next. I'll take the first flight I can get."

"I'm going with you," she said.

There was a long silence at the other end of the line. Angela pushed herself up on the couch. *Doesn't he want me to go?*

When Ricardo finally spoke, he said, "All right then. I'll call you back on arrangements."

Walt and she met him at the airport early the next morning. The two men shook hands and spoke briefly as they picked up tickets and handled the luggage. Later, she figured they must have talked at more length while she was in the rest room because Ricardo knew she was pregnant.

Seated beside her brother on the airplane, Angela felt suddenly shy, unable to find words to complete trivial sentences. Ricardo looked the same. Thinner, maybe, the crease between his eyes just a little deeper. His quick movements, too, were comfortably familiar, but there was a disturbing distance between them.

"I hope you have something to read," Ricardo said apologetically, "because I brought along some work and I'd better get to it."

In Mexico they took a bus from the airport to the little town of Los Palos. Angela sat stiffly, holding back a rush of feeling. She had made a trip like this before. At another time and another place. Still, there were differences, she reminded herself. They were not traveling on a hot and dusty desert, and *this* bus was crowded with people. The air was filled with the heavy scent of well-worn clothing and the clamor of children and babies. And above it all she could hear the threatening whine of the bus's tired-out motor.

In Los Palos, Angela registered at the town's only hotel. Ricardo had suggested that she come to Alberto's house with him, but she shook her head. "No. They don't even know I'm coming, Rico. They'll have Bonita and all her tribe; they won't have room for me."

Ricardo did not insist. He took her to the hotel and saw her settled.

Shortly after he left there was a tap on her door and a man with surprisingly blue eyes in a wrinkled brown face stepped into the room. He was carrying a five-gallon bottle of American drinking water on his shoulder. From the hall behind him a boy appeared, dragging an antique and battered stand for the bottle. "For the señora," the man said in Spanish, "from the señor with the serious face."

Once the bottle was in place, the blue-eyed man held a glass under the spigot and grinned up at her. "Like this," he said, filling the glass slowly, "but very, very carefully. It could go whoosh! And there it is on the floor."

She tipped them, closed the door, and sat on the bed, staring unhappily at the bottle of water.

In less than an hour there was another knock at the door. Alberto and Ricardo had come to get her. "So you came," Alberto said. "I wasn't sure you would."

Angela was glad to see Bonita. Her sister was plump and matronly and blunt as always. "I never thought we'd see you again," she said. "I just figured you'd be too busy with your new husband and your new life."

"I *am* busy," Angela said. Then, patting one of Bonita's children on the head, "And so are you."

Raquela kissed her and said, "I've missed you."

The funeral mass was early the following morning. Except for the family and a few curious strangers, the small church was empty. Dolores' gray metal casket (how much, Angela wondered, had that cost Alberto?) was at the foot of the altar. A florist's spray of delphinium and stock lay across it.

The priest had a few benign words to say about Dolores. They could have been said about anyone, Angela thought. Had he even known her? She glanced at Bonita's squirming children in the pew beside her. I'm their aunt, and I don't know them either. If I was asked to, what could I say about them except that one of them has lost two teeth and three of them have colds? How can I possibly be their aunt? Bonita was kneeling at the far end of the same pew. Angela stared at her, hoping to find a feeling of accustomedness, of old-shoe familiarity, and found none. In the pew in front of her, Alberto reached for a handkerchief and wiped his eyes as Raquela pressed his arm. Angela moved uncomfortably on the wooden bench.

After the service, when they were once more at Alberto's house, she felt even more separated from her family than she had in church. A faint mist seemed to hover between her and the others. She tried breaking through it by moving physically closer, by talking, but no matter what she did the mist remained. Beyond it was a circle of intimacy. She did not belong.

Late that same afternoon, Alberto said, "Hey, Angela, I'm going to show Rico my warehouse. Want to come along?"

My warehouse. How proud Alberto was of his new position. Six months after Angela's wedding, Raquela's father had offered him a partnership in a small exporting business and Alberto had jumped at the chance. Now he wanted to show her his plant.

Angela said, "I'm a little tired, Alberto. Do you mind? I think I'd better go back to the hotel and rest."

"Rest?" Bonita said. "Who has time for that?" She was wiping the noses of her two youngest children as she spoke. "You're just pampering yourself because it's the first one. Wait until you have five like I do."

Raquela was tactful. She said that things here were strange for Angela, and that was always tiring. Besides, losing one's mother was a deeply felt sorrow at any time. "And isn't it wondrous," she added, "how God takes one to Himself and gives us back another?"

Angela looked gratefully at Raquela. But even Raquela's kindness did not make her feel less strange. It was good to be back at the hotel.

At the airport in Los Angeles the next day, Ricardo found a comfortable place for her to wait while he grappled with their luggage. He carried the suitcases across the long, crowded room and put hers on the seat beside her.

"I'm going now," he said quietly. "I'm glad you came with me." Almost as an afterthought, he added, "When you want things to change between us, Angela, call me. Until then, I'll stay out of your way."

She started to say something, what she never knew, because he kissed her lightly on the cheek and was on his way out of the terminal before her words had formed. At the door he turned and waved, then he was gone.

A confusion of feelings stormed her then. Shock first, a heavy numbness like that of a limb fallen asleep. Then she felt the pinpricks, and they were anger. Ricardo didn't have to stay out of her way; she had no intention of coming near him. But she had. It was *she* who had said, I'm going with you, and *he* had thought it over before he agreed. At that thought, chagrin took over. She moved gingerly on the seat. Then her eyes misted as she thought of her brother's kindnesses on the trip and a softer feeling replaced her chagrin. In his usual rational way, Ricardo had stated a fact and presented her with the advantage of deciding when, or if, they should meet. She could see this clearly. She saw, too, that she would not use the advantage. As she waited for Walt, she thought of Ricardo's friendly wave at the door of the terminal, and she had felt strangely deprived.

One year later she received an announcement of Ricardo's marriage. That was like him. It would be against his nature not to let her know of something so important. Standing at the foot of the steps that led to her garage apartment, Angela's mind was filled with questions about her brother's bride.

She was a Latina. The announcement told her that. Elena Almada. Strange. She had never pictured Ricardo married to a Mexican girl. Angela stared blankly at the zig-zagging flight of a hummingbird around a hanging fuchsia plant. Maybe that was an unconscious hope. In any case, it had been fed by Ricardo's history with other-than-Mexican girls.

During Ricardo's high school years, there was Shirley King. She played the piano, classical piano, and, according to Armando, was forever dragging Ricardo to concerts. Later, a girl named Estelle Fine telephoned two or three times a week. Ricardo took those calls in private. She was a political science major, he said, needing his help on a campaign. But for a while the family worried. Would Ricardo marry a girl who wasn't Mexican? Then there was Leni, a Leni who wrote poetry. Angela had found a poem of hers stuffed into Ricardo's sweater pocket when she sewed a button on for him. The poem was about love, not lovers, about love as energy, and its lines were simple and moving.

Leni. Probably Elena. Maybe Elena wrote poetry. Maybe she played the piano too, just as Shirley had. Well, that was all right. Because Ricardo, she thought possessively, deserved the best. His wife should be intelligent and fair-minded and good-humored, and beautiful. Angela stared again at the hummingbird, avoiding the feelings that lay just beneath the thoughts. In a moment she crumpled the card in her hand and went up the steps.

Later that week she sent Mr. and Mrs. Ricardo Martín a crystal dish and a note of congratulations. She received a simple thank-you note in return. That was all.

A couple of times in the next few years she was tempted to send Ricardo a snapshot of Ken, because Ken as a baby already showed a resemblance to his uncle. As Ken grew into boyhood, the resemblance became remarkable, even to the untamed lock of hair. She never did send Ricardo that snapshot. And except for hearing his name on newscasts or occasionally running into it in the newspaper, she lost track of him.

Eventually Walt and she bought their place on El Mar Drive. There were several bad moments before the deal was completed, but once the move was made Angela breathed a deep sigh of satisfaction. It had seemed to her then that life could not help but be wonderful.

Chapter Nineteen

They bought The House when Gloria was two. Walt, content with their lives just as they were, had taken some prodding before he agreed to take moving seriously.

"Look, Walt," Angela said one evening in May, "we've put this off too long. Now's the time to buy a house. Ken's going to start first grade in the fall. He should start in his new school."

"What can we get with the money we've saved?" Walt said from behind his newspaper. And then, putting it aside, "Maybe we should wait. What I'd like us to buy is the house we're going to stay in once and for all. None of this moving into a bigger and better place every few years."

She nodded, knowing about his need to put down roots, to feel a sense of permanency in his life. But she was afraid that he was already spreading out roots right where they were. He treated the apartment as if it belonged to him, painting, adding bookcases, even planting a dwarf lemon tree by the back door. She liked their apartment too. It was large and sunny and had a small fenced-in yard for Ken and Gloria. Even so, it wasn't enough.

"We're going to have to buy sometime," she said. "Let's look. What harm can it do?"

"None," Walt said. "None, I guess."

When they started searching in earnest, Walt and she were like kids planning a treasure hunt. They poured over the newspapers during the week, sketched their itinerary, and, with weather and baby-sitters cooperating, set out on a Saturday or Sunday to find The House. They began by looking at homes they could afford to buy, then in the beach cities at some homes they could probably afford, ending up in Pacific Palisades, just for a lark, looking at houses they couldn't afford at all.

She could call to mind the precise moment when they saw the house on El Mar Drive. It was at the end of a long, disheartening July afternoon. The homes they had seen in the Pacific Palisades that day were of all kinds: rambling on the flat lots, contoured on the hillsides, split into two or three levels, and in most instances provided with all-electric kitchens. Walt and she were enchanted by the features and disenchanted at the prices. But there was a small consolation. They hadn't seen anything yet that they couldn't live without.

When they were once again in their car that afternoon, Walt started the motor and looked at his watch. "Maybe these places are too rich for our blood, but we *can* afford the babysitter for another hour. Let's drive up to the top of this hill. I'll bet there's a great view of the coast."

Angela was tired, eager to get back to an apartment that was looking better and better as their search got longer, but she agreed. They curved up the hill on a newly paved road, catching glimpses of the water in between trees and shrubs that grew beside the asphalt. Within a few minutes, they had reached the crest of the hill. They found themselves on a long, flat plateau on which streets had been laid and houses were rising in the last stages of construction.

"More houses," Angela said. "Shall we look at them?"

Walt shrugged. "They'll be too expensive."

"I know, I know. But let's just look at that one." The house to which she was pointing had dormer windows, faced east, and sat slightly higher than its neighbors. Angela didn't need a second look to know that she was home. Maybe it was the wide front porch with its graceful wrought-iron railing. Maybe it was the large bay window that would drink in the morning light. Whatever. As far as she was concerned, this was The House. In the next half-hour Angela would discover that French doors in the master bedroom led to a veranda that had a magnificent view of the Pacific. But that would be a bonus. She was already sold.

That night and the next morning, Walt and she struggled with the figures they had been given by the realtor, with their bank books, with interest charts, with credit possibilities, and returned in the afternoon to claim The House. They wrote a small check and had an option to buy. Then they walked to the edge of the plateau with the salesman.

"This is lovely," Angela said. "We can watch the sun set into the ocean every night."

"Probably not," Walt said. "Sometimes it will set behind the mountains. Depends on the season. Right, Mr. Harkness?"

"Well, yes," the salesman said, his trim gray mustache quivering slightly, "but either way the sunsets are spectacular. Keep in mind that Santa Monica Bay and Malibu are world-famous places. Your property can do nothing but rise in value." His voice took on a more confidential tone. "This is a great neighborhood. And you can rest assured it's going to stay that way. We sell only to nice family folks like you. No undesirables, like coloreds or Mexicans, will move in next door to you."

Angela drew in her breath in a sharp little gasp. She glanced at the men; they hadn't seemed to notice. For an instant Walt looked miserable and then he said evenly, "I wouldn't be so sure if I were you. Isn't there a law?"

The little man with the trim mustache hemmed and hawed as Walt steered him back toward the houses. Angela, her mouth dry, felt them go, but didn't follow. She stood staring blankly at the sea.

It was the moment she had always dreaded. Her past had come to stand with her on this point above the ocean. But she had passed the test, hadn't she? Because Mr. Harkness wasn't talking about her. Well, maybe...maybe in a way he was. He was talking about the girl from Twenty-eighth Street. He had called that girl an undesirable. No, he wasn't talking about her. She wasn't that little girl anymore. Angela listened to the rationalization going on in her mind and finally found her comfort.

Her shoulders slackened, the stiffness falling from them like a shawl. After this, she thought, Walt will have to see how right I am in refusing to acknowledge my background. And in keeping that knowledge from the kids.

When she brought up the subject of The House that night, Walt's mouth was a tight line, "There are other houses. I don't want to deal with that man."

"Oh, come on, Walt. Where do you think you can go to escape that attitude? Look, if it didn't bother me, why should it bother you?" She knew immediately that she had made a mistake.

"We'll talk another time, Angela."

On Monday night she waited for him to open up the subject, and he didn't. On Tuesday, Wednesday and Thursday, he was out of town on business. On Friday night after supper, Walt shook his head, put down the paper he was reading and said, "Go ahead, Gypsy. You'd better say what you're thinking before you explode."

She let out her breath in a great sigh of exaggerated relief. "Can't we look at the house once more before we make up our minds?"

"Why not?" Walt said. "And we'll talk to Harkness about the money we put into that option."

Late the following morning, Walt curved their car onto El Mar Drive and parked in front of The House. He made no move to get out, and they sat in awkward silence staring at the nearly completed houses that lined the street. Suddenly, the door of the neighboring house flew open and a small sandy-haired woman raced out.

She whirled around on the cement walkway and threw open her arms as if to embrace the house she had just left. Then she ran to an old, tired-out blue Ford. With her hand on the car door she paused, looked in their direction, and waved. Walt nodded. Angela waved back. And the woman walked over to their car.

"Hi," she said, "I'm Maggie Paul. We've just signed on the dotted line and this place is ours. You must be the Raines. That salesman, Harkness, described you pretty well. Not the jazz about being a distinguished couple..." She paused and looked at Angela. "He said you were a cross between the Mona Lisa and Cleopatra. Coming from that funny little man, that's almost poetry. Besides, he came close, although I'd say you're more like Olivia de Havilland than the Mona Lisa. But here I am carrying on and probably embarrassing you. It's because Donald—Donald's my husband—isn't here to stop me. Well, when are you moving in?"

Angela looked at Walt. He nodded and shrugged in a gesture of surrender. "It's up to Angela," he said.

Before they had been in their house one full month, they had chosen plants and shrubs to begin their garden. Later, when they could afford a swimming pool, the planting would extend down the hill. But in the meantime, they bought a television set and a second car. They had done it! The house was almost too large and definitely too expensive, but even though there were moments when Walt and she wondered where they had found the nerve to do it, they never regretted their decision.

Angela quickly took on the coloring of her surroundings. She joined the PTA. She accepted invitations to plasticware parties And she took bridge lessons. In self-defense, she told herself later when she remembered her first bridge game.

The invitation to that card game came on a sunny March morning. Angela, wearing worn cotton pants and an old sweater of Walt's, was on her knees on the north side of her house transferring impatiens plants from a flat into the earth beside the fence. She loved to garden for the pleasure of seeing things grow, but even more for the joy of digging in land that was now her own.

When she was done, she settled back and looked with satisfaction at the long row of plants and at the earth gentled around them. Each breath she took was rich with the scent of green things and the smell of the moist spring earth. She sighed contentedly as she rose and brushed the drying mud off her hands.

As she turned to go, she came face to face with a neighbor, a plump, round-faced blonde dressed in cotton clam diggers and a crisp striped shirt.

"Hi," the woman said. "Hope I'm not interrupting. I'm Grace Renfrew. I've been meaning to come meet you."

Angela drooped. I look a mess, she thought, and she...she looks like an ad for Color Bright bleach. What's worse, there's not even one hair out of line in her page boy. "Hi," Angela said finally, tugging at Walt's old sweater, "I've been gardening." And then, "Oh, I'm glad to meet you. You live around the corner, don't you?"

"That's right. The house with the used brick and the Brazilian pepper...and the three noisy boys."

"I've seen them," Angela said with a laugh. "All towheads, aren't they?"

Grace Renfrew nodded. "I've come to ask a favor of you. I hope you can do it."

Angela, surprised, said, "Well, yes, if I can."

"Oh, you can all right. That is, if you're free this afternoon." Angela said a doubtful "yes, I am," and Grace said, "Well, then, it's settled. I need a substitute for bridge. It's not for lunch, just dessert. Maggie's coming. You can walk over with her."

"But I don't play bridge."

"You don't expect me to believe that," Grace Renfrew said with a smile.

"It's true," Angela said, feeling annoyed or embarrassed, she wasn't sure which. "I don't know how to play bridge. I'd ruin your party."

"You'd do nothing of the sort." Grace's voice changed into a coaxing little whine, "Please come. I just don't know who else..." She caught herself and blushed fiercely. "I'd really love to have you. Besides, all you have to do is hold the cards."

"All right," Angela said, "all right. But I hope you know what you're doing."

After Grace Renfrew left, she put her gardening tools away and hurried into the house to take a shower and to make her hands and nails presentable. But first she called Maggie. "I've just done something stupid," she said. "Maggie, I need you."

When Maggie had heard her out, she said, "If we both hurry and dress, we'll have one hour. I'll come over with a deck of cards. Be ready."

During that hour Angela learned the value of the cards— and that was about all. "Why did I ever say I'd go?" she moaned. "I'm going to make a fool of myself. They'll all think I'm absolutely stupid."

Maggie laughed. "All they want is a body, Angie. And it's only a card game. Besides, I've taught you my 'Bridge Made Simple Method'. Pass, pass, pass! They'll think you're conservative. Even smart."

Angela survived the afternoon. But for a while, as she stared at the mammoth slice of chocolate mousse pie topped with whipping cream set before her, her stomach turned somersaults and she thought she was going to throw up.

She left wondering if she would ever enjoy bridge parties, thinking how much more she would have enjoyed the last few hours working in her garden. Still, underneath her doubt, she knew that she would soon take bridge lessons. If that was what the women here did, that was, of course, what she would do.

Except for minor setbacks, Angela's life on El Mar Drive went smoothly. She chose to maintain a low profile. Whatever social event she attended, she stayed in quiet, dark corners, away from the limelight. It wasn't that she felt inadequate. She had a B.A. in literature and history. She was a good conversationalist. But she wanted to observe her situation as well as live it. She liked to be drawn out, too. She enjoyed every part of her fresh, new life. Yet there were times when she would hear a strain of a sad Mexican ballad and a bittersweet nostalgia squeezed her heart, leaving her breathless with longing.

Not long after they moved to their new house, Angela, in downtown Los Angeles to pick out dining room furniture, ran abruptly into her past. She had ordered just what Walt and she wanted and was walking happily to the parking lot when she heard a call.

"Angelita!"

It was automatic, her whirling around expectantly, her searching through the faces in the closely packed crowd. I'm imagining things, she told herself when she found no one she knew. She felt foolish as she started walking again.

"Angelita!"

There it was again. And closer. She swung around as she felt a pressure on her arm and found a familiar face smiling at her. "Diego?" She felt a sudden surge of gladness. "Diego!" Except for graying hair, Cousin Teresa's husband looked the same. Small, thin, with the quick movements she remembered well. But why should he have changed? It was only a matter of ten or so years. Had she expected him to grow like a child? "Diego, how are you?"

"I am fine, just fine," Diego said, and hugged her. Finally, jostling passersby, he held her at arm's length. "And you grow more beautiful with the years."

Embarrassed, she stammered something and Diego said, "A cup of coffee, Angelita, that's what we must have for old time's sake." He pointed to a small restaurant on the other side of the street. "There. A cup of coffee, a cigarette, and all the news about you and your husband. *¿Bueno?*"

Angela drew back. "No, Diego. I have no time...my children..."

"Just one little cup," he insisted.

"All right," she said stiffly. "But just one cup, remember, and then I'll have to go."

At midafternoon the restaurant was almost empty. She relaxed and slid into a booth near the back of the long room. Diego, smiling broadly, sat opposite her. When their coffee came, he watched her as she sipped cautiously. He added cream to his, tossed it off in one gulp, and reached in his pocket for a cigarette. As he lit up, she thought, who would have guessed this morning that I would be having coffee with Diego? All her family ties had seemed completely severed. But here I am visiting with Diego.

He waved the smoke away from the table and said, "*Bueno.* Shall I begin, or you?"

"You, please," she said, enjoying the warm, friendly scent of coffee and cigarette smoke. Her one cup of coffee lasted over three of Diego's Old Golds.

He told her of Tía Lupe, of her remarkable good health and energy, of how she was now taking charge of a young neighbor family whose father had been killed in the Pacific. Alberto and Raquela, he said, wrote often. Raquela wrote, that is, and it was clear that she was very happy in Mexico near her family. She had two little girls to go with that boy of hers now. But, of course, that was old news to Angela, no? No? *Bueno,* certainly she knew that Bonita and José had moved from Guadalajara to Mexico City?

Diego smoked silently for a few moments, then said, "Ricardo's office, Angelita, is but a stone's throw from here." She nodded as Diego squared his shoulders. "Ricardo is a man of growing importance in this city."

She knew. She had seen her brother's name in the papers.

Diego said, "I am proud to be his cousin, even if not by blood." He paused and put out a cigarette stub that was about to burn his fingers. Slowly, almost ceremoniously, he lit another and said, "Ricardo would be glad to see you. Here, in this place, you are so near to him."

"No, Diego. I don't want to see him." She was surprised at her need to be honest with this man across from her. "Ricardo and I have nothing in common anymore except our past, and I'm trying to forget that."

Diego looked up sharply. "But he is your brother. The only one of your family living near you."

"It doesn't matter," Angela said. "I don't want to see him." She looked over Diego's head down the long room to the window that faced the street. Just last month Walt had said the same thing: "He's your brother, Angela. He's the only one left here." She brought her gaze back to the table, looked into her nearly empty cup, and then up at Diego. "I know he's my brother, but it doesn't matter. I live a different kind of life now."

"And is it a better one?"

"Of course it's better. How can you ask? You know what it is to be Mexican here."

"Ah-h-h, *that's* what it is. I think I understand now."

"I hope you do." With an impulsive gesture she reached out and squeezed his arm. "In any case, I'm a mother now, remember? I have to get home to my children."

"*Bueno,* that is as it must be." He snuffed out his cigarette and paid the check. They walked together into the afternoon sunlight.

"Goodbye, Diego."

"*Adiós,*" he said. After a few steps he turned and called, "Do not forget us all too quickly, eh, Angelita?"

❧

She had tried. She had pushed Diego, Ricardo, all of them from her mind, forcing them out with the energy of a new life and new activities. And now because she had nowhere to go on this stalled freeway, she was remembering. Of course, that wasn't hard to do. She could call to mind every tree on their block of Twenty-eighth Street and every creaking floorboard of their house, and even the gasoline and leather smell of the old Model T...if she wanted to.

She stared unseeingly at the outlines of the road-building machines on the darkening slope ahead of her and felt hot tears on her eyes. Angelita. The name rang sweetly in her mind, like Christmas bells. Angelita. Only her father and Diego had called her that, and then, for a few short days, her father's friend, Ramón Salgado.

Angela brushed tears off her cheeks and took a deep breath. *Forget! Remember!* What good had forgetting done? And remembering? She shook her head irritably and moved her eyes from the cluster of trucks and bulldozers to fields, to hills, to the cars surrounding her. There must be some way to turn off the memories. In any case, if she had to have a memory to make her miserable, it didn't have to come from so far back in the past. Just last Sunday with Walt, Ken, and Gloria would do. The sound of Gloria's reasoning voice would always taunt her...

❧

"If you want to go to Mexico because your roots are there," Gloria said, "I can understand that, Mom. But do you have to go now?" Gloria paused and then, looking at her brother, added, "This isn't how we agreed to do it, Ken, I know. It just spilled out."

Ken shrugged in a gesture of acceptance. "Go ahead."

"We weren't going to tell you, Mom," Gloria said. "Not for a while. But now, with all this, we figured we'd better."

Angela, trying to figure out what this new twist was, suddenly had the answer. Roots. Gloria had said roots. Only a few minutes before, she had seen the look of fear on their faces, the distrust in their eyes. *Mom is off her rocker. We've got to* do something about it, and they had proposed a psychiatrist. Now Gloria had something else to say.

"I should've told you right away. God, I wish I had." Gloria's face was flushed. "It happened the last time I was up north." She looked at her brother, cleared her throat, and went on. "I talked to Ken about it because I didn't know what to do."

Ken said, "We didn't know *how* to tell you. We didn't know *if* we should tell you."

"For heaven's sake," Angela said. "What are you two talking about?"

Gloria swallowed hard and spoke hurriedly. "A couple of years ago, when Phil and I marched to the Capitol with the farm workers, there was this man. He showed up for the first time in a little town called Damon. He had come to confer with the leaders of the march. I couldn't take my eyes off him. It wasn't just that he was one of those people who inspire you. He was, but there was more.

"He had a particular attraction for me. So everywhere he went, I went too. It must have been very obvious because finally he came up to me and asked if there was something I wanted. I don't think I would've told him the real reason, except that Phil nudged me into it. So I told him that he looked a lot like my brother and that I was sorry I'd been staring."

Angela knew what was coming. Did Walt? There was no way to tell. All she could see of Walt's face was a furrow or two on his forehead. He was bent over, apparently concentrating on the section of rug between his feet.

Gloria inhaled deeply. "I guess that's all I would've said to him, but Phil kept on nudging. Phil knew what else was on my mind. So I told the man that it was weird that he looked like my brother, really weird because his name was the same as my mother's—Martin, Martín, what's the difference? And as far as I knew, my mother had no family. He was cool. He didn't so much as blink. He just turned around and motioned me to follow. Phil and I trudged behind him for a block and ended up in a truck stop having coffee and talking. That's how I met my uncle and his son David."

Angela stared at Gloria, bewildered. She had been expecting...she didn't know what, but not exactly this. Ricardo and his son David. She laughed nervously.

Gloria looked hurt. "This isn't easy," she said. "Please don't laugh."

"I know you're not laughing at Gloria," Ken said. "But it is serious, Mom. You kept him away from us. My God, for years. Why did you do it? Didn't you give us a thought? Didn't you think that in a way it was stealing? He belonged to us. He was part of our history. Ours. And you took it away from us."

"Cut it out, Ken," Walt said quietly, not raising his head. "You're pontificating."

"But he's right, Dad," Gloria said. "It *was* our history. When we were kids and asked about our grandparents, all we ever heard from Mom was that they'd died. Oh, sure, Mom, you showed us that beautiful picture of your mother and told us her beautiful name, but that was it. You were always too busy to talk if we asked anything more. Dad was always willing to answer us, but you..." Gloria stopped and bit her lip. "I'm sorry if I've hurt you, but I had to say it. Anyway, I don't want any more secrets between us. Not now. Not ever."

Ken said, "Sure, some of it was our fault. We could've insisted on knowing more. Dad kept saying you'd talk to us when you were ready." He threw up his hands in a gesture of impatience. "Oh, what the hell. I guess we were all pretty wimpy. But, Mom, you were such a wonderful mystery. And, in any case, you must've had your reasons."

Reasons? Angela looked down at her restive hands, anywhere but at her children. Still, it was mordantly funny. After all these years, after all the effort to keep them from feeling Mexican. Her fingernails dug into the cushion of her chair as she said, "Sorry. I didn't mean to laugh. Yes, I had a reason." And at that moment she discovered that her reason had been self-preservation.

Memories flooded back, and fear followed. What had Ricardo told Gloria? And Ken? For it was clear that Ken was involved too. And Walt? He looked up at her and shrugged and she turned her face away from them, fighting back hurt tears, certain that she had lived this moment before. But where? When?

Ken stretched his legs and said, "How's your supply of beer, Dad?"

The two men got up and left the room, and Gloria turned and stared out the window. In that interval of silence, Angela found her answer.

She remembered how when she was about eleven she had put together a thousand-piece jig-saw puzzle, carefully assembling it on a square of plywood that she slid under her bed each night. It was an autumn scene, a straw-hatted boy fishing in a stream that reflected the brilliant foliage of the trees, and she had put many hours over many days into completing most of it. The insignificant event came to memory in details as minute as the look of comfortable boredom on the fisherman's face. Before she had the satisfaction of fitting in the last few pieces, Bonita in one of her fits of pique (justified, maybe, she'd forgotten that) had swept the puzzle off the board, scattering its parts all over the room. Angela had been furious. She was sure she would have pulled Bonita's hair out completely if she had caught her. But when the fury was spent, she sat on the edge of her bed looking at the destruction of her idyllic scene, feeling only a deep sorrow for all the hours she had wasted.

In her white and gold living room last Sunday, Angela thought, yes, the feeling is the same. But squared. And today it's Gloria who's scattered the carefully placed pieces. She watched Walt and Ken return, each with a beer can in his hand. "So you kept that from me all this time," she said.

Gloria swung around on the couch, held out her hands palm side up, but said nothing .

"So we were stupid," Ken said. "We really thought you'd want it that way."

There was nothing she could answer. "That's it, then," she said, feeling shy and uneasy. She turned to glance at Walt. It had always been Walt to whom she looked for strength, for the support of clear thinking. But in this moment of stillness, which stretched into an awkward minute and then longer than a minute, she realized that he didn't know what to do or say. He looked miserable. She realized too, that the confusion with which he was struggling as he looked from her to Ken, then to Gloria, was the kind of thing with which he'd struggled on the night she told him that she was leaving. She stood up. Walt needed help, and there was one thing she could do for him.

"Relax, all of you," she said. "It's out now. And if it'll make you feel better, I promise to call Doctor whatever, the psychiatrist, tomorrow." Not that she expected him to do anything for her. Nothing was going to change. Too many pieces of this jigsaw puzzle were lost.

❦

Well, she had kept her promise. She had seen Doctor Verdon. And three or so hours after she had left his office, here she was on a freeway packed with motionless cars, staring at motionless trucks and bulldozers and going nowhere.

Chapter Twenty

At the moment that Angela switched off the ignition of her car and glanced at the road-building equipment, her daughter Gloria, eighty miles away, turned her car off the Harbor Freeway on to Gaffey in the Los Angeles port city of San Pedro.

She found her way to Sixth Street and swung into a diagonally lined parking place. She silenced the motor and sat staring blankly at the windshield. Phil had advised her against coming here, but she had ignored him. Something had happened to her emotions an hour ago when she had heard the frenetic note in her father's voice coming through the telephone.

"Heard from your mother today?" Casual words, but they had had a hurting edge.

"No, Dad. Why?" Even over the telephone wires she had sensed that he was debating his answer.

"Because she's gone, honey. I thought maybe she'd called to say goodbye."

"Gone, Dad? How can you be sure? She's probably just hung up in traffic."

"No. No, honey. Her suitcase is gone too, and some of her things."

"Oh." *Oh, Dad what're you going to do?*

" Well..." He coughed then cleared his throat. "Well...if you hear from her, let me know, won't you? Meanwhile, I have some thinking to do."

After talking to her father, Gloria had felt a desperate need to do something, and this had been it. But now that she was here, she was reluctant to move. She sat back, her gaze wandering from store window to store window. Directly in front of her was a decorating shop, wallpaper and paints; next, a barbershop; then Lida's, a bakery. Adjoining Lida's was her destination. She got out of the car and went into the bake shop. She bought a chocolate eclair and had it all eaten by the time she was outside. I'm nervous, all right, she thought, licking her fingers as she looked at the bright-colored banners and political posters in the window by the bakery.

She raised her eyes and faced herself in the glass, wondering if she shouldn't perm her hair and dye it too, since she had already gone all the way to hell and all the way off her health-food regimen by eating the impossible glop that made up the chocolate eclair. But, damn, it had tasted good! Wiping a crumb from the corner of her mouth, Gloria turned away from the glass and opened the door of Ricardo Martín's campaign headquarters.

Close to the entry at a huge battered desk, a slight young man was talking on the phone. He was extremely handsome, with dark wavy hair and large green eyes in an olive face that was saved from softness by the square-cut bones of the cheeks and jaw. He finished his conversation, dropped the phone on its cradle, and jumped up, saying, "Gloria, hey, Gloria, where've you been?"

He circled the desk, avoiding stacks of pamphlets and fliers on the floor, placed his hands on Gloria's shoulders and kissed her soundly on the lips.

Gloria pushed him away good-naturedly. "That's some welcome."

"My usual," he said, grinning, "for favorite cousins and volunteers. You here to stuff envelopes?"

"Not today, David. Another day, yes. Is your dad in? I called his office and they said he'd be here late afternoon."

"He's here," David said, his chin indicating a closed door in the back of the room. "But someone's with him. Shouldn't be long, though. Here, sit down."

He pulled at a chair by his desk and she took it gratefully. Her legs were getting rubbery. "Is this a bad time?" she asked.

David shrugged, dismissing her question. "He'll want to see you."

"God, I hope so. I need his advice."

David looked at her strangely. "You? It must be heavy. What is it? Your mother?"

She nodded, afraid to speak, afraid she might cry. Stalling for time, she looked around the small storefront room at the two other desks, one with a computer and printer, the second with a typewriter; at the two women behind the desks, who threw curious glances at her and returned to clicking the keys of their machines; at the long work table on which were stacked stationery boxes, a postage meter, heavy-duty staplers.

David said, "Benny sent his love."

"He did? How'd he know you were going to see me?"

"Easy. He figures you're one of the family now. And everyone in the family comes in and works on Dad's campaign." David grinned. "Benny's in love with you, Gloria."

"He'd better not be. I'm married. I'm his first cousin. And I'm much too...too mature for a sixteen-year-old."

"Well, let him down easy." David lowered his voice. "Okay. He's leaving."

A large man with a face drained of color marched out the door in the back wall, slamming it behind him. David jumped up. "Goodbye, Mr. Zvanich," he said. The man ignored him.

"Oh-oh," Gloria said.

"Nothing to worry about," David said, smiling. "He always leaves like that. Actually, Dad and he are good friends. Come on." He knocked on the door at the back of the room and threw it open. "Someone here to see you, Dad. She says it's important."

Ricardo, a deep furrow between his eyes, pushed a chair back from his desk and rose. "It doesn't have to be important," he said. "I'm always glad to see you, Gloria."

Gloria heard the door close softly behind her and said, "It *is* important, though." She pulled a chair near to him and sat down. "I need to talk to you about my mother."

Ricardo's chair squeaked as he rolled it closer to the desk and picked up a ballpoint pen. He turned the pen over and over in his hands. "Okay," he said suddenly, "what about your mother?"

"I told you about her operation." He nodded and she went on. "Well, even though the doctors have reassured her and us about her prognosis..."

"She'll be all right, won't she?"

"Yes, yes. Her doctor said it was all contained, that under the circumstances things couldn't have been better. But she's still terrified. We can't understand it. She's always handled things so well before, and now...she's like...well, like running scared. Maybe we made matters worse. Ken and I told her we'd been seeing you..." Gloria paused, frowning, then shook her head. "No. No, that didn't make a difference. Sure, she felt kind of wounded—I could see it in her eyes—but she had made up her mind before that. As a matter of fact, that's why Dad called in the troops. He thought we might persuade her to change her mind. But we couldn't budge her any more than he could. There was no explanation from her, no nothing. All she said was that she was leaving, going off to a place she went to when she was a kid..."

"Where?"

"A place called Punta de Cruces." When he made no comment, Gloria added, "I haven't a glimmer why. I thought you would, and maybe know what we might do."

Ricardo's dark eyes softened, but he shook his head slowly. "I'm not going to be any help to you, Gloria. First of all, we don't know why your mother is doing what she's doing. I have a guess—a bit more than a glimmer—but still only a guess."

"But why Punta de Cruces? What's there?"

"A lot of unhappy memories, as far as I can see. It doesn't make sense."

"What do you think we should do?"

"I can't tell you." He spread his arms out palms up on the desk. "I'm in a hands-off position where your mother is concerned. She's made that remarkably clear. However, I *can* tell you what I know. And this is it in a peanut shell: as a little girl, your mother arrived at some pretty warped conclusions about herself and her family, and she's been acting on them ever since."

Gloria stiffened, opened her mouth to interrupt him, but he held up a restraining hand. "I'm not blaming her, Gloria. In her mind she did what she had to do. There was no other alternative for her."

"How can that be? *You* didn't act that way!"

He shrugged. "Your mother and I may have spent our childhood years together, but my experience wasn't hers. I didn't feel what she felt. I didn't think what she thought. I'm sure I didn't even see what she saw."

"I guess that's true," Gloria said. "Ken and I remember some of the same things, but not in the same way."

Ricardo said, "I had my own anger, my own damn problems, and my own way of fixing them. What your mother did later—pushing us out of her life—made me pretty unhappy. It took years before I finally came to understand it."

Gloria was silent for a moment and then she said simply, "My mother's a pretty good woman."

"I'm sure of it." Ricardo stood up. "Look, Gloria, I may not be able to give you any good advice, but I can sure listen. Make yourself comfortable. I'll get us some coffee."

Ricardo walked behind a screen angled in the corner by his desk. An electric coffee pot was on a shelf along with mugs and a plastic container holding sugar. *Angela,* he shouted silently, *what are you doing?*

He thought of the last time he had seen her. He had not been surprised at bumping into her. He had known it would happen sooner or later. Only the place surprised him; it hadn't struck him that they would meet at something political.

From his vantage point he had seen Angela walk in that evening and wondered if, with so many people crowding the place, he would find a chance to speak to her. And then the pantomimist opened up a path for her that led right to him. It occurred to him immediately that he must tell her that he had met Gloria and Ken and that he saw them occasionally. But when her friend came along, Angela made it clear that she wasn't ready to hear that in some small way he had once more entered her life. He was boiling when he walked away. And yet not too far below that anger there had been pity. Almost the same feeling he'd had for her at their mother's funeral more than a quarter of a century before.

It had been so apparent that she was feeling uncomfortable and out of place with her own family. She had stayed at the edge of all their conversations, occasionally smiling like a hesitant stranger. She was not at all the confident girl who

several years before had announced her plans to marry Walt
and live a "different" life. At Mamá's burial, Angela seemed
more like the stunned little nine-year-old who had followed
him around silently the day after the Immigration men had
come and taken their father away.

On that day Ricardo had been restless and irritable. He
had been knocked unconscious the day before by a punch
delivered by an older man and, even more than his jaw and
cheekbone, his ego was badly bruised. He was tired, too, of
Tiá's hovering attention. He wanted to be alone. In midafternoon he escaped to a corner of the front porch, but he had
been there only a minute when Angela came and crawled into
the blue rocker beside him. And then it wasn't long until
Bonita, listless and grumbling about the heat, plopped herself
on the front steps. Before he had made up his mind where to
go to be alone, there was Tiá with a pitcher of cold lemonade
and more solicitude.

When Bonita went into the house, he stayed, hoping that
Angela would follow, but she didn't. She remained in the
rocker, curled into a corner, quiet and still. Finally she broke
her silence. "Why did those men take Papá away?" she wanted
to know. "What did he do?"

"Nothing," Ricardo answered grumpily.

"Then why?" she asked. *"Why?"*

"Just because," he had growled. "Just leave me alone!"

Just because. In his office, Ricardo filled the coffee mugs
and steam rose from them in soft elongated spirals. He shook
his head. *Just because.* What an answer to give a kid who was
hurting—and who really needed to know. But he hadn't been
more than a kid himself and, God knows he too was hurting.

Now, as he thought of that hot unhappy Sunday, he found
himself remembering something else. A conversation he had
overheard on that same Sunday night.

He had awakened slowly from an uncomfortable sleep. His
mouth was dry. He was thirsty. The house was dark and
silent as he slid out of bed. He found the kitchen flooded by
the light of a full moon, and he drank two glasses of water
without turning on the ceiling light. Then as he went by the

back door on his way to his room, he heard the soft murmur of voices.

"Are you sure you're not cold?" That was Alberto.

"I am sure." His mother. What was she doing outside?

"But your headache," Alberto said, "is it all right?"

"It is gone, son. I am fine. I simply needed some cool air."

Ricardo looked out the kitchen window. His mother and Alberto were sitting on the back steps.

"Well, if you won't go in," Alberto said, "I'll stay out here with you."

"No. You need your sleep. Remember, you are the only provider." A long sigh. "And now you are the man of this household."

"He'll be back, Mamá."

"Your father would be a fool to return. We are the ones who should follow him."

"Don't talk like that," Alberto said uneasily.

His mother shrugged. *"Bueno,* Alberto," she said. "Didn't you say he committed no crime? Didn't you say he was just trying to help everyone? So why did those men beat him yesterday and drag him away? In handcuffs, like an ordinary criminal. What was his crime, eh? I will tell you. He is a Mexican. And in this country, it is a crime to be a Mexican."

"Don't talk like that, please."

"You will see, you will see. You are a Mexican, and they will always hold that crime against you."

Alberto said, "You're tired, Mamá. You'll feel different in the morning. Come on, you'd better go in."

Ricardo turned away from the window and headed for the hall. At the door, he paused. There was someone in the hall ahead of him. A small someone who slipped quickly into the second bedroom. Angela. Angela had followed him into the kitchen. She had been listening too.

In his office by the steaming coffee mugs, Ricardo shrugged in a gesture of despair. Someone should have explained their mother's dramatic and pessimistic exaggerations to both of his sisters, especially to Angela. Well, it was certainly too late for that. His eyes narrowed and he frowned in concentration. Or was it?

He picked up the two mugs, brought them to his desk, and set one before Gloria. "Cream? Sugar?" he asked, and she answered, "Neither."

🐛

On the freeway, Angela drew her gaze away from the crimson-tinged road-building vehicles on the rise ahead of her. She looked over the lanes of stopped cars on her left, over the northbound lanes that were moving freely, beyond the railroad tracks that paralleled the road to the downy green fields of Camp Pendleton.

There was a blonde woman in the Mercedes now next to her, and that woman was pantomiming impatience, an exaggerated scowl, an up-and-down tantrum with closed fists, and directing it her way. The woman threw up her hands, tilted her head, and grinned. Angela allowed her lips to curve into a stiff, joyless smile. She turned away from the Mercedes as she heard a car door slam.

The driver of the camper in front of her had jumped to the asphalt. Her eyes followed his sneaker-clad feet as he strode to join two other men walking on the construction road beside the freeway. They looked at each other uncertainly, then stared into the distance ahead of them. Fools, she thought, nobody can see beyond that hill. Nobody knows what's ahead. And that's been true of this whole miserable trip—even before it started. Last night, for instance, who would have guessed that she would be in this tie-up? She had been so sure that nothing would go wrong.

Last night, as usual, Walt had come into her room to say good night. For the last couple of weeks she had been spending more and more time in the bedroom, sitting in the wing-backed chair by the terrace doors, looking out over the ocean. Now, more than ever, this was her room. On her return from the hospital, Walt had moved into the guest room, and neither one of them had made a move to change the arrangements.

Walt was already in pajamas. "Anything I can get you before I turn in?" he asked.

"Nothing, thanks."

He hesitated for a moment and then went and sat on the edge of the bed. "Still mad at me for calling the kids?"

She shrugged, showing unconcern.

"I had to, you know, Angela." She shrugged again, and Walt grimaced uncomfortably as he went on. "I know people do strange things for what seem to them to be good reasons, but you didn't even have a reason. You kept saying you didn't know why. That's what worried me. And giving up your medical treatment when Doctor Eichar and the others say things are looking so good. I couldn't let you do it, Angela. So I called the kids. I had to."

"I know, Walt. You've told me this before." And she thought, poor Walt. He's afraid I'm angry about the psychiatrist.

Walt pushed up from the bed. "Right. I guess I have. Anyway, thanks for changing your mind." He kissed her lightly. At the door he said, "Still want me out of here?"

She was caught off guard by his question. "Yes...yes, Walt. Just for another day or two." He nodded, closed the door, and she sank back in her chair. How could she have said that? She, who hated hypocrisy and lies. What had happened to her? In a day or two she wouldn't be here. And letting Walt think that seeing the psychiatrist meant that she had changed her mind. That, too, was a lie. But she couldn't open up the subject again. There was enough of an argument going on inside of her without creating an external one.

She pulled her robe around her and stepped through the French doors onto the balcony. In the distance below her the ocean glimmered with moonlight. Next door, the Pauls' Dalmatians sensed her presence and ran from their shelter, barking loudly.

"All right, all right," she said softly. The dogs gave a couple of friendly barks and were quiet. They miss Maggie and Don, she thought. Just as I do. She glanced at the empty house next door. I wish Maggie was here. If she was, we would talk and maybe I would feel better. Yet as those words formed themselves into a cohesive thought, another wove itself in and around them. This decision of hers had to do with something she had never discussed with anyone. And no other subject would be sufficient now; no other dialogue would hold her sincere attention, even if it was with Maggie.

It was remarkable that Maggie and she had lived in the same houses side by side all these years. But even more remarkable was the fact of their relationship. They had learned early in their acquaintance to respect one another, to accept and value their differences. Angela listened goodnaturedly to Maggie's chatter and to her questions, only some of which she answered. Maggie accepted Angela's reticence, only now and again scolding her for it.

During those years they had only one falling out, and it was over Joey. Her son was the luminary in Maggie's life, and any attempt to look at him directly resulted in temporary blindness. But when Angela caught him stealing from her purse, she dared to face Maggie with the fact. Maggie took a stubborn stand, defending her son at the risk of losing their friendship. Yet in less than a week Maggie admitted that that incident had been the end of her denial of Joey's drug addiction and the start of her painful acceptance. "Thanks," she had said, and they were back on their old easy terms with a stronger trust now drawing them together.

On her balcony Angela nodded slowly. It was just as well that Maggie was still in Spain. That very bond of friendship would give her neighbor the freedom to question and probe, making the leave-taking more difficult. Tomorrow, to avoid argument, she would say no goodbyes. Not to anyone.

She leaned against the wall of the house, her arms wrapped tightly around her, and stared at the luminous ocean. As she watched, dark clouds curtained the moon, and the water that had been alive and sparkling only a moment before became an opaque void. She shuddered and went inside, closing the door firmly behind her.

Maybe going to Punta de Cruces was a strange thing to do. But that was all right. If it seemed strange to others, that was how it had to be. Whatever else Walt and Ken and Gloria thought, the psychiatrist would make no impression on her, nor would he get her to change her mind.

Well, he hadn't. Angela, on the freeway, looking at the men who had left their cars to check out the construction road,

shook her head as she remembered. Doctor Verdon hadn't
even tried to dissuade her. He had merely suggested that they
examine her options.

Options. Instead of sympathizing with her (wasn't that
what shrinks were supposed to do?), Doctor Verdon had been
firm and insistent, his eyes unwavering as he suggested that
they look at all the possibilities.

She didn't understand the anger that had welled up in
her. He had been kind, putting her at her ease when she had
walked in and glanced uncertainly at the threatening leather
couch. She knew it was silly, but she had heard so many stories.

"Won't you sit down?" he said quickly, indicating the arm-
chair at the side of his desk. And they had talked rather comfortably for the first few minutes.

But a little later his words seemed dangerous, as if linked
together they could produce a chain of reasons to restrain her.
She didn't like his suggestion. "I've already examined the possibilities," she said firmly. "There's only one for me. To make
up for what I've done."

"And what was that?"

Through a window that faced her, Angela watched scattered gray clouds skim across the blue sky. My father loved
me and I threw him out of my life! she wanted to shout. I
know, I know. I thought I was doing the right thing. I didn't
want to suffer the way he suffered. And I didn't want my kids
to go through that either. But I was wrong. My son says so.
My daughter says so. So do Walt's eyes. And now so do I.

"What are you thinking?" The almost-whispered words
interrupted her thoughts.

Angela stared out the window, concentrating on the
clouds. "I don't want to talk about it," she said without turning. "What's happened, happened. Besides, there's no use in
talking. I'm the only one who can decide what's right for me
now."

"That's true," he said. "No one should make our decisions
for us. But that makes us all the more responsible for their
results."

She didn't want to hear that. She glanced at him across the desk and shrugged.

After a silent moment Doctor Verdon said, "Well, then, tell me about the trip you want to make."

"I'm going to the place where my father is buried because I want to be near him," she said defiantly. "Now you can tell me I'm crazy."

"No, you're not crazy," he said evenly. "But you *are* angry...and unfair to yourself. If your father's been lost to you, is there no other way to find him?"

How did he *know*? She clenched and unclenched her hands, telling herself that whatever he said, she didn't have to listen. And in a few moments she stopped listening. And in still another few moments she had left.

Angela shifted on the car seat and muttered, "Stop hounding me, Doctor Verdon." But the words of his question repeated themselves, seeming to have taken on life. "... is there no other way?..." Embodied, they scrambled into her mind to push against her skull "...find him, find him..." to stumble carelessly throughout her head until she wanted to shriek.

She glanced again at the men at the side of the freeway. "What are you doing?" she mumbled. "Don't you know? We're never going to get out of here." She leaned her head back and closed her eyes, shutting out the scene before her, trying to forget where she was. It was strangely still for a moment, and then far in the distance she heard a long plaintive whine. The sound was pulsating and shrill and familiar. Of course it's familiar, she thought. It's happening inside of me. Isn't everything? Back and forth, back and forth, the high-pitched cry tolled within her head like a bell striking the hour until she was so engulfed in the reverberating sound that she sat upright, opening her eyes to escape it. As she did, she heard the sound outside herself.

It sifted through the closed windows of her car, an urgent keening wail that she now had no trouble recognizing. It was an ambulance. Somewhere up ahead there must have been an accident. People would be lying on the highway or twisted into the wreckage of a car moaning with pain, waiting for help to arrive. She drew in her breath. Maybe they weren't merely hurt. Maybe they were dead. No, no! They were hanging on. And for what? Life was a fragile thread. Death happened so easily, and the stillness was forever.

She shivered. She, too, was expecting a death replete with agony. Suddenly, she was terrified. Her hands began to tremble. Then the trembling started in her knees and went up her legs, taking over all her body. She broke into a clammy, cold sweat. She hugged herself tightly, but the shaking wouldn't stop. What was happening? *Please. Stop.* Words. She was trying for words but made babbling sounds instead. *Please, stop!* The order now was imperative and little by little the trembling ceased. Her hands were limp as her arms fell on the steering wheel. Sighing brokenly, she pressed her face against her arms and at last the sobs pushed out.

Her crying ebbed slowly. She didn't know how much later it was that she surfaced to awareness. Above the whine of the ambulance there was a more demanding sound. An automobile horn was blaring, its loudness swelling close by. She buried her face deeper. Then over the blasting of the car's horn she heard the rumble of angry voices. Had everyone gone mad? Protected by the darkened circle of her arms, she tried to ignore the sounds.

Outside, the voices grew louder. There was a rapping on the glass beside her.

"Go away," she muttered, refusing to raise her head.

The rapping continued and a man's voice called, "Angela!"

Angela? Had he said Angela?

"Angela!" the man called once more.

Angela ran her arm across her eyes and a long shuddering sigh escaped her. "You came for me," she said, and attempting a smile, raised her head to look into a puzzled face pressed against the car window.

Chapter Twenty-One

Angela stared at the face on the other side of the glass and thought, this is wrong. He doesn't belong here. The shock of the unexpected face sent prickles of irritation across her back and she wriggled her shoulders uncomfortably. She was annoyed, too, by her feelings of confusion. Whom had she been expecting? And if this man was not the one, why did he seem familiar? His face was angular, ruddy. His wiry brown hair curled above the collar of a dark blue shirt, and that seemed known too. Who was he?

She frowned as she looked over his shoulder to the driver of the camper who stood a few feet behind, his face florid and frowning, his jaw thrusting toward her; to the three-pointed pink scarf on the head of a woman leaning out of her car, staring wide-eyed; to the blonde coming around her Mercedes, throwing her arms out in an angry gesture, calling something vaguely heard but not processed in Angela's mind; back again to the face on the other side of the glass. Her confusion grew. What was this all about?

The man by the window scowled and signalled, open it.

She daubed at her face with a tissue and lowered the glass. "What do you want?" she said. "Is anything wrong?"

"You tell me, lady. What the devil do you think you're doing leaning on the horn that way?"

Leaning on the horn? She looked stupidly at the leather-covered rectangle centered on her steering wheel and dimly saw the wet smudges her tears had left on it. My God, she had been the one. "I'm sorry," she said. "It was...it was a mistake." What else could she say? And then she thought of something. "You called me Angela. Why?"

"Your plates," he said, gesturing to the rear of her car.

"Oh. Yes. I should have known." If she had been thinking clearly, she *would* have known. She shook her head furiously, trying to shake off the sluggishness, the daze that was blurring everything. She fixed her eyes on the man's face. "Should I know you?" she asked.

Instead of answering, he rubbed his hand across his chin. "Say, lady, are you okay? I've been directly behind you for a lot of miles and you...well, you've been driving kind of funny."

The man in the gray truck. She had seen him so many times in the rearview mirror. No wonder she seemed to know him. She bit her lip, embarrassed. "I'm sorry about that. But I'm fine now. Fine. I won't bother you anymore. So...so you can go away."

He stepped back, hooking his thumbs on a belt that undergirded his belly, and his face deepened in color. "Okay, lady," he said, "but don't be in such a hurry. You're not going anywhere right now." He swung his arm to include the group behind him. "None of us are. Not till they clean up those accidents down at Carlsbad."

A picture of bodies writhing in pain shot into her mind again. "Were there a lot of people hurt?" she asked, her voice as thin as eggshells.

The truck driver nodded. "That's what they tell me."

He must have been talking to other truckers. Why hadn't she thought to turn on her radio? "Will it take long for them to...to take care of things?" she asked.

"Could be minutes," he said, "could be hours."

Angela slumped down in the seat and groaned.

The truck driver, who had started to turn away, stopped. "Say, lady, what's wrong? Are you sick or something?"

She shook her head.

"You sure? Can I do anything for you?"

"If you were God you could. You could get me off this freeway."

The man scratched high on his head and scanned the area adjoining the highway. "Oh, I can get you off the freeway, if that's what you want," he said, pointing to the construction road. "I can put your car over there."

"What good would that do?"

He shrugged. "You won't be able to go anywhere, but maybe you can rest there. Get out and stretch your legs. Maybe you won't feel so bogged down."

"I...I don't think so."

"Suit yourself," he said and swung around. The others who had been standing behind him began to drift back to their cars.

As she watched the truck driver walk away, Angela was struck with a surprising remorse. She leaned out the window. "Don't go!"

The truck driver turned. "Talking to me?"

"Yes." She opened the car door and slid her feet to the ground. "I've changed my mind. I do need help."

"Yeah? Like what?"

"Will you move my car?" she said in a voice close to a whisper.

"Sure. We'll get your car off this freeway. You'll be better off there." His tone was conciliatory, reminding her of Doctor Verdon and, earlier today, Walt. She went around to the passenger's seat and the man got in beside her.

He smelled of tobacco and faintly of peppermint as he curved the car backwards and then forward across the shoulder of the freeway and around a mound of earth to the well-packed soil of the construction road. He put the car in a place with easy access to the freeway's shoulder and got out.

"Maybe you shouldn't drive for a while," he said, leaning into the window. Then seeing the quick lift of her chin, "But when you're ready to be on your way again, be sure you're moving fast off the shoulder."

"I'll remember. And...and I'm sorry I was rude."

"Forget it. Think you'll be okay?"

"I'm fine."

He gave her a skeptical look. "There's an off-ramp in a couple of miles, just in case. Gas station and a Seven-Eleven, too. Now all you have to do is wait."

"That's all I've been doing."

"I know," he said. "But you're not the only one. My schedule's gonna be screwed up for days. Well, if that's how it is, that's how it's gotta be."

"I'm glad you can be so patient."

"I didn't used to be," he said. "The wife taught me to cool down." He smiled slowly, his mind elsewhere. "That wife of mine. Always coming up with something. Says life is a game. You know, a grab bag."

"I guess it is."

"Well," he said, a softness spreading over his face, "she says this is a game with only one rule. And the rule is that you gotta keep what you get. You see?"

"I see," Angela said, eager now to end the conversation.

But the truck driver went on. "She says the winner's the one who knows what to do with what he gets. Sounds simple, huh?"

Angela, feeling annoyed and not knowing why, said, "I guess so."

"Well, there you are," he said abruptly, and Angela sensed that he was embarrassed. "Better get back to my rig."

"Thank you," Angela said. "You've been very kind."

He nodded and walked away. After a few steps he glanced over his shoulder and said, "Take care."

She watched him stride to his truck and swing up into the cab and then she settled back on the seat. She stared at the outlines of the road-building machines on the rise ahead of her, watching their darkening shapes absorb scarlet tones from the sun. Then she opened the windows and let the ocean air fill the car. She gulped it in. This was better. For hours she had been trying to escape the trap on the freeway, the nightmarish inability to move, while memories pursued her. And now she had been released. Thanks to a truck driver who was also a down-home philosopher.

In the distance she heard again the wail of an ambulance. It grew louder for a few minutes and then diminished. Another one. So the wait would be long. She got out of the car stiffly, stood a moment unsure of her legs, unsure of her purpose. At the side of the freeway, the blonde from the Mercedes and the shaggy-haired driver of the camper were staring at her. The young man pointed in her direction and said something. The blonde laughed, nodded, and then shrugged. They turned back to their cars. Angela forced a frown away from her face. *I don't care what they think.*

She glanced once more at the stalled cars on the highway, reached for her purse, and picked her way across the fields.

The damp ground felt firm as she plodded up a slope toward
the sea. Halfway up the incline she paused, listening. The
strident sounds of the freeway were left behind, only a muted
hum reached her, and in the near silence there was a huge
emptiness.

She pressed on up the slope and in a few moments she
was at the top of the rise and the ocean was spread out before
her. She trudged downward and soon was at the edge of the
cliff, looking below to a sandy cove. The emptiness was gone
now, filled by the sound of the surf.

A voice rose above the breaking waves. Another. And
laughter. Angela turned, her eyes circling the cove. She saw
two boys climbing the bluff on the opposite side. When they
reached the top, they stopped, breathing hard, two-dimen-
sional figures against the sky. One started to run. "Beat you
home!" he shouted. "Who? You?" And the other boy sprinted
after him.

The echoing voices, the sun vividly exiting into the sea,
the smells of rained-on earth and walked-on grass all com-
bined into a rare event, a flash of something once known and
held close and, like the spirited colors of the declining day, lost
in an inescapable sequence. There were the days when her
father had lived. The days when she had found Walt, and
Walt had meant the answer to a search. The days when her
hopes were reborn, transferred to Ken and Gloria. But that
was before Walt and she had become hesitant strangers, their
closeness drifting away like a cloud, and long before Doctor
Eichar had stood at her hospital bedside trying to reassure
her.

The breeze blew her hair over her face. Chilled, she shivered and pulled her jacket close around her. If now she were
to look only at the twilight sea, ignoring reality, and she could
with a single wish return to one of the times that was gone,
which would it be? She knew the answer of course. Frowning,
she brushed the hair away from her eyes. Of course she knew
the answer. Yet it was eluding her, scurrying through a maze
of confusing thoughts.

Impatiently, she spun around. The glow from the freeway
lights outlined the slope before her. The exhilaration of a few

moments before was gone. She climbed slowly. At the top she paused and glanced at the idle strings of cars in the south-bound lanes. Instead of going on, she dropped her purse and sat on the damp ground beside it.

Her thoughts were aimless, blown here and there by the whisper of a word. "...lost...lost..." *Leave me alone, Doctor Verdon! I don't want to listen to you now any more than I did earlier. I've made my choice. And it's mine alone to make.*

At the edge of the point, distinct against the gray-red sky, a clump of mustard weed swayed in the breeze. A thin stalk swung toward her, stabbing the air like an accusing finger. Your choice alone? Really, Angela. How about your son, your daughter? And how about Walt? Her shoulders slumped. Wrestling with arguments wearied her. She lifted her face to the sky and bit by bit the weariness drifted from her shoulders to her waist, to her legs, down to her feet, uncurling her drawn-up toes. Limp, she thought. Sagging. Run down like a wind-up toy. I don't want to be here, I don't want to be here, and I'm too tired to move. She closed her eyes. She could pretend for a while. Instead of wandering around an unknown field near Oceanside being hounded by the words of a psychiatrist and an insolent mustard weed, she could be wherever she chose.

She pretended that she was back on El Mar Drive when Ken and Gloria were still little. It was twilight; they were looking for the evening star. With her eyes squeezed tight she pretended and she thought that she heard their laughter and their childhood voices making wishes. And for an instant she was sure that life was still spread out before her in uncountable hungry years that waited only to be filled with living.

Then she opened her eyes and she was alone on a bluff on the way to San Diego, and the day was gray-red and dying. She sighed and dropped her head on her knees. Ken. Gloria. She hadn't said goodbye to them. She had said goodbye to Walt, and he had said, "Good luck." Only Emilio had said goodbye to her. Waving his tattered grass hat as he stood in the driveway, he had called, *"Vaya can Dios."*

A few minutes before that he had said something else. "Is this not a day for miracles, Mrs. Raine?" And his voice had stood out cheerfully against a backdrop of sadness. Yes, that was like Emilio.

Cheerful against a backdrop of sadness. But not only Emilio. There had been someone else. There had been another comforting voice. Angela tilted her head, listening. The past whispered. Of whom was she thinking? The past whispered again, and she knew.

"I know what little girls like," he had said with a smile. "Hidden behind these others, I have a bottle of strawberry soda." Señor Salgado.

Chapter Twenty-Two

Señor Salgado. After forgetting him for so many years, he had returned to her mind in details as exact and unimportant as the threadbare edges of his coat sleeves, as biting as the smell of his cigarettes, as warm as the touch of his hand on her shoulder. He seemed almost as real as the firm earth on which she rested. His essence surrounded her and for some unknowable reason she tried to push it away. She turned abruptly, her eyes wandering over the bluff.

In the distance the silhouettes of the road-building machines stood gaunt and deserted. Then a light flickered and moved slowly around them, a flashlight beaming on a truck, a bulldozer, finally disappearing. She clutched her purse, ready to run, looking for somewhere to hide, and almost as quickly sat back feeling foolish. She turned once again toward the ocean, aware that she was searching for something. A boulder. Of course. A flat-topped boulder near the edge of the cliff. And although there was none, the feeling that there should be persisted.

In Punta de Cruces on the day of her father's funeral, she had spent long hours near that boulder. From its top she had been able to see both the bay and the grave, and as the hours had gone by she had felt that there was nothing in the world except for the sound of the surf crashing on the rocks below, the cloud-filled blue sky, and her. Then, just as it was getting dark, she had become aware of something else: two dim lights moving on the bumpy road toward the cemetery. When they disappeared beneath the hill, she slid to the ground behind the big rock, more scared than she had ever known she could be.

Within minutes she heard someone walking toward the bay. Then there was silence, and in that silence she heard her own breathing, loud and furious as a windstorm, giving her away. She tried holding her breath but quickly gave up and, in a burst of daring, peered around the edge of the boulder.

Against the sky she saw the outline of a man. He reached into his pocket and struck a match. In its glow she saw the face of Ramón Salgado.

"Angela," he called. "Angelita, it is I, Ramón. I have come for you."

She exhaled in a torrent of relief and scrambled on to the flat top of the boulder. When he came and sat by her side, she said, "I'm sorry if I've been trouble, señor, but I *had* to stay right here."

"Your father would be unhappy if he knew."

"Do you think so?" she said. And then, hungry to share the thoughts that had built up during the day, she talked and talked. And he listened silently until she said, "More than anything, señor, I wanted to tell him I was sorry."

Ramón Salgado coughed and she heard him fumbling in his pockets. Soon she heard the crinkle of paper and rustling sounds, the smell of tobacco. He lit a cigarette and in the burst of match light she saw that he looked deeply tired. He drew on his cigarette, exhaled and pressed her hand.

"Your father is not here, Angelita. You must believe that."

She pulled her hand out from under his. "Don't say that!" she cried angrily. "He *is* here! He's right here, sleeping forever!" She turned her back on him, peering through the darkness toward her father's grave.

Ramón Salgado shook his head slowly and sighed.

She waited impatiently while he smoked, her eyes following the glowing red tip of his cigarette as it moved from the level of his head down to his knee where his hand rested and back again. She wanted him to stop smoking, to say something that would assure her that he wasn't mad. She kept looking at him and wishing that she hadn't pulled her hand away, that she hadn't shouted at him, wishing that there was something she could do to make it up to him. And then she remembered the shell in her pocket.

She dug it out and tugged at his sleeve. "Look, señor," she said, holding out her hand. "Have you ever seen such a shell?"

He drew on his cigarette once more. In the sudden glow the sand-colored shell looked coral. He lit a match and examined it carefully. He smiled as he turned it over in his hand,

and she relaxed. It was all right.

"A fine shell," he said. "I have never seen one better."

"Hold it up to your ear the way Papá showed me. Do you hear? Do you hear?"

"Ah, yes. I can hear the ocean clearly."

"How can that be, señor? That the ocean sounds are in the shell?"

He shrugged. "I am a simple man," he said, flipping the burning cigarette to the ground. "I have not studied such things. I only know that it is so." He reached for her hand and curved her fingers around the shell. "You and I can call it the miracle from the sea."

She put her hand up to her ear. Yes, the sound was there, filling the empty shell with music. Music from the sea, her father had said. Suddenly she was very lonely, and she had to hug herself tightly to keep from crying.

Ramón Salgado, seeming to sense her struggle, said nothing for a while. After a bit he started to speak, but stopped. Finally, he cleared his throat and said, "We are all like your pretty shell."

"Who? People?"

"People."

"Even me?"

"Even you. It is like this," he said, speaking slowly as if looking for special words. "The shell was part of the sea, no?" She said yes, and he went on. "And it is also true that you are a part of your father."

Yes, she knew *that*, but what did it have to do with the ocean sounds? She was tired, and she was hungry, and her stomach had started to gurgle. She wriggled uncomfortably as he went on talking.

"*Bueno.* You and I know that even if that shell is taken far away, it will always carry the sounds of its ocean parents, the wind and the water. Is that not so?" He did not wait for her t answer. "We know that is so," he said. "So, why not you? After all, you have much of your father in you. Some of his ways, some of his sounds..."

She stiffened. That was a strange thing for him to say, but what if it was true? "Do you really think I do?"

"I am sure of it." He tilted his head as if listening and then said close to her ear, "If we are very quiet, it could be that something will tell us so."

She looked up into his face, trying to see if there was teasing there, but she could make out only a shadowy outline in the darkness. Still, his words had been serious. She had no reason to doubt him, so she sat silently beside him, not daring to breathe for what seemed a long time. She gasped when she heard a little noise. "Señor!" she whispered. "Is that it?"

He shook his head.

Then, because she realized that what she had heard was only a stone rattling across the ground when Señor Salgado had moved his foot, she chuckled. Quickly, she put her hand over her mouth and, now contrite, listened intently again. After a few moments, above the surf sounds and into the almost intolerable silence between them, came the loud rumbling and gurgling of her stomach.

Angela leaned over, covering her mouth, trying to control herself, but she laughed. And the more she tried not to, the louder she laughed.

Ramón Salgado sighed loudly and patted her shoulder. "There, Angelita. There it is!"

"But it's just my stomach growling," she said. "It's because I'm hungry, señor."

"Not that, not that. It is the laughter, Angelita. That is what we were waiting for. Manuel often laughed like that."

"Yes!" she said, pulling in her breath. "Yes, he did! He *always* laughed like that!"

"*Bueno*," he said. "There it is. His sounds from you."

She nodded slowly. It was a kind of a miracle. Even her father had told her it would be this way. "Am I not always in your heart?" he had said earlier this summer. "Well, then, I will always be with you, no?" And she had been as comforted on that sunny day with her father as she was on this dark one with Señor Salgado.

He pushed himself down from the rock, stretched out his arms and lowered her to the ground. "Come, Angelita, your mother is waiting. Let us go home now."

They picked their way carefully across the rocky point. When they neared her father's grave, she hesitated, but Señor Salgado urged her on.

"There is no need to stop here," he had said gently, "is there?"

Now on the bluff near the freeway, Angela watched the darkness descend over the ocean. That memory had lain hidden all these years like a deep underground spring waiting to push upward, now fresh and clear. Behind her she heard motors starting and she got up. With a gentler breeze blowing her hair, she walked once more to the edge of the cliff. Tears welled into her eyes.

Sounds. "Am I not always in your heart?" A few feet away a late-homing gull flapped its wings awkwardly and then soared over the edge of the bluff. Sounds. "There it is, Angelita. Your father's laughter." Below her the surf rushed into the cove, the sand drank thirstily, the water receded. Sounds. "There is no need to stop here, is there?" Angela swallowed tears as she turned and trudged up the slope. Señor Salgado was right. She had pushed away her family, thinking that somehow she had washed away her heritage. She was wrong.

A feeling of distance held her as she walked, a sense of being in a remote place, one never known before. She was deeply tired but at peace, as if a storm had caught her in its vortex, whirling her around and around and finally tossing her on to a sheltered, tranquil spot.

Halfway to her car she stopped. Her gaze circled the bluff, beginning where she had seen the two boys emerge, past the clump of mustard, dimly outlined now, and then to the slope on which she had sat. Above her, two pale stars flickered, and on the freeway the rear lights of southbound cars began to move in ruby chains. Maybe life had to come to a standstill to be grasped at all. Maybe life had to come to a standstill in order for it to start. She pulled up her coat sleeve and looked at her watch. My God, it had gotten late.

"Who says it's too late now?" Walt had been pleading with her. "Who says it's too late, Angela?"

She turned and hastened down the incline toward her car. Gratefully, she slid into the driver's seat and turned on the ignition. She straightened her shoulders and glanced at the freeway. The traffic was still moving slowly as she drove her car from the dirt road into the first lane. Within minutes she had reached the off-ramp, and she took it with no hesitation. To her left, high above the traffic, was the bright orange globe of a Union Station, and at the bottom, facing the ramp, was the familiar low structure that was the Seven-Eleven.

As she made her boulevard stop, she scanned the area and found the telephone at the far end of the gas station. She parked by the phone and dug in her purse for change. After she dialed, she closed her eyes and pictured Walt sitting in his leather chair in the den. He would jump up and be across the room in two strides when he heard the telephone ring. But what if he wasn't there? Her shoulders sagged at the thought. Answer, Walt, please answer.

He picked it up on the first ring. "Hullo!" he said, and the sharp sound of worry shot through the wire.

"Walt, it's Angela." That was all. How could she say more now of what was just beginning?

"Angela! Good God, Angela, where are you?"

A sense of sureness filled her when he spoke, and she imagined that she felt the firm grasp of a hand on hers. "Not too far away," she said. "On my way back home."